Nora Roberts

Visit her online at www.juliaquinn.com
www.facebook.com/AuthorJuliaQuinn

Eloisa James is:

'Extraordinary'
Lisa Kleypas

'Romance writing does not get much better than this'
People

Visit her online at www.eloisajames.com
www.facebook.com/EloisaJames

Connie Brockway is:

'Delightfully witty and dazzlingly imaginative'
Booklist

'Simply the best'
Teresa Medeiros

Visit her online at www.conniebrockway.com
www.facebook.com/Connie.Brockway
www.twitter.com/ConnieBrockway

The Lady Most Likely

Julia
Quinn

Eloisa
James

Connie
Brockway

PIATKUS

PIATKUS

First published in the US in 2011 by Avon Books,
An imprint of HarperCollins Publishers, New York
First published in Great Britain in 2012 by Piatkus
This paperback edition published in 2021 by Piatkus

1 3 5 7 9 10 8 6 4 2

A CIP catalogue record for this book
is available from the British Library.

ISBN 978-0-349-43062-1

Printed and bound in Great Britain by
Clays Ltd, Elcograf S.p.A.

Papers used by Piatkus are from well-managed forests
and other responsible sources.

Piatkus
An imprint of
Little, Brown Book Group
Carmelite House
50 Victoria Embankment
London EC4Y 0DZ

An Hachette UK Company
www.hachette.co.uk

www.littlebrown.co.uk

*This book is dedicated to all the
wonderfully funny, cheerful people who visit
Connie's, Eloisa's and Julia's Facebook Fan pages.
We have so much fun with you—
we hope you have fun reading this book!*

The Lady
Most Likely

Chapter 1

August 20, 1817
The London town house of
the Marquess of Finchley
14 Cavendish Square

After years of inducing giggles, squawks, and outright bellows of laughter, Hugh Theodore Dunne, Earl of Briarly, understood perfectly well that an older brother exists primarily for the amusement of his younger sisters. After all, his parents had endowed him with four such sisters. They had the heir; they needed a spare; all they had managed to produce were girls who turned poking fun at their brother into an art form.

"A list!" his oldest sister Carolyn was saying, practically hooting between words, she was laughing so hard. "Georgie, did you hear what Hugh just said?"

Perhaps he shouldn't have issued his demand in front of his sister's best friend, since Lady Georgina Sorrell was practically convulsed with laughter.

"What's so damned funny about it?" he demanded, starting to feel irritated. "It's not as if you haven't warned me a thousand times that I have to get married unless I want Slinky Simon to inherit my title. Here I am, bending over to put my head in the parson's noose, and you're falling all over yourself because it's so hilarious."

"I *do* think you should get married," Carolyn replied. "I'm sure I have said so a thousand times. But now that you've finally decided to do it, you want me to pick you a wife?" Laughter bubbled out of her again. "You want me to make you a *list*?"

"I'm sorry," Georgina said, gasping a little. "I certainly don't mean to poke fun. I should allow the two of you to speak in private. I'll leave."

Hugh couldn't help grinning as giggles burst from behind her fingers. He'd always liked Georgie, even back when she was in pinafores, and she didn't smile enough these days.

"Be serious," he commanded the two of them. "I don't have the time for fiddling around in a ballroom and doing this sort of thing myself. You're always running around those places; you know the cattle; just point out a woman with good bloodlines and good teeth."

"He's in the market for a Hereford," Georgina said to Carolyn.

"Not a cow," Carolyn said. "A horse. You know Hugh; the only thing he thinks about is horseflesh day and night."

"I'm sitting right here in front of you," Hugh pointed out. "Scoff all you like, but I'm still waiting for a list."

"Hugh," Carolyn said.

He raised an eyebrow.

"You're serious?"

It was a mystery to him why his sister would think he wasn't serious. "I don't have time for wife-hunting," he pointed out. "I'm breaking in a new stallion, Caro. He's a —"

"Wait a minute," Georgina broke in. "What happened to make you decide to marry?" All the laughter was gone from her voice as if it had never existed.

"What happened is that he's finally growing up," Carolyn said blithely. "And at twenty-eight, it isn't a moment too soon."

Georgina waved her hand impatiently. "Something brought him here, Caro." She turned to Hugh. She had a delicate jaw, but damned if it didn't take on a bulldoggish look. "What happened?"

Hugh stared at her. He'd known Georgina since she was five years old. Their mothers were close friends, so they spent their summers together. Not that he'd seen her much in the past five years . . . in fact, he hadn't had a proper conversation with her since her husband's funeral. And that was, what, two years ago?

"Hugh?" Carolyn asked, the mockery gone from her voice as well.

"There's no need to make a production of it," he said, wondering exactly when Georgina's eyes had grown so grave. She had spent her childhood falling about laughing, yet now she was so clearly a matron. A widow, even though she couldn't be older than twenty-five since she was the same age as Carolyn.

She was sitting bolt upright, her eyes focused on his.

"Richelieu threw me," he admitted.

Carolyn gasped. "But you get thrown all the time."

The corner of his mouth twitched. "It goes with the territory. You can't break in a horse, let alone the particular horses I fancy, without cracking a bone now and then."

"But obviously this was different," Georgina stated. "What happened?"

"I've been out," he admitted reluctantly.

"Out?" Carolyn echoed. "Out of what?"

"Out of my mind. Flat out. In a coma, or so they call it."

"For days?" Georgina put in. Her voice was steady, calm. Of course, she had watched her husband die. And it took the man months . . . even a year.

"A week," he said, resigned. "I was out a week."

"Why didn't I know?" Carolyn cried. Her big blue eyes were filling with tears, which was precisely why he hadn't meant to tell her at all.

"Peckering has explicit instructions what to do in case of an event like this. And he followed them."

There was a moment of silence in the room.

"Peckering is your groomsman?" Georgina asked.

"Valet," he said. "I'd trust him with my life."

"Did he even call for a doctor? Was that in the plan?"

"Of course. There was nothing they could do. You know that. After a kick in the head, you either wake up, or you don't."

"And if you do wake up, you might well be injured for life," Georgina said. She was very white in the face, so white that her freckles stood out. She'd always had pale skin. It went with all that fiery red hair.

"I'm not injured," he said shortly. "I'm fully *compos mentis,* as you can see." Not that he hadn't feared just that, particularly when his vision didn't come back at first. It was during the day, when he lay in the dark after waking, that he realized the time had come to produce an heir. That or stop training horses. A wife was infinitely preferable.

"Oh, Hugh," Carolyn said with a wail. "I can't bear it!"

He went over and picked her up as if she were still a little girl, then sat down with her in his lap. "I'm fine, Caro," he said, patting her back. "You know that training horses can be risky. You've seen me fall off a hundred times."

"I don't understand why you can't just hire someone to do the dangerous part," she said, leaning against his shoulder. "Other people hire stable masters." He had a sudden memory of holding his sister like this when she was much smaller, and she used to suck her thumb. That would be after their mother died, he guessed, when he was nine, and she was only five or six.

"Working with horses is my life," he said simply. "I do have a stable master. Hell, I have three of them because of the stables in Scotland and Kent. But when a horse like Richelieu comes along, I'm the only one to touch him."

"Why can't you work with normal horses, then?" she cried. "Why must it be these terrible Arabians? So violent and uncontrolled?"

"They aren't violent by nature," he said, picturing the gorgeous animals he spent his life with. "Richelieu is high-spirited, and it's a game for him to try to best me. If I kill his spirit, I kill his ability to win."

"I don't know a single other earl who spends his days in such a dangerous manner," Carolyn said, starting to scold, which meant that she was feeling better.

He stood up, put her on her feet, and grinned down at her. "There's my shrewish little sister back."

"It serves you right if I'm a shrew. You drive me to distraction, Hugh. I hardly ever see you, and then you nearly die without even telling me, and—I *worry* about you!"

"You've been pestering me to marry for years. Ever since I turned eighteen, and that was ten long years ago. Just think about how happy you'll be. It shouldn't take me long to manage the business."

"Did it hurt?" came a quiet voice.

He turned and met Georgina's eyes. She had remarkable eyes, sort of dark lavender. The kind of flower his housekeeper hung in the stillroom. And she looked at a man steadily, without playing the coquette. Of course, she wouldn't play that with him. He was like a big brother to her. "No," he said.

And then: "Yes." He didn't want to lie to her. "My head hurt like the devil when I finally woke up. Something about the light, I think. But I was all right after a few days."

Carolyn ran to the door with a little sob. "Piers, it's the most awful thing—Hugh was in a coma for a week, and he didn't even let us know!" She flung herself into her husband's arms.

"Finchbird," Hugh greeted his brother-in-law.

The Marquess of Finchley didn't bow since he had an armful of marchioness, but he nodded. "Hoof to the head?"

"Unfortunately."

"He looks all right to me," Finchley told Carolyn.

"He almost died," she said, catching her breath on a sob.

Hugh's brother-in-law shot him a look that said, clear as shooting, that he never should have told his sister.

"I didn't mean to," Hugh said, sitting down again. "Georgina ferreted it out of me."

Georgina was still sitting bolt upright. "He came over to offer himself as a sacrifice at the marital altar," she said dryly. "I thought it would take at least a brush with death to bring him to that point."

Finchley nodded. "It would have to be something disagreeable to get Hugh out of the stables."

Hugh rather resented that. In the last ten years, he had tripled the estate his father had left by importing and breeding Arabian thoroughbreds. If he wasn't traipsing around ballrooms, it was only because . . . it was because there was no life for him outside the sweat and the thrill and the pure joy of the stable. "Well, here I am," he said shortly. "I plan to marry, so if you want to jeer at me, Finchbird, get it over with now."

Finchley's arms tightened around Carolyn's waist, and he smiled an odd lopsided smile over her head. "Why would I do that?"

Of course, theirs was a love match. Hugh wouldn't have had it any other way; Carolyn had always been the most softhearted of his sisters. She needed to be taken care of, and the marquess was just the man for it.

"He's asking Carolyn to produce a list," Georgina explained.

"What sort of list?" Finchley asked.

"A list of women to marry," Hugh said, feeling as if his idea had been a stupid one. Now Finchbird would take the piss out of him as well.

"I find that one wife is more than enough," his brother-in-law said, grinning.

"Thanks for the sublimely intelligent advice," Hugh said. "Could you stop hanging on to your husband and jot down a name or two, Caro? I thought I'd go to Almack's tonight and take care of this."

"Almack's? In case you didn't notice, Hugh, the season is over. It ended more than a week ago."

Georgina's voice had a sweet thread of laughter again. He hated to see that sadness in her eyes. Damn her husband for dying anyway.

"Does that mean I can't meet women simply because it's not the season? Caro, you seemed to be at Almack's almost every night the year you came out."

"Almack's is only open once a week, during the season. And how would you know how often I was there?" Carolyn asked tartly. "Aunt Emma kept hoping that you would escort me one night, and you never bothered, not even once."

"Brothers never—"

"Don't even try that," Carolyn interrupted. "I myself saw your closest friend, the Earl of Charters, at three or four balls this season with *his* sister."

"Poor Alec," Hugh said, amused. "Shall I ask him to make me up a list instead? He must have seen every woman on the market if he's been spending his time in ballrooms."

"If anyone is to make you a list, I'll be the one," Carolyn stated. "*I* will behave in a sisterly fashion by attempting to find you a spouse even if *you* completely neglected to help me in the same endeavor!"

"You came out the year I brought Monteleone over from Arabia," Hugh said. "Richelieu, the horse I'm working with now, comes from his line."

"I made a bundle on Monteleone when he won the Ascot," Finchley said with satisfaction. He pulled his wife over to a sofa and sat down with her.

"So you see? Finchbird managed to find you without my help, and if I'd been gadding about in a ballroom, Monteleone wouldn't have won," Hugh pointed out.

"And if Monteleone hadn't won, no one would want his issue, and you wouldn't nearly have died at the hoof of Richelieu," Georgina put in.

"Georgie," he said, reverting to her childhood nickname, "for God's sake, throw me a bone, here!"

Carolyn sniffed and straightened up. "So whom should he marry, Georgina?"

They both stared at him for a moment. Hugh waited.

"Gwendolyn Passmore?" Georgina said, with just a touch of doubt in her voice.

"That's just what I was thinking," Carolyn said, but then she shook her head.

"Why not?" Hugh demanded. Then he realized he had no idea who this Gwendolyn Passmore was. "I don't want to marry anyone walleyed," he said hastily. "Or with spots."

"Gwendolyn doesn't have spots. She's easily the most beautiful debutante of the year. Gorgeous pale red hair, the kind with a perfect curl," his sister clarified.

"I love red hair," Hugh said. "Didn't you just say that the season is over? So why didn't this paragon marry someone?"

"She turned down three offers that everyone

knows of, and I'm sure there were others. The word is that she's waiting for the Duke of Bretton to declare himself."

"Betting is running strongly against the duke's future liberty," Finchley put in. "He danced with her twice at the McClendon ball."

"No stables to speak of," Hugh said with a shrug.

"It's not stables that will win a woman," Carolyn said, frowning at him. "Bretton has great address."

"And he's *very* handsome," Georgina put in.

"I'm not?" For some reason, it nettled him to hear that from Georgina. Granted, he didn't swan about in ballrooms, but the woman he'd—ahem—befriended never showed any lack of appreciation. In fact, he had the distinct impression that his broad shoulders and muscled body were highly regarded.

"She's above your touch," his sister said. "Too beautiful, too desirable."

"I don't agree," Georgina said, knitting her brow. "Gwendolyn would be lucky to get Hugh. After all, he has your hair, Carolyn."

Carolyn grinned. "My finest feature!"

Hugh peered at his sister's hair. It was the same brandy brown as his own, not that he'd ever given the subject much thought.

"But I don't know that she would want him," Georgina continued.

"Why not?" he demanded.

"She's a bit shy," Georgina said.

"You have the social graces of an elephant," his sister said briskly. "Besides, Gwendolyn really is a smash hit."

"She's the Carolyn of her year," Finchley put in. He was holding his wife tightly against his side.

Hugh eyed him. Whatever happened, he didn't want to end up as lovesick as his brother-in-law. All the same . . . "If you won the top debutante, I can certainly do the same," he said pointedly.

"There's a perfect comparison," his sister said. "Piers knows how to dance. He *courted* me, Hugh. He wooed me. He sent me violets every morning for three weeks in a row. You couldn't do all those things. You don't even—no. Just put Gwendolyn out of your mind."

"What about Miss Katherine Peyton?" Georgina asked. "She's so adorable, and she does come from the country. She understands stables."

Carolyn tapped her chin thoughtfully. "I heard her ask Lord Nebel how many sheep he was running on his estate. He didn't even know he was running sheep."

"I have sheep, but from the look of it, all they do is eat. No running," Hugh said. "I think I'd rather have Gwendolyn. Look how well it's worked out for Finchbird."

"What has?"

"Going for the best woman on the market," he said promptly. "I know you don't like the comparison, but it doesn't strike me as so different from buying a horse. There's always one foal that everyone thinks will breed a winner. Gwendolyn's it this year, so she's the one I want."

Carolyn rolled her eyes. "You can't just buy Gwendolyn, Hugh."

He knew enough to keep silent about that. But he had a shrewd idea that Gwendolyn's father, whoever he was, wouldn't be unhappy to learn that the Briarly estate was now one of the richest in all England. And if he offered to throw in Richelieu as a bridal present . . .

"Kate is absolutely charming," Georgina said. "An adorable laugh and a charming figure. Plus, she has beautiful teeth."

He didn't like it that Georgina, of all people, was choosing a wife for him—and poking fun at him while she did it. Her own teeth were very white, as he could easily tell since she was laughing again. What was the matter with liking good teeth? No one would want to marry a woman who had a snaggletooth in front.

"I agree that Kate Peyton is a brilliant idea," Carolyn said. "Don't you think so, Piers?"

His brother-in-law shrugged. "No use planning these things."

There Hugh disagreed with him. "Just give me one more name," he said. "I've got Gwendolyn, Kate, and—"

"Georgina," Finchley put in. "Why not Georgina?"

Carolyn and Georgina burst out laughing, which nettled Hugh even more.

"As if I'd want my dearest friend to spend the rest of her life trying to woo her husband out of the stables!" Carolyn exclaimed.

He narrowed his eyes and waited until Georgina stopped laughing. "You *are* on the market, aren't you?" he asked pointedly. "After all, it's been two years since your husband died."

"Yes, it has," she said, the laughter running out of her like air from a punctured balloon.

A pang of guilt hit him. "I'm sorry. I never should have reminded you. Damn it, but I'm as careless as a stableboy."

"It's quite all right," Georgina said, producing a smile that curled her lips but didn't touch her eyes. "I'd rather not be on your list if you don't mind. I have a fancy not to marry again."

"Never marry again?" he asked, stunned. "Ever?"

She shook her head. "Richard's estate was not entailed. I have no need for the protection of a man's income."

"That's not the point," he said. "What about someone to be with? What about children?"

A shadow crossed her eyes, and he knew he had put a finger on the weakness of her argument.

"Even I can remember how you dragged around that raggedy doll summer after summer," he pointed out. "You were always putting her to bed and feeding her leaves and generally carrying on."

"We never fed our dolls leaves," Carolyn said indignantly. "Acorns, yes, leaves, no."

"When we weren't trying to sail them down the stream," Georgina said. "Give way, Caro. I'm afraid that our treatment of our poor dolls would only prove our unfitness for motherhood. I am sorry that no children came of my marriage. But I can't imagine myself marrying just for that reason. I shall never marry."

"I don't agree," Carolyn said. "You simply haven't met a man who is a true grown-up. We'll find you someone who's a real man, like my Piers. Perhaps someone in the military."

Hugh opened his mouth—and shut it again. It was none of his business, after all. "Where the devil am I to meet this Gwendolyn if Almack's is closed?" he asked his sister.

"We'll have a house party," she said promptly. "I'll send out the invitations for a fortnight from tonight. I'll invite Gwendolyn *and* Kate. Oh, and some other debutantes as well. Once I drop the word in a few mothers' ears that you'll be there, I'll have every nubile maiden you could possibly want."

Hugh grunted. He was vaguely aware that he was the subject of matchmaking fervor; one could hardly miss it given that he was regularly besieged at the races, especially Ascot. But he'd never paid the least attention before. "They don't have to all be maidens."

"Well, that's very liberal of you," Carolyn said with a sisterly smirk. "But since I can hardly hand out a questionnaire as regards their experiences in that regard, we'll have to leave it there."

"I mean that I'd be happy to marry an older woman," Hugh said. "A widow. Not Georgina, since she's apparently marked out for the uniformed crowd, but what I'm saying is that I'd just as soon my wife wasn't sixteen years old."

"No debutantes are sixteen this year," his sister said comfortably. "Seventeen, perhaps. But the fashion at the moment is to wait for a bit before debuting. I do believe that Gwendolyn is near twenty."

"She sounds better and better," he said.

"And since I can't invite only women," Carolyn said, "I know just whom I'll invite for you, Georgie."

"For *me*?" Georgina exclaimed, looking less than thrilled, somewhat to Hugh's pleasure.

"She just said she didn't wish to marry," he pointed out.

Finchbird gave him a look that told him it was useless to add anything to the conversation and, sure enough, Carolyn talked right over him. "Captain Neill Oakes. He's a war hero with a lovely estate—not that you need it—and most of all, he's just so *manly*. I don't even like uniforms, and I shivered all over when I watched him being presented to the queen."

Georgina wasn't so quick to scoff at that idea, Hugh noticed. "You'll want to be careful there," he said, in his role as big brother. "The war can do terrible things to a man."

"He has these fabulous jet-black eyes that just look right through you," Carolyn said dreamily.

Hugh could tell that Finchbird wasn't enjoying the description any more than he was. His arm tightened on his wife, and it seemed to wake her up.

"I'll also invite the Duke of Bretton," she continued. "Otherwise, Gwendolyn's mama will never accept the invitation. I heard it said that she has her heart set on her daughter becoming a duchess. And who can blame her?"

"You'll hold this party in a fortnight?" Hugh said.

"Yes. We'll be at Finchley Manor, of course. The

household is already scheduled to move tomorrow."

"We have the best grouse hunting south of Scotland," his brother-in-law put in. "You've never been with us in September."

Hugh could hardly say that he disliked nothing more than tramping around the woods trying to kill something. Especially now that it had been established that war heroes made the best husbands.

"Plus it's my twenty-fifth birthday," Carolyn said smugly. "Piers has promised me a particularly wonderful present, Hugh. So you can learn from him how to make a woman fall in love with you."

"You're lucky you're sitting all the way across the room," Hugh said. "I'd love to pinch you."

The marquess grinned at him. "Don't worry, old man. I'll give you some pointers . . . if you give me the next foal from Monteleone's line."

"Don't even dream of it!" he said rudely. But that reminded him. "I'll be bringing Richelieu, of course," he told his brother-in-law. "Will there room for him in your stables?"

"Absolutely!" Finchley replied. "Everyone is talking about Richelieu, and no one's seen him yet."

"I can't leave him, even for a week or two," Hugh said. "I know he has the passion for racing. Something might happen to his mouth if I allowed someone else to finish his training."

"Richelieu is *not* invited to my house party," Carolyn said pointedly. "I'm only inviting males of the two-legged variety, and they all have to be housebroken."

Hugh was about to tell her that he wasn't coming in that case when Finchley gave his wife a little shake. "You can't get the Duke of Bretton to come to the country just because there's a beautiful debutante in the offing. *She* may have decided to marry him, but I'll warrant that Bretton isn't so hellfire keen to tie the knot." He met Hugh's eyes, and the knowledge passed silently between them that Bretton's new mistress, an opera singer cheerfully known as Delicious Delilah, would likely keep him in London.

"But if Bretton knew that Richelieu was training at my estate," Finchley continued, "he would come. And the other men too. *That's* the lure that will bring in gentlemen."

"Bretton would be there in a sodding minute," Hugh agreed. "He has tried to buy Monteleone from me five or six times."

"You don't want Bretton to come," Georgina said, looking amused. "He's your competition for Gwendolyn's hand, remember?"

"The day that Bretton provides competition for me is the day that I—"

"What?" his sister interrupted, laughing. "Throw in the towel? Declare that you'll stay single forever?"

She burst into giggles, and they were right back where the conversation had begun, so Hugh managed to get himself out of the room.

Chapter 2

When Gwendolyn Passmore was eighteen, she slipped on a muddy lane and broke her leg. The doctor did a splendid job setting the bone, but Gwen was required to stay off her feet for eight full weeks. Normally, this would have been utter torture. Gwen was a walking sort of girl; she loved nothing more than to slip out of the house when the dew was still fresh on the grass and walk for miles and miles, until the hem of her dress was soaked.

But she broke her leg in April, which meant that she had to forgo what was to be her first London season. Her mother was devastated.

Gwen was ecstatic.

When she was nineteen, her brother was killed

at Waterloo. The family went into mourning, and Gwen's season was postponed by another year.

Gwen had got to do all her lovely, long walks that spring and summer, but half the time she found herself sitting under a tree, crying. Her brother Toby had been the only person in the world with whom she had felt completely at ease. And now he was gone.

When Gwen was twenty, she broke no bones, and no one died, and so in late March, she found herself being measured and poked and fitted and examined, and then she was taken off to London where she was measured and poked and fitted and examined by women with French accents (which somehow made the experience remarkably different although no less miserable).

As her parents were the Viscount and Viscountess Stillworth, she received invitations to every important party, and on one chilly night in April, she was trotted out before the *ton* to make her debut.

To her horror, she was an instant sensation.

"I told you she looked like Botticelli's Venus," her mother said proudly to her father, after a fourth gentleman had commented on the resemblance. And indeed, with her wavy titian hair, alabaster skin, and sea-green eyes, Gwen did bear a striking resemblance to the goddess as interpreted by the Italian master.

But each time someone commented on it, she could do nothing but stammer and blush because she knew as well as all the rest of them that Venus was standing in her clamshell with her hair covering only one breast.

And so, less than a week into the season, Miss Gwendolyn Passmore was heralded the undisputed beauty of the *ton*. Sonnets were composed in her honor, the newspapers had taken to calling her Venus of London, and she had been asked to sit for a portrait by Sir Thomas Lawrence himself.

Gwen's mother was ecstatic.

Gwen was miserable.

She hated crowds, hated having to talk with people she did not know. She did not enjoy dancing with strangers, and the mere thought of being at the center of anyone's attention was terrifying.

She spent a great deal of time standing in corners, trying not to be noticed.

Her mother was forever telling her to, "Smile! Smile a bit!" and "Be more cheerful!" Gwen wanted to please her parents, and she would have loved to have been one of those girls who laughed and flirted and was the life of every party.

But she wasn't.

By June, Gwen was counting the days to the end of the season. In July, she gazed at her calendar, thinking—*so close, so close.* And then August (so tantalizing), and September, and—

"I have wonderful news!" her mother exclaimed, rushing into her room.

Gwen looked up from her sketch pad. She wasn't terribly good at drawing, but she liked to do it nonetheless. "What is it, Mama?"

"We have been invited to a house party!"

Little fingers of dread began to uncurl in her belly. "A house party?" Gwen echoed.

"Indeed. We have been invited by the Marchioness of Finchley. Isn't that splendid? It is to be two weeks hence."

"I thought we were going home next week." It did not matter that the London residence bore her family's name; to Gwen, home would always be Felsworth, the huge, rambling estate in Cheshire where she'd grown up.

"Finchley Manor is in the Yorkshire Dales. It is almost directly on our way to Felsworth," her mother explained. "We shall stop off on the way. It will be a lovely diversion. So nice to break up the journey."

The journey wasn't so long as to require breaking up by anything more than a few nights at inns, but Gwen didn't bother pointing this out. Nor did she ask how, exactly, Yorkshire was on the way to Cheshire. There was nothing to be gained by it; her mother had made up her mind, and there would be no budging her.

A house party, Gwen thought miserably. She supposed it couldn't be worse than a London season.

"Lady Finchley writes that Bretton will be there," her mother said, holding up the letter as if it were a legal document. "I do think we have him close to proposing, Gwennie. This may be our opportunity to bring him up to scratch."

It was at times like these that Gwendolyn wondered if she and her mother inhabited the same world. Because in her world, it was quite obvious that the Duke of Bretton wasn't anywhere *near* to proposing marriage. Although she would probably say yes if he did. She rather fancied being a duchess. As far as she could tell, duchesses got to do anything they wished.

It might be rather entertaining to be an eccentric.

And the duke seemed pleasant enough. Quite handsome, and terribly intelligent.

"I shall have to write to Lady Finchley to see who else is coming," Gwen's mother said, her eyes taking on a terrifying strategic gleam. "Perhaps her brother—he is Lord Briarly, you know."

Gwen knew. She had memorized *Debrett's*. It made talking to people a bit easier, knowing who they were and how they were all connected.

"I wonder who else," her mother mused. "I cannot think of anyone with whom Lord Finchley is friendly. Although one would think it is his wife who is composing the guest list." She leaned forward and patted Gwen's hand. "I know you don't like these things, darling, but this won't be so terrible, I promise. A house party is much different than London. It's much more intimate. By the end, you shall be great friends with everyone."

Based on her experience with the young ladies of the *ton* thus far, Gwen thought tartly, she highly doubted it. She looked down at her sketch pad. She'd been drawing a rabbit. She decided to give him unpleasant teeth. Vicious little bunny. Excellent.

"Now then," her mother continued, "we shall have to get you a new riding habit, and perhaps three new day dresses as well. And oh, I am just so *so* pleased that Lady Finchley thought of this. I am so grateful for this last opportunity for you to meet a few gentlemen."

"I've *met* all the gentlemen," Gwen insisted. It was true. She'd been introduced to every gentleman in London. She'd danced with most of them, and she'd received offers of marriage from four. Two had been rejected out of hand by her father, one had been nixed by her mother ("I know his mother," she had said, "and there is no way I am subjecting my only daughter to that."), and the last—Lord Pennstall—she had almost accepted.

He had been very kind, and he was rather handsome, too, and only eight years her senior. There had been nothing wrong with him at all—until she found out that he wished to make his primary

27

home in London. He was very interested in governmental issues, even extending beyond his seat in the House of Lords.

Gwen just couldn't do it. The thought of spending the rest of her life in London, acting as his hostess, giving parties and arranging salons—it was unbearable.

And so with some regret, she declined, explaining her reasoning to Lord Pennstall. (She could not imagine refusing an offer of marriage with anything less than complete honesty.) He had been disappointed, but he understood.

Gwen knew that this meant she would have to endure another season unless she somehow managed to find the perfect husband back home. Still, one more season in London was infinitely preferable to a lifetime as a political wife.

But she'd thought she had earned a respite. She'd thought she'd be free of this for another year. She looked over at her mother, who had apparently just composed a song called "A House Party La La La."

Freedom, it seemed, would be delayed.

Alec Darlington had been the Earl of Charters for two years, but he still had not grown used to the name. "Charters" was his father, a gruff and strict old man who had never met a bit of his son with which he did not find fault. Alec had always enjoyed being "Darlington." It was a roguish, devil-may-care sort of name, perfectly suited to a man who spent his life in the pursuit of pleasure.

Alec had enjoyed living up to his name when he was Darlington.

Charters, on the other hand, was dull. Charters made charts. Looked at ledgers. Acted responsibly.

And it wasn't so much that he wished to be irresponsible again. He'd simply have liked the option of it.

But the carriage accident that had taken his father had also taken his mother, whom Alec had deeply and honestly mourned. And Alec had quite suddenly found himself entrusted with the care of his two younger sisters. He'd got Candida married off the year before, to a well-connected second son who worshipped the ground she walked upon. All in all, it had been a most satisfying arrangement.

This left Octavia, who, at twenty, had just completed her second season with nary a proposal, despite the perfectly respectable dowry he'd settled upon her. She'd done everything right, or so their great-aunt Darlington (who had acted as chaperone) had told them. Her clothing had been from the finest of modistes. She danced like an angel. She could sing, and draw, and paint watercolors. In short, she could do everything a young lady of her birth was supposed to do.

But for whatever reason, she did not "take."

Maybe she wasn't ravishingly pretty, but he did

not think she was plain. Her teeth might be a bit prominent, but that was all, really. And her eyes were quite lovely, the same color as his, actually—a clear, crisp gray. He'd certainly received compliments on his eyes. Why the hell didn't Octavia?

The men of London were a pack of idiots. It was the only explanation Alec could think of.

"Do you know who will be in attendance?" Octavia asked him. They were in his carriage, nearly to the end of the long drive that led to Finchley Manor.

"Briarly, of course," Alec said, peering out the window. He'd never been to Finchley despite his long-standing friendship with Hugh. "The marchioness is his sister."

Octavia nodded. "Yes, but I can hardly set my cap for him. He's practically my brother."

Alec nodded absently. "I'm sure Carolyn has assembled quite a guest list. She's very thoughtful about these things."

Octavia sighed. "It's just that—*Oh no!*"

"What is it?"

She let out a beleaguered breath. "Look," she said, jerking her head toward the window.

Alec looked out but saw nothing out of the ordinary. Just another carriage at the entrance to the house, depositing its owners—a young woman and her parents, from the looks of it.

"You don't see her?"

"Who?" he asked.

"Gwendolyn Passmore," she groaned. "This is the *worst* news imaginable."

"What's wrong with Gwendolyn Passmore?"

"Alec, no one will even so much as *look* at me if she is in the room."

Alec had been introduced to Gwendolyn Passmore once or twice, and he had to admit, she was rather amazingly beautiful. Still, Octavia was his sister, and so he said, "Don't be ridiculous. I can think of a thousand reasons why a gentleman would rather spend time with you."

"Oh, really," she said. "A thousand. Do tell."

He groaned inside. Sisters and sarcasm were a lethal combination. "You have much more personality," he said.

She looked stricken.

"What did I *say*?"

"That I have 'personality'?" she nearly cried. "Don't you know that's what gentlemen always say about the ugly girls?"

"I never said you were ugly!"

"You didn't have to," she sniffed.

He stared at her for a moment, then said, "I just want to verify that there is no correct statement I could make at this point, yes?"

She gave him a grudging nod.

This, Alec thought, was why he was not married. Clearly, a man could manage dealings with only one female at a time. He couldn't even consider taking a bride until he had his sister off his hands.

He shook his head, then put his hand on the door handle. They had come to a stop, and he was eager to hop down and stretch his legs.

"Don't!" Octavia said, yanking his hand back.

"What is it now?"

"Wait until she goes inside."

He looked outside. "Miss Passmore?"

"Yes."

He looked outside again. "Is she that bad?"

"I don't want to walk in beside her."

"For heaven's sake, Octavia."

"I shall look like a pudgy little hen next to her."

"Oh, for the love of—"

"*And*," Octavia added with great emphasis, "she's very standoffish. If *I* had been declared the pearl of the season, I would be a great deal more friendly to the other young ladies."

Alec took a breath. He didn't want his sister to feel uncomfortable, but this was ridiculous. And uncomfortable. For him. He'd been in the bloody carriage for four hours. He wanted to stretch his legs. "I will count to ten," he said. "If she is not inside by then, I am getting out."

"Please, Alec. For me?"

Luckily for both of them, Miss Passmore entered the house when Alec reached nine, and he did not have to force the issue. But still, he could not walk with anything approaching his normal speed. Octavia clamped her hand on his elbow with what had to be superhuman strength, then positively bolted her feet to the ground.

"Now what?"

"Give her time," she ground out.

"You would prefer to stand out here like a lackwit than cross paths with Gwendolyn Passmore?"

From Octavia's expression, the answer was clearly yes, but she must have had some pride because she allowed him to nudge them forward at the same pace he'd used when he'd given Candida away at her wedding the previous year.

"I am beginning to realize," Alex murmured, "why people always hope for sons. It has nothing to do with producing an heir."

"That was unkind," Octavia said, not sounding the least bit insulted.

"Females are a prodigious amount of work."

"I'm told that we're worth it."

This time Alec halted in his tracks. "Who told you that?"

Octavia opened her mouth to speak, but before she could make a sound, he said, "What the devil has Candida been telling you?"

"We haven't a mother, you know," Octavia said primly. "Someone must explain to me how things are done."

Alec felt his whole world drop by two inches. Or maybe it was just his belly. He felt ill. Exhausted. "She was supposed to wait until you married," he grumbled.

"Sisters don't have secrets," Octavia said gaily, and then she sailed inside with a wide smile on her face. Alec was impressed. She gave no sign of her recent distress.

Lady Finchley was waiting in the foyer, greeting her guests with a basket of scones.

"Carolyn," Alec said, giving her a polite bow and a sly smile. "You look positively pastoral."

"Don't I?" She held up the basket as if displaying a costume. "Everyone has been in town for so long, I thought it only right to be as rustic as I could. We are here to celebrate fresh clean air and morning dew and all that, aren't we?"

"Do I have to awaken in time to enjoy the dew?"

"Absolutely not," Carolyn assured him.

"Then I agree completely."

She gave him a smile that was really half smirk. "You need a wife."

"You are not the first to say so."

Her brows rose, and then in flash she dismissed him with a wave, turning to his sister with a grand smile. "Octavia Darlington," she said, with enough delight that one would think they hadn't seen each other just one week prior. "How nice to see you!"

"Thank you for inviting me," Octavia said, bobbing a polite curtsy.

Carolyn leaned in and spoke in a conspiratorial voice, although it was difficult to understand why as Alec was the only other person nearby, and he could hear perfectly well. "I have invited many eligible young gentlemen," she said to Octavia. "You, my dear, are going to have a splendid time."

She turned back to Alec, one of her brows arching in question. "I'm told you were in London for the season, but I hardly saw you."

"He pawned me off on Great-Aunt Darlington more often than not," Octavia said with a grin.

"Well, don't tell Hugh," Carolyn said to Alec. "I told him you took Octavia everywhere." To Octavia, she added, "I needed to make him feel guilty about something. I do hope you don't mind."

"Not at all," Octavia said, clearly pleased to have been included in Carolyn's subterfuge.

"Now then," Carolyn said, clearly ready to move on, "where *is* Great-Aunt Darlington?"

"She was delayed in London," Octavia explained. "Her bimonthly meeting of the Society of Bird Collectors was the day we left. She'll be along this evening."

"She collects birds?"

"You should ask her about it sometime," Alec said.

"Don't," Octavia put in, flashing him an aggravated look. "Not unless you *really* want to hear about it."

"I confess to a curiosity . . ."

"She stuffs them," Alec said.

"She does *not*," Octavia exclaimed. She looked at Carolyn. "He is a nuisance. A blight on society."

Carolyn laughed. "Brothers often are. I tell you, I don't know what to do with Hugh these days."

"Is he here yet?" Alec asked. He hadn't seen his good friend in months.

"In the stables," Carolyn said.

"Of course."

"Of course." She rolled her eyes, then slid back into her role as hostess. "Winters will show you to your rooms. Octavia, I've put you with Great-Aunt Darlington. The room is exceedingly pink. I hope you don't mind. Alec, you're off near Hugh." She gave a little wave of her hand as if to indicate some specific portion of the massive house.

"I believe I'll go find Hugh," Alec said. He looked over at Octavia. "You'll be fine without me?"

Octavia looked peeved that he would embarrass her with such a question in front of Carolyn. "Of course."

"There is already a small group of young ladies gathered in the west salon," Carolyn said. "Gossip abounds."

Octavia grinned. "Then I shall proceed there directly."

"And I shall make my escape," Alec said, wondering if there existed any greater nightmare than a pack of young ladies in one room, engulfed in a cloud of gossip. Luckily for him, he would not have to find out. He headed back outside, striding across the drive toward the stables. It would be good to see Hugh again. They had been fast friends at Eton, then at university, but after that, their meetings had been sporadic. Alec was more often than not in town, and Hugh was, more often than often, wherever his horses were. Which wasn't usually in town.

Alec hummed to himself as he approached the massive stables. The smell of hay and manure wafted toward him on the breeze, and he smiled, even as *eau de* sweaty horse mixed itself into the scent. He liked riding just as well as the next man, and he'd certainly run in his fair share of races and hunts, but he'd never quite understood the passion for horseflesh that gripped Hugh. Still, he liked that Hugh liked it. He wouldn't be the same if he weren't so cowheadedly obsessed with his cattle.

"Hugh!" Alec called out, pushing open the door. He heard a whinny from a rear stall, followed by an expletive. Followed by another whinny, which he assumed was the horse's version of an expletive.

"Hugh?" he called again.

A head popped out from the stall. "Darlington," Hugh said. "Good to see you."

"And you." Alec didn't bother to correct him about the name. He rather liked that Hugh still called him Darlington. There was something lovely and familiar about it, as if they were boys again, their only responsibilities to their tutors and their friends. He walked closer and peered in. "Is this the stallion that has half of London aflutter?"

"The intelligent half," Hugh answered.

"Robespierre?"

"Richelieu."

"Of course," Alec murmured.

Hugh got back to work, which was—well, quite honestly Alec wasn't sure what he was doing, but the horse didn't seem to like it. Alec took a step back. He'd seen men kicked by horses before. He did not aspire to the experience.

"What are you doing here?" Hugh asked, not looking up.

"You invited me."

"Eh?"

"Your sister. By extension, you."

At that his friend raised his head and gave him a frank stare. "Will our sisters ever not be, by extension, us?"

"I don't think so," Alec said regretfully.

Hugh pressed his fingers to his temples, an action Alec would not have endorsed, considering the state of his gloves. Still, the poor man did look as if he was battling a ferocious headache. "One more," Hugh said. "One more to get married off, then I'm done."

Alec thought of Octavia, off gossiping with her brethren. "We shall have a party, you and I."

"Do you ever think of taking a bride?" Hugh asked.

Alec blinked at the surprising turn of the conversation. It was damned odd. Men didn't talk about marriage. Not the way women did. "Er . . . No?"

"You'll have to eventually, won't you?"

"Well, yes." But not yet. What the devil had got into him?

Hugh let out a sigh. Or maybe a groan. "I've been thinking of taking one on myself."

"A wife?" Alec asked, just to clarify. *Taking one on* seemed an odd way to phrase it.

Hugh nodded, then jumped back when the horse let out an aggressive snort. "It's time."

Was it possible that Hugh needed to find an heiress? He'd not heard of difficulties in the Briarly family finances, but that did not mean they did not exist. Hugh was a private man, and he did not go to town; his estates could be falling apart without anyone knowing a thing about it.

"Is there something you'd like to tell me about?" Alec asked carefully. Something wasn't quite right about Hugh. He was far too serious. Not that he'd ever been unserious, but this was different. He looked guarded. Worried.

Hugh never worried about anything that wasn't equine.

"Everything's fine," Hugh said with a grunt. "It's just that I have responsibilities." He looked up. "As do you."

It didn't *exactly* sound as if Hugh was scolding him, but it felt like it, all the same. Alec paused, lest he reply in a manner he might later regret.

"Don't look at me like that," Hugh said, giving him a lopsided smirk. "Where does *your* title go if you don't reproduce? You don't have a brother."

"First cousin," Alec said, a bit peeved that Hugh could defuse his irritation with so reasonable an argument.

"Do you really want that? Mine goes to Simon Carstairs."

Alec blinked. He knew Carstairs. He wished he didn't. "You're related?"

Hugh nodded grimly. "Third cousin."

Alec considered this. "Your family really does have difficulty producing boys."

"It's a problem."

"Very well, you *should* marry. Quickly."

"My sisters call him Slinky Simon."

Alec chuckled.

"It's only funny if he's not your cousin."

"It's funny because it's true."

Hugh did not look amused. "I had them make me a list."

Alec stopped chuckling. "What?"

"A list. Of women. I had my sisters make me a list of possible brides. I can't be expected to figure this out on my own."

"The rest of us generally do."

Hugh gave him a powerfully irritated glare. "I'm busy." He waved an arm toward the stallion, which, Alec had to admit, had calmed down remarkably during the conversation. Whatever it was that Hugh was doing to the beast, it was working.

"Very well." And then Alec had a provident thought. "D'you want my sister?"

"Octavia!" Hugh gaped at him. "Isn't she twelve?"

"She's nineteen."

"I can't marry her. I'd keep picturing her as twelve."

"She doesn't look twelve any longer, Hugh."

Hugh shuddered, looking vaguely ill. "All the same. I can't do it."

"Damn." There went a perfectly good husband prospect.

"I'm thinking about Gwendolyn Passmore."

Alec looked up and let off an exhausted groan. "Double damn."

"What's wrong with Miss Passmore? I'm told she's lovely."

"You haven't met her?"

"When would I have met her?" Hugh asked with a shrug.

Alec shook his head. He adored Hugh, but honestly, he was sometimes so far removed from normal British life it was scary. "She's beautiful," he said. "Insanely so."

Hugh cocked his head to the side and tilted the corners of his mouth as if to say, "That'll do."

"Octavia hates her," Alec went on.

"She's probably jealous."

"Of course she's jealous. She admits it freely. But she also says she's haughty."

"Miss Passmore?"

Alec gave a nod.

"Damn." Hugh released a pent-up breath. "I can't tolerate a snobby female. Ah, well, I suppose I'll give her a go, anyway. Ought to judge for myself."

Give her a go. Alec wasn't so sure Hugh understood the difference between winning a female and taming a horse. "Who else is on the list?" he asked.

Hugh blinked. "Do you know, I can't remember."

Alec smiled. There was Hugh for you. "I wish you well with Miss Passmore, then."

But Hugh was already back to Richelieu, whispering something as he rubbed an ointment into his flank.

A really, incredibly, viciously foul-smelling ointment.

Alec shook his head as he left the stables. He hoped Miss Passmore liked horses.

Chapter 3

$\mathcal{D}$inner was at eight, Gwen was informed, with guests meeting for drinks and conversation during the hour prior. Gwen had pleaded fatigue and begged her mother to allow her to arrive at the drawing room at ten minutes to eight. Her mother had agreed, but Gwen suspected this had less to do with her arguments and quite a lot more with her mother's dreams of a dazzling grand entrance.

In truth, Gwen was just trying to limit the time she'd be forced to mingle with the other guests. Supper she wouldn't mind. Conversation at the dining table was rarely unbearable. One wasn't standing about, thinking that one's feet were hurting or worrying that one might perspire through one's corset. At the table, everyone was stuck firmly in place, which meant that no one was looking over someone else's shoulder, wondering if there was a different crowd to join, with better people.

And if it still turned out to be wretched, at least the soup would probably be good.

"I am famished," Gwen said, as she and her mother made their way down the elegant front staircase of Finchley Manor.

"Don't eat too much tonight, dear," Lady Stillwell murmured. "You know you have a delicate stomach."

Gwen was trying to figure how best to reply to that, since her stomach wasn't the least bit delicate, but they'd reached the entrance to the drawing room, and her mother had moved on to a whispered, "Stand up straight, my dear."

Gwen swallowed and followed her mother into the room. She supposed one couldn't say it was crowded, as it was one of those terribly long, rectangular salons with at least a half dozen separate seating areas, but it still felt as if there were a bevy of people in attendance. She glanced around, trying to see if she could find a friend. Oh, there was Kate Peyton. Gwen had always admired her. She was so outspoken and direct. And there was—*oh dear*—Octavia Darlington. Octavia did not like her. Or at least Gwen was fairly certain that she didn't. She always seemed to have a pinched-up smile when Gwen approached. And on a few occasions, Gwen was sure that Octavia had very much on purpose pretended not to see her. It had not been a cut direct; Octavia would never have done anything so obvious. But Gwen had known what she was up to. And she supposed she did not have the right to be upset about it; she herself was an expert at pretending not to see people.

She suspected, however, that the motives had been different. Octavia Darlington was not the sort of young lady to hide in corners. Gwen rather envied that about her, actually.

"Miss Passmore," came the lovely, musical voice of their hostess, Lady Finchley. "I was beginning to fear you would not make it down in time for supper."

"I'm terribly sorry to be late," Gwen said, giving a curtsy.

"Lady Stillworth," Lady Finchley said to Gwen's mother, "may I steal your daughter away for a moment?"

Gwen's mother agreed, and Gwen soon found herself with her arm tucked firmly in Lady Finchley's elbow. "I am so eager for you to meet my brother," Lady Finchley said.

"Your brother?" Gwen asked with some surprise. She had met Lady Finchley on several occasions, but she had not got the impression that she had become enough of a favorite that she should wish to attempt to match her with a brother.

"My brother Hugh is an earl. Briarly."

"Yes, of course," Gwen said.

"What a relief that you know of him. He never goes down to London, you know. I'd feared the world had forgotten him completely."

"He never goes to London?" Gwen asked. And her delight must have shown in her eyes because Lady Finchley gave her a shrewd look, and said, "You're a country girl, then?"

"Oh, very much so."

"I'm a complete dilettante myself. When I'm in London, I miss the country, and when I'm in the country, I declare myself bored. It's really a vexing way to be."

Gwen smiled and nodded, hoping that would suffice as a comment.

"My brother is the same way," Lady Finchley said, then added, "as you, not me. He hates town."

Gwen nodded again, happy that Lady Finchley didn't seem to notice that she was contributing very little toward the conversation.

"I suspect the two of you have a great deal in common," Lady Finchley said. "Ah, here we are. Hugh! Hugh!"

A tall man with thick brandy brown hair turned around. He was quite pleasant looking, Gwen thought, and quite obviously related to Lady Finchley. She liked that his hair was not neatly trimmed. And that his face was a bit tanned. Although . . .

She took a discreet step back. There was a spot

47

of something brown on his boot that she suspected might not be mud.

"Caro," he said. "Good God, are we going to eat anytime soon?"

"Hugh," his sister said pointedly, "this is Miss Passmore."

Gwen smiled and curtsied.

Lord Briarly blinked twice, then said, "Of course. I am pleased to make your acquaintance." He took her hand and kissed it, the elegant motion somewhat out of place on so rough-hewn a man.

"I am honored to meet you as well, Lord Briarly."

He stood for a moment, his brow furrowing. Gwen had the distinct impression that he was thinking of something else.

"Hugh," his sister said, not sharply, but nearly so.

"Right," he said. He looked at Gwen, cocking his head to the side, almost as if he were examining her for . . . well, for something. "I understand you're from the north, Miss Passmore?"

She nodded. "Felsworth, in Cheshire. We go home directly from here. I am very much looking forward to it."

"Miss Passmore prefers the country," Lady Finchley said, without an ounce of subtlety.

Lord Briarly nodded approvingly. "Better for the horses, too. I know there are some who feel they can be stabled properly in town, but I must say, I'm against it."

Lady Finchley turned to Gwendolyn. "My brother is mad for horses."

"Do you ride, Miss Passmore?" he asked.

"A bit," she answered. She had a mare, of course. She'd always had a mare. But she much preferred walking to riding. One couldn't see anything from atop a horse. Not close enough to get a good look, anyway.

"I do think the country is the only place for children," Lady Finchley said gaily. "I have such fond memories of Highcross, with my brother and sisters."

"Highcross," Lord Briarly said, nodding at the memory. He turned to Gwen with a bit of a grin. "Have you siblings, Miss Passmore?"

"I have—I had," she corrected, "three brothers."

"Did you misplace one?" Lord Briarly chuckled.

"He died," Gwendolyn said quietly.

There was a horrible, horrible silence.

"Please pardon my brother," Lady Finchley said, leaping into the chasm. "We trot him out only for special occasions."

Gwendolyn wished she knew how to act at such a moment because she knew that the earl had not meant to cause her distress, and now *she* was feeling guilty that he looked so embarrassed. But she didn't know what to say, couldn't even summon a smile.

"Oh, look!" Lady Finchley said. "There is the Duke of Bretton. Let me call him over."

Gwendolyn stood awkwardly, waiting.

Lord Briarly stood awkwardly, looking at her feet.

"Here we are," Lady Finchley said. "Miss Passmore, you know the Duke of Bretton, of course."

Gwen curtsied as the duke told her how delighted he was to see her again although Gwen didn't think he really meant it because he immediately launched into something about a horse named Richelieu with Lord Briarly.

"Miss Passmore?"

She turned. It was another young gentleman. No, two of them. George Hammond-Betts and Allen Glover. She had met both in London, several times. They had known her brother Toby at Eton. Sometimes they told stories, and Mr. Glover, in particular, could do such a good imitation of Toby that it always made her laugh.

Funny that. She'd have thought it would make her cry, but it didn't.

"What a splendid surprise," one of them said. "I had not realized you would be here."

"Nor I," said the other.

"Do you plan to stay the entire week?" the first asked.

"I should love to escort you to Parsley," said the other.

"Parsley?" Gwen echoed, completely lost now. Were they talking about food?

"As would—"

"It's the name of the village," someone new said. "The inn is called the Sage and Thyme. Isn't that droll?"

"Er . . ." No. It wasn't, but Gwen would never say so.

"Miss Passmore."

Gwendolyn lurched back slightly, turning her head to the right, then—

"Miss Passmore."

—to the left. "Good evening," she managed to say as two more gentlemen nosed in. There really wasn't quite enough room for everyone, and Gwen found herself edged up against the back of the sofa. There were five young men now, all vying for her attention, plus Briarly and the duke, who remained standing next to her, even though they were still arguing about a horse.

Gwen swallowed, trying to smile and nod at all of them, but it was difficult, and she thought she might be nodding in the wrong direction, and not smiling at all, and she really wished they wouldn't stand so close, although she knew it wasn't their fault; there wasn't much empty space in this little corner of the room.

"Yes, yes," she said, when one of them commented on the weather, but then she realized that he'd asked her a question for which that was certainly not the correct answer, and she could only imagine that they must think her the most absolute dimwit, nothing but an empty head with long red hair.

She wasn't an idiot, she thought miserably, she just acted like one.

She took a breath, trying to focus on the words swirling about her. She really wished that people would take turns talking. But Mr. Hammond-Betts was nattering on about a book of poetry he'd recently read, and Mr. Glover had taken to arguing with him about it, and the other men were saying something about the color of her dress, which Gwendolyn frankly thought was rather ordinary, and if that weren't enough, Briarly and Bretton were still going on about that horse!

Not for the first time, Gwen wished she possessed a flair for drama. This would be the perfect moment for an extravagant swoon.

With quiet desperation, she glanced over at the clock. It was three minutes past eight. Surely Lady Finchley would lead them into supper soon.

Her stomach growled.

Please. Please let her be the prompt sort of hostess, not the *We're having such a lovely conversation; supper can wait* sort of hostess.

She spotted Lady Finchley, who was deep in conversation with a gentleman Gwen did not know, or at least could not recognize from behind. She showed no indication of looking at the clock, or Gwen, or any of her guests for that matter.

Supper, apparently, would wait.

Alec had been playing the dutiful big brother, moving about the room with Octavia on his arm, but finally he declared himself in dire need of a drink, so they'd stopped their amblings and were presently standing near the decanter, Alec with brandy and Octavia with nothing.

It was not the first time Alec had reflected upon how glad he was not to have been born a woman.

"Oh, will you just look at her," Octavia said disgustedly.

"Lady Finchley?"

"No," Octavia returned, with the type of exasperation women reserved only for men who shared their last names. "Gwendolyn Passmore."

Right. The raving beauty. "What did she do this time?" he asked.

"Nothing. That's the problem. She just stands there, and all the gentlemen flock to her side."

Alec had to admit that the little swarm surrounding Miss Passmore did look a bit like sheep. Especially Hammond-Betts, whose blond hair had always been a bit fluffy.

"It isn't fair," Octavia sighed.

"Jealous, are we?" he murmured.

"Of course I'm jealous. She doesn't even *try*."

Alec looked down at his baby sister. Could it be that Octavia was trying *too* hard? There was nothing wrong with her, nothing at all. She was friendly and intelligent, and she had a charming smile. She might not resemble Botticelli's Venus, as Miss Passmore did (with what Alec found almost alarming accuracy), but there was absolutely no reason why she should not be considered a splendid catch for any young gentleman.

And honestly, did Hammond-Betts and whatever the others were named *really* think they had a chance with Miss Passmore?

He set his drink down. "Come with me," he said, grabbing his sister's hand.

"What are you doing?"

"Getting you a flock."

"What?"

He stopped and looked at his sister solemnly. "You deserve sheep, Octavia."

And then he hauled her off again, until they were right in the middle of the Passmore passel. "Octavia, dearest," he said, "would you introduce me to your friend?"

Octavia's eyes widened with shock, and embarrassment, too, the ungrateful chit, but she recovered (there was a Darlington for you!) and she introduced him to Miss Gwendolyn Passmore, whose eyes had also widened, although if he read her right, hers were with alarm.

"Miss Passmore," he said elegantly, bowing over her hand. "I have heard so much about you. How can it be that we have never been introduced?"

"I . . . er . . ."

As she stammered, he recalled that they *had* been introduced. Right, well, she was polite at least. Either that or forgetful, because she made a pretty remark in return.

He took her arm, earning him lethal glares from the other gentlemen. No matter. He was giving them Octavia. If they couldn't see that she was every bit as appealing as Miss Passmore, to hell with them.

"Octavia has spoken so highly of you," Alec said, and he led her away, right past Hugh and Bretton, who paused in their equine argument for just long enough to stare at him with unconcealed curiosity.

"There," he declared, once they were off in a corner. "I have rescued you."

"Rescued me?" she echoed.

"You didn't really want to spend the rest of the evening with Hammond-Betts and the other one, did you?"

Her lips parted with surprise, and for a moment he had to wonder if perhaps she was a little dim.

She didn't seem able to form replies very quickly. But then something in her eyes changed. It was remarkable. One moment her face was an utter mask, and the next . . .

It was not.

Her eyes deepened; he didn't know how else to describe it. They were the most amazing shade of seafoam green, and he'd thought them rather blank, but now he couldn't imagine how he'd thought that. Because they weren't blank. They were anything but. Her eyes were oceans, two oceans of—

Good God, he thought disgustedly. No wonder his sister hated her. He'd been in her presence for less than a minute, and already he'd gone completely stupid.

"Thank you," she said, and she smiled.

And then—heaven help him, it happened again. He was not being fanciful, he was *not*. He was a full-grown, perfectly reasonable and intelligent earl of the realm. He'd taken a good Second at Oxford, a really good Second. And yet he could not tear his eyes off her mouth. Because he would swear that the smile she'd just given him was not the smile that had been on her face two moments earlier.

Octavia, he reminded himself. This was about Octavia. He had behaved like an idiot, practically dragging a young lady across the room, which was not a recommended behavior for an unmarried, un-marriage-minded gentleman. The gossips would be all over this one. It would be in London by week's end. The betting book at his club would have him marrying her by Christmas.

He looked over at Octavia. Was she enjoying herself? She had damn well better be.

Then he turned back to the ravishing Miss Passmore, who was standing beside him, utterly quiet, with an expression of serene patience upon her face. He realized that he, too, had been quiet, unsociably so, and so he said the first thing that came to his mind, which was the astoundingly pedestrian, "Fine weather today."

Idiot.

"Oh yes," she replied. And then, when he was quite sure she wouldn't say more, she added, "I think autumn might be in the air."

Alec nodded, then scowled at Hugh and Bretton, who had apparently stopped arguing about Richelieu in favor of watching *him*. He turned, getting himself back to facing Miss Passmore, who was still standing there quietly, except her expression was different. Her lips were pinched at the corners. It was not unattractive; Alec rather suspected she could howl like a monkey and look not unattractive.

She didn't look angry, either. Rather, she looked . . .

Bored.

His brows rose. This would not do. He leaned forward, intent on making mischief, and whispered, "I hear you're thinking of marrying Bretton."

Her face went utterly slack with shock, and he saw her swallow before she replied, "I don't think he's thinking of marrying *me*."

Alec glanced back. Bretton and Hugh were back at it, their conversation of sufficient vigor to dissuade anyone from interrupting. "I fear you may be right," he said to her. "To be honest, I think he simply wants a horse."

"It's why he came to the house party," she replied.

Alec blinked.

"He wants the horse," she explained. "He's been talking about it all summer."

Alec found himself a little nonplussed by her direct reply. "Well, it *is* a fine animal."

She gave a little shrug, one he found impossible to read.

"Why are you here?" he asked her.

She didn't answer right away, but she did look at him rather oddly. Finally, when he returned the expression, she said, as if it should be obvious, "My mother insisted."

Actually, it should have been obvious.

"You're not delighting in the festivities and fresh air?" he murmured.

She shook her head. "I was looking forward to going home."

Alec studied her for a moment. She was holding herself very still. She wasn't one of those fidgety girls who always seemed to be twisting a handkerchief. And she was quiet, very quiet. But she did not strike him as standoffish, and he could not imagine her giving anyone the cut direct.

Was it possible that Octavia had misjudged her?

What was he thinking? Of course, it was possible. Octavia was a dear, but she was nineteen years old and thinking of Octavia. The last thing she wanted in her life was a staggeringly beautiful rival who was not conveniently evil.

His silent study must have stretched too long for comfort because Miss Passmore started inching to her left. "I think my mother is calling me."

Her mother was most definitely not calling her. Her mother, whom Alec could see out of the corner of his eye, had found Great-Aunt Darlington, who had just arrived on the scene. Their conversation appeared to rival Hugh and Bretton's in animation and fervor.

"I'd better go," Miss Passmore said. "My mother, you know."

He nodded. It was probably safe to let Venus de Passmore go; Octavia had snagged the attention of two gentlemen, including the fluffy-haired Hammond-Betts. And he meant to step aside, he really did. But just when his brain was directing his foot to move, she looked up at him, and she smiled, and for once it wasn't hesitant. It probably should have been, since he'd all but dragged her across the room.

But instead she smiled.

He understood in an instant, in a bloody quarter second, why Octavia hated her so much. Because when Gwendolyn Passmore smiled, the world quite simply stopped spinning.

And so he reacted just as any male of the species would do upon coming face-to-face with a female he found attractive: He pulled her hair.

Except he *couldn't* pull her hair. He was nearly thirty years old; one really couldn't get away with such behavior past ten. But he did the adult equivalent of a hair-yanking, which was to stand there and glower at her forbiddingly. Because if he *looked* like he was unaffected by her smile, then she would not realize that, in actuality, he was in an utter panic because somewhere deep down inside he'd realized that his life had just changed forever.

Not that he was thinking quite so clearly. For the most part, he just thought he had indigestion.

Gwendolyn had known who Lord Charters was, of course. There wasn't a debutante in London who was not aware of his existence. He was not the biggest matrimonial catch of 1817 (that would be the Duke of Bretton), but according to the young ladies with whom Gwen sometimes visited, he was number two.

There were not many titled unmarried gentlemen under the age of thirty with no debts and all of their teeth. Add in thick, dark hair, an athletic physique, and a devilish smile—well, it was no wonder that only a duke could edge him out for the top spot.

But Lord Charters did not often bother with soirées and musicales, and if he'd been to Almack's, she had never seen him. His sister was more often accompanied by a maiden aunt. His sister, who Gwendolyn was certain had *never* spoken highly of her.

Clearly he was up to something, barging over like he did and yanking her away, but then, to her utter surprise, he'd said something about rescuing her, and she wondered—was it possible that someone had finally noticed that she didn't like attention? That what she really wanted was to sit quietly at the wall, watching everyone else?

No. No, as a matter of fact, it wasn't possible. Because then he'd gone and made that awful comment about her planning to marry the Duke of Bretton. What was he thinking? You didn't say such a thing to someone's face, you said it behind her back.

At any rate, he'd turned perfectly horrid. She'd

tried to be polite, giving him her sweetest smile as she attempted to escape, and he'd returned the gesture with an angry glare.

She did not understand men. She did not understand most women, either, but she truly did not understand men.

She was still trying to figure out how to extricate herself when she was finally saved by the arrival of Lord Briarly, who had stomped over to their side.

"The supper bell's rung," he said.

"It has?" Gwen hadn't heard it. But really— *thank heavens.*

"My sister tells me I'm to take you in," Lord Briarly said to her.

Lord Charters shook his head. "You are a paragon of charm and grace, Briarly."

Lord Briarly gave him a blank look.

"I would be delighted to accompany you," Gwen said enthusiastically. Too enthusiastically, it seemed. Lord Briarly looked stunned.

She smiled again, beaming at him.

Lord Charters gave her a very queer look.

Gwen continued smiling, starting to feel as if she were trapped in a theatrical tableau, and no one had given her her lines.

Or informed her of the plot.

It was at that moment that Lady Finchley came sailing over, Kate Peyton's hand tucked firmly in her own. She took one look at Gwen gazing worshipfully at her brother and practically floated off the ground.

"Alec, darling," she said with steely determination, "you're to escort Miss Peyton in. Here you are." She then physically lifted Kate's hand from her own and placed it on Lord Charters's arm.

"Gwendolyn," Kate said. "So nice to see you."

"And you," Gwen murmured, utterly relieved to see her. She and Kate Peyton were not close, but Gwen knew her well enough to know that she did not dissemble; nor did she have patience for double entendre.

The party began their procession into the dining room, promenading four across, and Gwen found herself next to Kate.

"Are you hungry?" Kate asked, leaning in just a touch.

"Famished."

"Oh, me too," Kate practically sighed. "I thought they would never call us in. I shall count the evening a success only if I am able to claim an entire hen."

Gwen laughed, then pressed her lips together when she realized that Lady Finchley and both earls had turned her way.

"I think you should aspire to greater ambitions," Gwen murmured to Kate. "Perhaps a pig."

"In its entirety? I don't want to seem greedy."

"We could share."

"Only if you take the snout," Kate demurred.

"Oh, no, you must, I insist."

Again they laughed, and again the rest of the crowd stared. But, for once, Gwen didn't care. It was far too lovely to share a joke with a friend.

All in all, by the time Gwen crawled into bed, she realized that the evening had been quite pleasant, after all. The soup had been good, the meat even better, and once she exited the drawing room, she hadn't had to talk to Lord Charters even once.

Chapter 4

$\mathcal{G}$ wendolyn woke early the next morning. She dressed, left a quick note to her mother to inform her that she was going for a walk, gathered her sketchbook and pencils, and slipped out of the room.

The house was quiet; clearly, most of Lady Finchley's guests did not share her love of dawn and the morning dew. She peeked into the breakfast room, which was empty save for a footman, who looked extraordinarily surprised to see her. After assuring him that she did not require a full meal at half six, she managed to obtain a small loaf of bread, which she thought she might split between herself and the ducks on the lake she'd spied on the drive in.

It was a lovely morning, crisp and cool, with the sort of mist that one knew would disappear within the hour. Gwendolyn adored such mornings. It was as if she had the world to herself. Just her and the great outdoors. Gwendolyn Margaret Passmore and a million blades of grass.

Something ran past her feet.

Gwendolyn Margaret Passmore, a million blades of grass, and a small rabbit.

She smiled.

Humming softly as she walked, she followed the path Lady Finchley had described to her. The bread had not been warm when it was handed to her, but it smelled fresh and new, and she broke off a piece and ate it.

Lovely. The ducks might have to go without.

After about a quarter of an hour, she reached the edge of the lake. It was more of a pond, really, with quite a few trees at the edges and a marshy area across the way. It couldn't be even half as big as the lake at home. She popped another piece of bread in her mouth and looked around for a dry spot to sit. The ground didn't look too wet, but it was kind of squishy. She let out a breath. She'd better find a rock.

She hummed some more, switching from the Mozart she'd been practicing on the pianoforte to a more jaunty tune, origin unknown but probably inappropriate. The early-morning sun was bouncing off the surface of the water, and she tilted her head to the side, trying to capture the exact angle of the light. She felt alone. She felt happy.

Her mother had never understood that, that Gwen had always found joy in the quiet moments. It was so strange how someone could love another person so much and so well and still not understand what made her happy.

There was a large flat-topped rock about ten feet away, so Gwen took a bite straight from the loaf and ambled over. She patted the damp surface, decided it wasn't too wet, then sat down. The mist was already starting to burn off, and the air was warming, so she pulled off her gloves, took out her best pencil, and began to sketch.

She started with the tree across the way, but then for some reason added a squirrel, even though she hadn't seen any running about. She paused, examining her work. Was that squirrel perhaps a bit large? Or maybe . . .

Not large enough.

She flipped a page and started over, quickly getting the tree down, then adorning it with a monster squirrel. Now that was more like it. She grinned, giggled even, as she added huge, furious claws.

She could never let her mother see this. Never. Never never. She'd never recover from it. The shock alone might do her in.

The picture needed something else, though. The

squirrel shouldn't be *evil*. "You're not a monster," she murmured, "you're monstrously huge." And then she started drawing a girl squirrel, who, it turned out, looked exactly like a boy squirrel wearing a fancy hat.

This was definitely one of her worst drawings ever.

And quite possibly her favorite.

Still, she'd have to burn it. If anyone saw it, they'd think her mad, and—

Splash.

Gwen froze. Was someone in the water?

Of course someone was in the water. The question was who, or actually, no, the question was: Could Gwen pack up her things and leave before anyone noticed her?

She didn't want to talk to anyone just then. She was having a perfectly lovely morning on her own. Not to mention that whoever was in the water would be, quite logically, wet.

And thus indecently attired, if attired at all.

Her face burning, she grabbed her gloves, shoved her sketchbook under her arm, and hurried to her feet. She started back the way she came, going as quickly as she dared, but the ground was still damp, and the stones mossy and wet, and she was far more scared than she was careful.

"*Yah!*"

There was no way she could avoid screaming.

Her feet flew out from beneath her, and she had the awful sensation of flying through the air before coming down—hard—on her bottom.

"Ow," she moaned. Oh, that hurt. It really hurt. And her heart was racing, and her stomach felt as if it had been twisted inside out, and—

"Who's there?"

She swallowed. It was a male voice. Of course it would be a male voice. No woman would jump in a lake at this time of the morning.

"Is someone there?"

Maybe if she was very quiet . . .

"Reveal yourself."

Oh, she didn't think so. She got her feet under her and slowly—very slowly—started to rise. Her coat was dark green, so she ought to blend in with the trees quite well, and—

"Miss Passmore?"

Or not.

"Miss Passmore, I know it's you."

She swallowed again, slowly turning back to the pond. The Earl of Charters was standing in the middle of it, the water up to his chest. She said nothing, trying not to focus on the fact that she could see his shoulders, and his chest was quite bare.

She swallowed, then squeezed her legs together tightly, although, really, she had no idea why. Unlike him, she was completely covered under her dress. Still, it seemed like the thing to do.

"Your hair," he said. "It gave you away."

Gwen cursed under her breath. She did not often resort to profanity, but with three brothers, she'd learned enough of it to satisfy a moment like this.

"Lord Charters," she said, determined to be polite despite—Well, despite everything.

"What are you doing out at this time in the morning?" he demanded.

"I went for a walk. What are *you* doing out at this time in the morning?"

"I went for a swim."

Insolent wretch. She hugged her sketchbook more closely to her chest. "I shall leave you to your privacy, then."

But before she could go, he asked, "Do you always roam the countryside unaccompanied?"

She couldn't tell if he was scolding her. His tone wasn't sharp, but no one asked that sort of question for mere curiosity. Still, *he* was one to talk. She felt her brows rise as she regarded him, half-naked in the water. "I did not expect to meet anyone."

"No one ever does, when she is foolish enough to venture forth unaccompanied."

Gwen drew back with outrage. "I am not the one half-naked in the lake."

"Oh, I'm not half-naked."

She gasped. She made a sound that was not even remotely dignified. She might have even barked his name. "Good day," she finally bit off, turning sharply on her heel.

Except the ground was still slippery. She ought to have known that, considering she'd just taken a tumble a few moments earlier. But she was not accustomed to men in lakes who were, as he had put it, not half-naked, and really, could she be blamed for not having the presence of mind to learn from her mistakes?

She lost her balance, then lost her sketchbook when it flew from her hands, then lost her dignity when she landed, her entire left side hitting the ground with a bone-jarring thud.

It hurt considerably more than the time before.

She swore again.

And then again. Because she'd tried to move, and her wrist *hurt*.

She paused, took a breath, and made one more attempt to push herself up into a sitting position.

"Don't try to move." It was Lord Charters's voice, alarmingly close to her ear.

Gwen let out a shriek and squeezed her eyes shut. She had no idea how he'd emerged from the water so quietly, but she was quite sure that he hadn't had time to don his clothing.

"Where does it hurt?" he asked.

"Everywhere," she admitted. Which was more or less the truth. "But most of all, my wrist."

"Can you sit up?"

She nodded, still keeping her eyes closed, and allowed him to help her into a sitting position. He took her hand and gently palpated it, murmuring, "Here?" when she winced.

She nodded again.

"It's a little swollen," he said, "but I don't think it's broken."

"It's not broken." She knew what a broken bone felt like, remembered precisely the awful *snap* she'd heard—no, felt. No, heard. No, both. She'd heard it through her body, if that made any sense.

"Nevertheless," he said, "you'll want to put a splint on it."

She nodded yet again, still not daring to open her eyes. He had a very nice voice, calm and gentle, and if she hadn't had such an unpleasant encounter with him the night before, she would have felt very much reassured and at ease.

"You can open your eyes," he said.

"No, thank you."

He didn't chuckle, but she could have sworn she heard him smile.

"I give you my word," he said softly. "I am well covered."

Slowly, and not without doubts, she opened one eye. To her great relief, she found that he wasn't lying. He had pulled on a shirt, and although it stuck to him in places, he was not indecent. His breeches were soaked through. Clearly, he'd been wearing them in the water.

"I said I wasn't half-naked," he said with a wry smile. "I didn't say which side of *half* I was on."

She pressed her lips together but was unable to muster irritation. "That was very devious of you."

He shrugged, and his expression grew devilish. "It's the sort of thing men do."

"Be devious?"

"It's easier than being clever."

She laughed. She didn't mean to, but it bubbled right up and out before she realized it. He smiled along with her, and somehow the moment became . . .

Easy.

It was easy.

It was the sort of description that would be meaningless to most, but for someone who did not enjoy crowds, or new people, or strange experiences, *easy* was a marvelous thing. *Easy* was the best kind of moment there was.

"Do you often go for morning hikes?" he asked her.

"Are you going to scold me?"

He looked down at her mud-stained skirts. "I think you've been punished enough."

She gave him a scowl, then said, "I love mornings. I walk at home all the time. It was just awful two years ago, when I broke my leg."

"So you do know what it's like to break a bone?"

She nodded grimly. "The sound is the worst."

"You can hear it?" he asked with some surprise.

"You've never broken anything?"

"Not on my own body. Nor on anyone else's," he added quickly, upon seeing her eyes widen, "but . . ." His expression grew sheepish and yet at the same time more than a bit proud. "I *have* done some damage to furniture. And dishes. And, oh, can one break a tree?"

Gwen tried very hard to maintain a serious mien. "I think one can."

"Then I've broken one of those, too." He held up a hand. "Don't ask. It was an extremely convoluted boyhood game involving balls, swords, and a sheep."

She took a moment just to stare at him, trying to see if he was joking. She didn't think so. "Please say you didn't break the sheep."

"The sheep never left the ground," he assured her.

And while Gwen was trying to digest that, he added, "Not for lack of trying."

She had no reply. Really, she wasn't sure there *was* a reply to such a statement.

His head tilted to the side, and his eyes grew distant. "Actually, I think there might have been a catapult involved, too."

She shook her head. "I find it astonishing that any of you survive to adulthood."

"Boys, you mean?" He snapped back to the present and gave her a grin. "Yes, well, we're beasts. There's no getting around it. We play foolish games, drink too much, start wars, and that doesn't even begin to . . ."

But Gwen didn't hear the rest of his statement. His mention of war had brought a vision of Toby to her mind, except that his face was growing fuzzy around the edges, and that seemed the saddest part of all. She was forgetting her brother's face. It was as if he'd had to die twice, only the second time stretched over years.

"Let me see that wrist again," Lord Charters said, taking her hand in his.

"No, no," she assured him, horrified by the catch in her voice. "I'm fine."

"You looked—"

"I was just thinking of someone, that is all."

"Someone?" he asked quietly.

"My brother," she said, because she did not see any reason to hide it. "He died at Waterloo. I still miss him very much."

To her surprise, Lord Charters did not offer his condolences, nor did he make some completely uninformed statement about Toby being a hero. Gwen hated when people did that. What did *they* know about how he'd been killed? *She* didn't even know how he'd been killed, just that he was dead. The family had got a letter, then a visit from an officer, but no one had actually witnessed the death.

Instead, Lord Charters looked at her with compassion and said, "A year is not such a very long time when you loved someone."

She could not help but think—*he knows. He knows what it is to lose someone.*

She said nothing, not a hint of her thoughts, but he answered the question anyway. "My mother," he said quietly. "Two years ago."

"I'm sorry."

"So am I." He drew a deep breath, then let it out. "It was a foolish accident. A carriage that had not been maintained properly."

Gwen didn't say anything, just nodded in sympathy. He looked at her, and she knew, she simply knew, that they were the same in this; that he, too, appreciated quiet, honest sympathy.

He had nice eyes, she thought. Gray, but not entirely so. The outer edges were rimmed with dark, dark blue. She wondered how she had not noticed this the night before.

Then he stood, clearing his throat and breaking the moment. "Aside from your wrist," he said briskly, "how are you? Are you able to walk?"

She was already sitting up, so with the aid of his arm, she rose carefully to her feet, testing out her weight on each of her legs in turn. "I think I'll be fine," she said. "I didn't turn an ankle."

"You're limping," he pointed out.

"I'm just a bit achy from the fall. I'm sure it will go away."

"May I escort you back to the house?" he asked politely.

"Yes," she said, "I would appreciate it very much." However unpleasant he had been the night before, he was not so now, and Gwen decided it was much easier to begin anew than to agitate over the past. She took a step, then remembered—

"Oh! My sketch pad." She twisted around to see behind her. It had fallen near the water's edge, but thankfully had managed to stay dry.

"I'll get it for you." Lord Charters carefully disengaged his arm from hers and retrieved the pad. "Were you drawing the wildlife?" he asked, returning to her side.

Gwen considered her monster squirrels. "Er, of a sort."

He gave her a curious smile. "What does that mean?"

"Nothing," she said, wishing he'd hand her the sketch pad.

"May I have a look?"

"I would really rather you didn't."

"Just a peek?"

Gwen could not imagine anything more mortifying. "No, my lord, I—"

"You're not drawing nudes, are you?" he cut in, eyes sparkling.

"No!" she exclaimed, feeling her cheeks go instantly crimson. Good heavens.

He made like he was going to look, his index finger sliding between the pages. "Please?" he murmured, and she almost gave in. Something very strange and unfamiliar began to unfurl within her. It was as if her insides were light-headed. And her heart was not beating quite properly. It wasn't racing, and it wasn't pounding . . .

It was dancing.

Singing.

That was it, she was going mad. She must have hit her head. She hadn't felt anything, but maybe that was only because she'd been so focused on her wrist. Her wrist, which really wasn't hurting quite so much any longer, so shouldn't she now feel the injury to her head?

"Miss Passmore?" Lord Charters said softly. "Is something wrong?"

She blinked, then looked over at him, then decided that must have been a mistake, because his gray eyes were looking at her with such kindness and concern, and somehow that made the whole thing with her heart that much worse.

"Yes, I mean no," she stammered. "I mean I'm fine. Just a bit dizzy coming to my feet."

He did not comment on the fact that she had been on her feet for at least a minute before her dizzy spell, for which she was quite grateful. And then, to her great surprise, he pulled his fingers from inside the pages of her sketchbook and held it firmly closed. He held it forward, as if to hand it to her, then said, "I would be happy to carry it back for you if it would make it easier for you to walk."

"You're not going to look?"

He regarded her with a serious expression. "You asked me not to."

Her lips parted with surprise.

One corner of his mouth tilted up. "Did you think I would disobey?"

There was no way to answer truthfully without insulting him. "Er, yes," she said, giving him a rueful look.

To her relief, he only smiled. He held out his free arm for her to lean upon and turned her toward Finchley Manor. As they walked up the gentle slope, he said, "You're rather more forthcoming than you were last night."

She did not answer right away, and when she did, she kept her eyes ahead of her, on the path. "I don't enjoy crowds," she said softly.

He looked at her for a moment, then came to a stop, forcing her to do the same. "You must have hated the season."

"Oh, I did," she said, the words rushing from her mouth. It was such a *relief* to say it. She looked up at him, finding unexpected comfort in his eyes. "It's a *terrible* time for someone like me. The whole season, all I wanted was to be home."

"I don't believe I have ever heard a young lady say that."

"Do you often speak with young ladies?"

He blinked. "Of course. I—"

"Not to," she cut in, "*with*."

His brows rose, but his gray eyes retained their humor. "Do you imagine me standing at the front of a room, offering a lecture?"

"No, of course not. But . . . Well, you must admit, it is very rare to have a conversation of any consequence while at a social event. And where else would you have spoken with a young lady?"

He started to say something, but she broke in with: "Your sister does not count."

For a moment she thought she might have offended him. He did not immediately reply, just looked at her in a considering sort of manner. Then he said, "I thought you were shy."

"Oh, I am," she replied. Except, amazingly, with him . . .

She wasn't.

Oh my.

Chapter 5

$\mathcal{A}$lec was not generally one to rise with the sun. At home, he kept his curtains heavy and drawn tight. If the morning light could not invade his bedchamber, then he could happily sleep all day. If the sun hit his face, however, he woke instantly, and there was no point in trying to get back to sleep.

The minute he saw his room at Finchley Manor, he knew he'd be awake at dawn. The windows were broad and tall, with curtains that could, at best, be called light-filtering. And so, not one to tolerate a lack of sleep, he'd made a point of turning in on the early side. Which was why he was in a surprisingly cheerful mood when he sat up in bed at half five.

This was cause for some note. Half five awakenings were not normally accompanied by a cheerful mood.

He knew that most of his acquaintances did not share his freakish inability to sleep while the sun shone, and so he had not been surprised by the quiet house when he slipped outside for a quick dip in the pond. He had, however, been surprised— very much so—when, as he burst back through the surface of the water following a spectacular cannonball entrance, he heard someone shriek.

Who would have thought that Miss Passmore would have turned out to be an early riser?

Or, he thought with some alarm, that she'd somehow manage to be even more beautiful in the morning light. Weren't women supposed to look puffy and blotched in the morning? His sisters looked wretched before their morning toilette and hairdressing.

Said with the greatest of affection, to be sure.

But no, Miss Passmore, even while gritting her teeth in pain, rivaled the Mona Lisa. It couldn't possibly be fair to the rest of humanity.

He supposed it wasn't her fault that she was so bloody beautiful, though, and she *was* hurt, so he hauled himself out of the lake and managed to pull off a respectable show of being a gentleman. He inspected her injuries, and she was perfectly pleasant. Rather kind, actually, with a quiet sense of humor he suspected she did not often show.

"Do you like horses, Miss Passmore?" he asked quite suddenly. Because if Hugh was setting his cap for her, she had damned well better like horses.

She turned to look at him, a bit surprised by the sudden change of topic. "I don't dislike them."

"But you don't love them."

"Well . . ." She grimaced, just a bit, clearly unsure of how to respond. "I suppose I love *my* horse."

"You suppose."

"Well, it is a horse." And then she gave him a look as if to say—*You do realize this, don't you?*

Alec stared at her with something approaching alarm. She could not marry Hugh. Alec could not imagine a more miserable pairing.

"Is something wrong?" she asked.

"Not yet," he said ominously.

Her lips parted. She looked concerned. Or maybe wary.

Sensible girl. Even Alec had to admit that he sounded like a half-mad buffoon.

"I fear I owe you an apology," he said.

She looked at him again with surprise, and he knew exactly how she felt because he was quite certain he had not meant to say that.

But he realized he meant it.

"I don't understand," she said.

"I misjudged you."

She was very quiet, then she said, "People often

do. I—" She looked to the left and right, as if she were making sure no one else could hear. Which was absurd, because they were completely alone. But somehow it looked like the correct thing to do, and something about it warmed his heart. Because whatever it was she was going to say . . .

It was for him. Just for him.

She leaned forward, but just the tiniest bit.

Alec's heart skipped a beat. That quarter inch . . . That tiny sliver of space that she'd eliminated between them . . .

It took his breath away.

And then she pulled back. "It's nothing," she said, and she looked down, embarrassed by whatever it was she had not been courageous enough to say.

"No," he said, with a fervor that surprised him. "It's not nothing."

Her eyes rose to meet his. Those amazing seafoam eyes. How could anyone have been born with eyes like those?

"It's silly."

"Let me be the judge of that."

"I was just going to say . . . It's really rather obvious." She looked off to the side, then down, and then back at his face but not quite to his eyes. "You said it already."

He could not help but smile. "What did I say?"

"People think I'm cold," she said, "but I'm not.

It's just that I don't know how to talk to most people. And crowds . . . They terrify me." She looked down, frowning at the damp grass, and then back up, her brow still furrowed. Looking as if she'd never before uttered the words aloud, she said, "I'm shy."

Alec, who had never stood nervously in a corner or felt sick to his stomach before entering a room, said, "It's not a fault."

She smiled regretfully. "It is in London."

"But we are not in London."

"We might as well be," she said, giving him a vaguely condescending look. "There is no one here at Finchley Manor I have not met before. Except Lord Briarly, of course."

Alec thought of Hugh. Single-minded, horse-mad Hugh. He loved Hugh. He did. He'd have thrown himself in front of a carriage for his friend, and in fact on one memorable occasion had done so, saving Hugh's life in the process. It was a miracle that Alec had escaped with only a bruised rib.

But Hugh could not marry Miss Passmore. Forget what it would do to Hugh, shackled to a woman who did not share his passions. Alec was now thinking of *her*. She would be miserable.

And as he watched her face, her lips curving into a secret smile that spoke of intelligence and hinted of mischief, he realized that he could not allow her to be miserable.

"I think I'm going to kiss you," he whispered.

She looked stunned. He *felt* stunned. But it was the most obvious thing in the world. If he didn't kiss her, *now,* on this field, in this mist, at this moment . . .

It would be tragic.

He touched her chin, tipped her face up to his, and for a moment simply drank in the sight of her. Her hair caught the early-morning light, and he had to fight the urge to reach behind her head and pull out her hairpins. He wanted to see it long, wanted to know the texture of the curls. He wanted to examine the gorgeous mass of it strand by strand, to see how such an amazing red-gold color could possibly exist.

He almost whispered that she was beautiful, but she had to know that already, and he realized, as she gazed up at him, her eyes filled with the same wonder that he felt in his own heart, that this breathless feeling wasn't about her beauty.

She needed to know that it wasn't about her beauty.

And so instead he said nothing, just shook his head in amazement, then leaned down and kissed her.

It began softly, just his lips brushing hers, and he had every intention of keeping it that way, of being gentle, and reverent, and everything else a man was supposed to be with the woman he . . .

The woman he . . .

He drew back, staring at her again, as if the moment were brand-new.

Her lips came together, and he knew she was about to say, "My lord."

"Don't," he said, touching her lips with his finger. "Say my name."

She looked as if she might say something profound, but then she whispered, "I don't know your name."

He froze. He didn't breathe. And then he burst out laughing. He was falling in love—hell, he'd quite possibly already fallen—and she didn't know his given name.

"Alec," he said, unable to stop the ridiculous grin that was spreading across his face. "My name is Alec, and I don't want to hear you use anything else ever again."

"Alec," she murmured. "It suits you." She smiled, and it lit her whole face. "I am Gwendolyn."

"I know," he confessed. He had a sister, after all, who'd told him all about her, most of which he suspected was wrong. But her name—that, he knew.

"Some people call me Gwen."

Gwen. He liked that. It was simple. Plain. Charming.

It was *her*.

"My mother wanted to name me Guinevere," she said, "but my father said it was too fanciful."

"He was right," Alec said firmly.

She smiled, laughed a little. "Why do you say that?"

"I don't know," he admitted. "I just know that it is true. You are a Gwen. No, you are *the* Gwen."

"*The* Gwen," she repeated, sounding highly amused.

"*The* Gwen." And when she quirked a brow, he added, "It's important to say it correctly."

"And you're sure that's the correct way?"

"Oh, absolutely," he murmured. "It's blindingly obvious."

"Blindingly, you say."

He smiled slowly. "Blindingly."

She smiled back, but this time she looked devious. He decided he liked when she looked devious.

"I think you should kiss me again," she said.

He decided he *loved* when she looked devious.

He took her hand, twining their fingers together, and tugged her toward him, slowly, playfully, until she was just a breath away. "You want me to kiss you, hmm?"

She nodded.

"Here?" he murmured, kissing her on the nose.

She shook her head.

His lips found her forehead. "Here?"

She shook her head again.

"Here?" he said softly, the word warm on her lips.

"Yes," she sighed.

88

He moved to the corner of her mouth, then the other. "Here? Here?"

She didn't speak, but he could hear her breath coming faster, could feel it warm and moist as it brushed against his skin. He grew bold, lightly running his tongue along the soft inner skin of her lower lip. "Here?" he teased gently, once he was done.

Again, she didn't speak, but she used her body to say yes. Her hands came around to his back, and she swayed toward him, resting her body against his. His pulse jumped at the contact, and suddenly he was fighting himself. His hands, his arms, his soul—everything wanted to reach out and crush her against him. He wanted to kiss her, touch her. He wanted to worship her.

He wanted her to know how it felt to be worshipped.

He kissed her again, and then again, in what he was certain was the longest, deepest, most exquisite kiss in history. It was the stuff of legend, of song. Somewhere, he thought, poets were weeping. No verse could rival this single, perfect kiss.

Alec drank her in, absorbed her scent. He held her against him, imprinting her body to his. By the time he was done, he knew her completely, had felt the very essence of her soul.

And he hadn't even seen her naked.

Good *God.*

Alec pulled back, coughing like mad. Where had *that* thought come from? He was being a gentleman. A romantic. This was Gwen. *The* Gwen. She was a delicate flower, a priceless treasure. He was not supposed to be fantasizing about her with her clothes off, never mind the fact that he regularly thought about women with their clothes off.

Wasn't that what men did?

But not about *her*, he berated himself. Not about the girls they were going to marry. Not that he'd decided to marry her although, really, now that he thought of it, it sounded like a bloody good idea. But still, regardless, she was the type of woman one married, not the type one fantasized in various stages of undress.

She was better than that.

Although . . .

Dear God, she'd look amazing in *any* stage of undress.

Alec started having trouble breathing.

"Are you all right?" she asked. She sounded concerned, but he didn't dare look at her. If he did, he'd only start thinking about her again . . . *that* way. Which would have profound and quite possibly painful effects on certain parts of his body.

Oh, very well, the parts in question were already well and good affected, but if he could just stop thinking about her, and how she might feel if he put his hands—

This had to stop.

Now.

"I think we need to go back to the house," he choked out.

"Now?"

He nodded, not exactly looking at her. He knew his limits. He swallowed. "Perhaps you should go ahead of me."

"You want me to return by myself?"

"No," he said, even though he was nodding.

"You . . . *don't* want me to return by myself."

He *wanted* to reach out and yank her back to him. He *wanted* to peel the clothing from her body and kiss her again, this time in unspeakable places. He *wanted* to hear her moan with passion, then he *wanted* to . . .

"Lord Charters? I mean, Alec? Are you all right?"

She sounded concerned. Worse, she sounded as if she might reach out to touch him.

She was definitely going to have to return by herself. *He* was jumping back in the lake.

Chapter 6

$\mathcal{A}$s first kisses went, Gwen was well aware that hers had been spectacular.

She had nothing to compare it to, of course, and there had been no one to impart wisdom or relate the details of other, more inferior first kisses. She had no sisters, and as far as she knew, none of her friends had been kissed, or at least not by anyone of note. But she knew—oh heavens, she knew—that hers had been the first kiss to end all first kisses.

She was fairly certain that Lord Charters—*Alec*, she reminded herself—had been similarly affected. But then he'd broken it off, and turned away, and now, to be completely frank, he sounded ill.

Which meant that she probably would be by nightfall, as well.

She smiled even though he would not see it, turned away as he was. No, she probably smiled *because* he would not see it. It was cruel to grin in front of someone in such distress. But she could not help it. All she could think was—

What a *wonderful* way to catch a cold.

"Alec?" she said softly. He had not responded to her previous query, when she'd asked if he was all right. "Alec? Is there something I can do to help you?"

She thought she might have heard him groan, then, with a haggard breath, he turned back to look at her. "Gwen," he said, looking quite uncomfortable as he crossed his arms, "do you know what happens between a man and a woman?"

Her eyes widened, and she shook her head.

"If you don't go back to the house this minute," he said hoarsely, "you will."

For a moment she could but stare, then, in a single ridiculous flash, she understood. "Oh!" she yelped, jumping back a step.

"You catch my meaning," he muttered.

"Not really," she stammered, "but, also . . . yes?"

He uncrossed his arms, then recrossed them, then clasped his hands together in front of him. She did not think she had ever seen him look so ill at ease.

"We are not far from the house," she said.

"No."

She swallowed. "I should just get my sketch-book." She motioned to the grass, where her pad had fallen, completely unnoticed by either of them.

He didn't move, and she didn't either, not at first. Finally, aware that one of them had to break the awkward spell, she scurried forward and grabbed it, stepping back and hugging it to her body.

"I shall see you later," he said, still holding his hands stiffly in front of him.

"Of course. I shall look forward to it."

He motioned toward her with a tilt of his head. "Perhaps you will show me one of your sketches."

Gwendolyn thought of her gigantic squirrels, with their vicious teeth and festive bonnets. And for once, she saw no reason to be embarrassed. "Perhaps I shall," she murmured. "Perhaps I shall."

Several hours later, Alec was feeling much refreshed and renewed. His second dip in the lake had proven quite useful, and he was feeling almost human again by the time he returned to Finchley Manor.

Wet, but human.

A hot bath and a fresh change of clothing completed the transformation, and he was almost ready to head down to breakfast when he heard a knock at his door. He started to say, "Enter," but the door began to open before he could complete the word, which meant, of course, that it had to be his sister.

"Alec!" Octavia said, rushing in. "Where have you been?"

He thought about that for a moment. It could not be possible that she had been looking for him. He knew Octavia's sleep habits, and there was no way she'd been up early enough to have noticed he was gone.

"Everyone is already down at breakfast," she continued.

Ah, so that was what she meant. "Why are you not there, then?" he asked.

She pressed her lips into a peevish expression. "I came to find you."

He adjusted his cuffs, straightened his coat, and gave a nod to his valet that he might depart. "Since when have you been unable to eat eggs and bacon without my exalted presence?"

"*Alec.*"

"Very well, what is it?"

"It is Miss Passmore," she said, and he grew instantly alarmed at the gleeful note in Octavia's voice.

"What about Miss Passmore?" he asked carefully.

Octavia leaned in, her eyes glowing with the promise of gossip. "Apparently she was out walking early this morning."

"Apparently?" He hated the word *apparently.*

"I didn't see her," Octavia admitted. "But others did."

"I don't see anything wrong with a morning walk," he said, trying to nip the conversation off at the bud. "I would permit you to go out walking at home had you any inclination to do so."

If Octavia had noticed the subtle scolding he'd just given her, she made no indication. Instead, she continued as if he had not spoken. "Emily Mottram has reason to believe she was not alone."

Emily Mottram? Who the hell was Emily Mottram? And what did she think she knew? Alec was quite certain that he and Gwen had been alone that morning. No one could have seen them. No one.

"Emily saw her when she returned," Octavia said. "She was very rumpled."

"Miss Mottram?" Alec said testily.

"No. Miss Passmore. Emily said she looked as if she'd been rolling about in the mud."

"Well, perhaps she was," Alec snapped. "It rained last night, and it's slippery. She could have fallen."

"Oh, please," Octavia said dismissively. "That would never happen."

Alec nearly threw up his arms in exasperation. "What are you talking about?"

Octavia let out an irritated snort. "She's so graceful. She would never just *fall.*"

"You really must get over this jealousy," Alec said sternly. "It is most unbecoming."

Octavia drew back, her mouth opening indignantly. "What a stodge you've become."

"My stodge to your shrew," he shot back.

She gasped. "You're calling me a shrew?"

Alec saw no reason to respond to that.

"Why are you defending her?" Octavia demanded.

"I'm not," Alec shot back, although he rather thought he should be. "I am merely pointing out that *you* are gossiping, and it's extremely unattractive."

"Alec!" she exclaimed, and he half expected her to stamp her foot.

He just crossed his arms.

"You don't understand," she insisted. "I will never find a husband with her nearby. Never."

If this was how she conducted herself in public, Alec thought, then she was probably doing a fine job repelling her prospective suitors on her own. He wasn't so cruel as to say so, however, and so he tried to gentle the sentiment. Not quite resisting a roll of his eyes, he told her, "You can't blame your woes on Miss Passmore."

"Oh, yes I can," Octavia retorted. "And before you call me whatever arch and dignified insult you think of next, let me assure you that I am not the only young lady who feels this way."

"Octavia, I have spoken with Miss Passmore

myself. Last night, as a matter of fact, when I removed her from a flock of young gentlemen so that *you* might have an opportunity to attract their attentions."

"Thank you for that," Octavia said grudgingly.

Alec shook his head. His sister was going to be the death of him. "I found her a most amiable and kindhearted young lady."

"That's because you're a man," Octavia practically spat.

"It's because I'm a person. Good God, sister, what has become of you? When did you become so mean-spirited?"

"When did *you* fall in love with Gwendolyn Passmore?" she shot back.

"I'm not—" He cut himself off, because the truth was, he had no idea if he was or wasn't in love with Gwendolyn Passmore. He was certainly in love with the idea of her. Of Gwen. *The* Gwen, with the laughing eyes and quiet smile.

And the kiss. The perfect, amazing, soul-shattering kiss.

Never in his life had he felt so instant a connection to another human being as he had with her, mere hours earlier.

"Octavia," he said, trying to sound reasonable, "you have no reason to believe that Miss Passmore has done anything other than take an early-morning walk. I can only deduce that you are spreading rumors about her out of spite. And I cannot begin to tell you how ashamed of you I am."

"I can't believe you are saying this to me," Octavia replied, her lips parted with shock and dismay. "You are my brother."

"Indeed." He crossed his arms and gave her a stony stare.

"I'm going to find out who she was with," she said in a low voice.

"I'm warning you," he said. "Leave well enough alone."

"But—"

"Stop," he commanded, unable to listen to another word of this. "Has it ever occurred to you that Miss Passmore might simply be shy? That she holds herself apart because she is hoping that *you* might make an overture?"

Octavia stared at him for a moment, then said, "No one who looks like that would be shy."

"It's not a choice."

But Octavia had formed her opinion and would not relinquish it. She shook her head, and said, "It doesn't matter if she is shy. It is unkind of her not to consider the feelings of the young ladies who do not attract as many suitors as she does."

"Good God, Octavia, what has Miss Passmore done to hurt you? Is there even anyone here at Finchley you might wish to court you?"

That seemed to silence her, at least for a moment.

After a few seconds of grinding her teeth, Octavia mumbled, "There is Hugh."

Oh Lord, the morning only needed *this*.

"Hugh's not going to marry anyone who won't be delighted to give birth atop a horse," Alec snapped. "And besides that, he's not interested. He still thinks you're twelve."

"You *talked* to him about me?" Octavia said, aghast.

"He told me he was thinking of getting married. I mentioned you."

"You *what*?" she practically shrieked. "How could you *do* such a thing?"

Alec let his head fall back and groaned. He had to find her a husband. Soon. He couldn't take much more of this.

"How will I face him?" she moaned. "He will think I have set my cap."

"Haven't you?"

"No!"

"Fine. Tell me who you want. Hammond-Betts? The other one? Don't say Bretton because even I can't scare you up a duke."

"The other one's name is Mr. Glover," she said in a small, petulant voice.

"Do you like him?"

"I don't dislike him."

Hadn't he already had this conversation this morning? About a horse?

"I will see what I can do to have you seated together this evening," he said. Preferably far, far down the table from him.

Octavia's eyes widened. "What are you going to do?"

"Oh, for heaven's sake, I'm not going to paint a sign. I'll ask Carolyn. Very quietly. She'll be happy to do it. She's a ridiculous matchmaker."

Octavia pressed her lips together, clearly trying to decide if she could trust her brother with such a critical endeavor. Finally, she must have concluded that she had no choice because she said, somewhat curtly, "Thank you."

He said nothing for several seconds, then asked, "May I go down to breakfast now?"

She nodded, then followed him to the door. But before he could depart, she let out a quiet exclamation and put her hand on his arm. "Just one more thing, brother."

He turned wearily. "What is it?"

"There are to be games today. Archery, badminton, and hide-and-seek."

"Don't shoot Miss Passmore," he said immediately.

"*Alec.* I'm not going to—" She let out a ladylike snort and shook her head, obviously deciding there was little point in defending herself. "I was just going to ask if you might do me a favor. Will you play hide-and-seek?"

"Am I *three*?" he asked sarcastically.

"Everyone will be playing," she told him, ignoring his jibe. "Will you partner Miss Passmore?"

He straightened. Now *this* sounded interesting. Except—"Since when are there partners in hide-and-seek?"

"There aren't. But could you pay her some attention?" Octavia made a flitting motion with her hands. "Take her off to the side or something. Distract her."

"Remove her from the rest of the group, you mean."

"*Yes*," Octavia said, as if she'd just got through to a slow student. "If she's not there, the gentlemen might actually pay attention to the rest of us."

"What makes you think she will wish to spend time with me?" Alec asked.

Octavia looked at him as if he were an idiot. "Because you're—Oh for heaven's sake, all of my friends are in love with you. Even I'll concede you're handsome."

"My heart swells at your show of sisterly affection."

"*Don't* act like that," she warned him.

"Like what?"

"*My heart swells*," she mimicked. She snapped out of her caricature, and said sternly, "Women don't like to be on the receiving end of sarcasm."

"They only like to give it," he drawled.

She didn't even pretend to be insulted. "Please try to keep Miss Passmore away from the rest of us this afternoon. Can you do that for me?"

Alec rather thought he could.

Chapter 7

"R ules, everyone!" Lady Finchley called out. "There are rules."

Gwen waited patiently as her hostess attempted to gain the attention of her small crowd of guests. Everyone seemed to have broken off into smaller groups. Gwen supposed she was in the Lady Finchley-Lord Briarly-Duke of Bretton group, if for no other reason than accident of location.

"No one listens to me," Lady Finchley said to her brother, who was standing directly next to her, looking as if he'd rather be elsewhere.

Gwen watched them with interest. She loved watching people. Besides, it helped her keep her eyes off Alec, who was several yards away, dutifully attending to his sister, who appeared to have set her cap for Allen Glover.

She was being a bit obvious about it, but Allen did not seem to mind. In fact, he was blushing and giddy with the attention. Gwen was happy for him; like her, he was shy, and it was nice to see him having such a good time.

"Everyone!" Lady Finchley trilled again. "Your attention, please!"

But Octavia Darlington kept chattering on to Emily Mottram, who was making eyes at George Hammond-Betts. Gwen's mother had attached herself to an older woman who Gwen thought was Alec's great-aunt, and the pair of them were having an impassioned discussion about waterfowl.

Gwen hoped that Mrs. Darlington was not a great champion of birds; her mother's opinion of ducks was that they were best stewed in sauce.

Off to the right, the Duke of Bretton was talking with Lady Sorrell, probably about that horse he was trying so hard to buy from Lord Briarly. Lady Sorrell was nodding and even seemed to have something to offer the conversation, which Gwen found interesting. She herself didn't have much interest in cattle, but she'd found that most men did not give much value to a woman's opinion on the subject.

"Does anyone want to know the rules?" Lady Finchley tried.

No one did, apparently.

"Hugh," Lady Finchley sighed.

Lord Briarly put two fingers in his mouth and let out an amazing whistle.

Conversation ceased.

"Well done, Hugh," Alec murmured. Gwen, too, was impressed.

Lady Finchley acknowledged this with a pretty smile. "My brother is a man of unique talents."

"I am occasionally useful," Lord Briarly said in a droll voice.

"Now that I have your attention—Thank you, Hugh"—Lady Finchley dipped her head toward her brother—"perhaps I might set out the rules."

"Are there rules to hide-and-seek?" someone asked.

"There are at *my* home," Lady Finchley returned pertly. "First of all, no one is to wander off the property. Our neighbor to the north is most unpleasant, and he has terrible eyesight. He's likely to mistake one of you for a grouse."

Several young ladies gasped.

"It's a joke," Alec told them.

"Oh, no it's not," Lady Finchley said, not even taking a breath before continuing. "If it rains, the game is canceled, and we shall convene in the drawing room with brandy and biscuits."

"Is there a reason we cannot cancel right now

and move straight to the brandy?" the Duke of Bretton murmured.

"I think I see a cloud," someone else said hopefully.

"Hush, the both of you," Lady Finchley continued. "We shall have two seekers, but they may not work together. The rest of you shall hide, and—"

"The rest of *us*?" her brother cut in. He turned on her with suspicion in his eyes. "What about you?"

"Oh, I shall be supervising." She waved a hand through the air as if motioning to a large canvas. "Someone must monitor all the details."

"That person could be me," he pointed out.

"When you are found," she continued to the crowd, rather determinedly not looking at her brother, "you must return to the house and tell me which of our seekers found you. The winner shall be whoever is last to be found, with the consolation going to the more successful seeker."

She was met with silence.

"You win if no one finds you," she said briskly, "and come in second if you find more people than the other seeker."

This seemed to be a more effective directive, especially after Mr. Hammond-Betts asked, "Are there prizes?"

"Of *course* there are prizes," Lady Finchley exclaimed. "What good are games without prizes?"

She flashed the crowd a wide smile. "I shall tell you all about the prizes just as soon as I decide what they are."

"Carolyn!" someone groaned.

"Oh, call me unprepared," she said with a wave of her hand. "I'm doing my best."

"I'm still voting for the brandy," the Duke of Bretton drawled.

"Just for that," Lady Finchley said, "*you* shall be one of the seekers."

She turned to Gwen, presumably because she was the closest female. "It means he cannot escape the game quickly by choosing an obvious location and getting himself found in the first five minutes."

"Very clever," Gwen said.

"Yes, I thought so. I would make you a seeker, too," she said, turning to her brother, "but I think it should be a woman." She scanned the crowd, her eyes falling first on Gwen, who gave a silent plea not to be picked. Lady Finchley must have seen the panic in her eyes because, after moving her outstretched arm through the air like a protractor, she stopped at Alec's younger sister, and said, "Miss Darlington! You shall be our other seeker!"

Octavia clapped her hands together in delight, cooing something at Mr. Glover that Gwen couldn't quite hear. Gwen couldn't imagine wanting to be the seeker in such a game. To have to roam the grounds *looking* for people—how awful.

Gwen was already plotting how she might get her sketchbook before she went out to hide. If she found a good spot, she could win the game and have hours of blissful solitude.

Although . . .

She stole a glance at Alec, then looked away when she saw that he was stealing a glance at her. She couldn't help but smile, though. Maybe blissful solitude wasn't what she wanted right now. She was so used to spending parties trying to escape that it hadn't even occurred to her that this time there might be someone she did not wish to escape from.

This time, there might be someone she wished to escape *with*.

She could feel her face grow warm, and she kept her gaze on the grass, afraid to look up with her cheeks so obviously pink. Any hope she had of remaining unnoticed, however, was dashed when she heard a warm voice in her ear say, "You're blushing."

"I'm not," she lied, but she knew that her cheeks had grown even pinker, just at the sound of Alec's voice.

"Liar," he murmured. "Whatever can you be thinking about?"

Gwen raised her head to reply, but before she could speak, Octavia Darlington joined them. "Do your best, brother," she said with a grin at Alec. "I'll find you."

"Please do," he replied. "I'm looking forward to savoring my brandy while Bretton slogs through the mud."

"It's not that muddy," Gwen said.

"It will be with those shoes," Alec replied, nodding toward his sister's slippers.

"Oh, these old things?" Octavia said. "They are quite well-worn. I was nearly ready to dispose of them."

"Is it any wonder my bills are so high?" Alec murmured.

Gwen bit back a laugh, then quickly sobered her face when Octavia shot her a scowl.

"Your sister doesn't like me," she said, once Octavia had departed.

"Right now I don't much like my sister," Alec replied tightly.

Gwen didn't know how to reply to that. She was probably supposed to be all sweetness and light and cry out something like, "Oh, don't say that!" But Octavia Darlington had been scowling at her for four months now, and Gwen was frankly sick of it.

"She's just jealous," Alec said. He let out a tired sigh, then quickly buried the unpleasantness with a shake of his head. He turned to her with a smile, and said, "She has always wanted titian hair."

Gwen rolled her eyes.

"It's true," he insisted. "Green eyes, too."

"I don't believe you."

"Oh very well, I lied about the eyes, but I know I've heard her moan about her hair."

"She probably wants more curl," Gwen said. Most young ladies did.

He looked mystified by the entire conversation. "Whatever it is she wants, it isn't what she has."

"Your sister is lovely," Gwen said. It was true. Octavia had gorgeous thick hair and very fine gray eyes. Rather like Alec's, which Gwen had recently become quite partial to.

"Not as lovely as you," Alec said quietly, "and I'm afraid she knows it."

Their eyes met, and Gwen almost allowed herself to sway toward him. The moment seemed to call for a kiss, and as she gazed up—

"Stop," he said in a strangled voice.

"Stop what?"

"Looking at me like that."

Gwen swallowed nervously and stepped back, hastily looking about to see if anyone had noticed her staring at him like a lovesick cow. Lady Finchley was looking their way, but Gwen couldn't be sure if she was watching them or the Duke of Bretton, who was leaning against a tree, counting aloud with a great show of exaggerated patience.

"Thirty-four . . . thirty-five . . . One hundred, you say?"

"One thousand," Lady Finchley said with a wicked grin.

"Shall we hide?" Alec whispered.

Gwen looked at him in shock. "Together?"

"There is nothing in the rules saying we can't."

"I seem to recall failing in maths at Eton," the duke said. "Something about triple-digit numbers."

"It's a difficult concept," Lady Finchley said, "but I'm sure you'll catch on."

Gwen laughed at the sight of England's most eligible bachelor, slouched against a tree, counting like a schoolboy.

"I don't know what he was thinking," Alec said, shaking his head. "He should know better than to try to outwit Carolyn Finchley."

"You've tried, then?" Gwen asked.

"Oh, many many times," Alec said, as they wandered off behind the house. "I have known her since she was in pinafores. Her brother is one of my closest friends."

"Lord Briarly seems like a very nice man," she said.

Alec looked at her sharply. "You're *not* to marry him."

Gwen very nearly choked on her own tongue. "Excuse me?"

"He's looking for a wife. I am not sure what has brought it on with such urgency, but . . ." Alec paused, then said, "Can you keep a secret?"

"I can," Gwen confirmed.

"He has made a list. Or rather, his sisters have done so. Of prospective brides."

Suddenly, many of the previous day's events began to make sense. "Am I on it?" Gwen asked with a frown.

"Of course," Alec replied. He was rather matter-of-fact about it, so much so that Gwen found herself nonplussed. He turned to her with surprise. "Did you think you wouldn't be?"

"I—I don't know."

"It does not matter. If he asks, under no circumstances should you accept."

Gwen could not help but wonder if he might have alternate plans in mind, but before she could even lament her lack of boldness (she could never bring herself to ask, never), Alec shook his head and said, "You would be miserable."

"I would?" And then some devil within her made her ask, "Why?"

He gave her a very stern look. "Hugh lives and breathes horses. He'll not have time for any wife who does not share his passions."

"Some women would find appeal in such an arrangement."

Alec looked at her intently. "Would you?"

Gwen swallowed. "I suppose it would depend upon my husband."

They had reached the edge of the clearing and

113

were now stepping into the woods. A shadow fell across her skin, and she shivered.

But she wasn't so sure it was because of the cold. Alec had stopped walking, and one of his hands had found hers. Their fingers entwined, and he tugged her toward him. She looked up at him, and her breath caught. He was watching her with such intensity; surely, she thought, he could see straight down to her soul.

"What if I were your husband?" he asked softly. "Would you want such an arrangement?"

Silently, she shook her head.

"Nor I," he murmured, bringing her fingers to her lips. "A husband and wife should share their passions, I think."

Gwen smiled. She felt feminine. She felt bold. "We're not talking about horses any longer, are we?"

"Definitely not."

"Books? My father is passionate about his library."

"Some books," Alec said, his voice so seductive that Gwen could only wonder what books he was thinking of.

"Embroidery?" she teased. "My mother is very passionate about her embroidery."

"I am only passionate about embroidery as pertains to what may be worn on your body."

Her cheeks burned, and yet the rest of her felt rather anxious. Anxious and delicious.

He leaned down and kissed the corner of her mouth. "I am more passionate about embroidery as pertains to what may be removed from your body."

"Oh my," she whispered. "I don't think we're nearly far enough into the woods."

He let out a huge peal of laughter, then grabbed her hand and pulled. She ran after him, her legs having to add a hop to her run, just to keep up with his longer stride. She was laughing all the way, blissful and breathless, leaping over tree roots, and ducking under branches.

"Stop!" she pleaded, just barely dodging a bramble that was jutting out onto the path. "I can't—oh!"

He'd stopped.

She slammed into him, their bodies meeting with sudden, thorough force, then—It couldn't be stopped. He didn't say a word, and she didn't want him to. His arms were around her, and her hands were in his hair, and whatever they'd done earlier that morning, it was nothing like *this*.

Gwen did not know what had come over her, could not have even dreamed that she might feel such a sense of urgency. But when she crashed into him, her body pressing up against the hard length of his, something inside of her had broken free. She wanted—no she needed—to feel him, to kiss him, to *show* him that she was not just shy little Gwendolyn Passmore. She was a woman, a woman with passions. And she wanted *him*.

She moaned his name, pulling him more tightly against her. She felt powerful. She felt fierce. She wanted to take charge of her life. Of this moment.

Of the world!

She laughed. She threw her head back and laughed.

"What is it?" he asked, panting.

"I don't know," she admitted, barely catching her own breath. "I'm just so happy. I feel like . . . I feel . . ."

He pulled her back to him, but he didn't kiss her again. He just held her close, gazing down into her eyes.

"I feel free," she whispered.

Chapter 8

$\mathcal{A}$lec had not meant to kiss her.

 Very well, that wasn't true. He *had* meant to kiss her. He just hadn't meant to kiss her like *this*. But now . . .

He couldn't have stopped if the king himself arrived on the scene and ordered it. For the first time in his life he was moved by something beyond desire, beyond even need. She was his. He had to make her his. He had to *show* her . . .

Hell, he didn't know what he had to show her. He just knew that he had to . . .

That was it. He didn't know anything. He didn't know anything except her and him and this moment and this kiss and the wind and leaves and scent of wet earth and—

"You're so beautiful," he whispered. He had to say it. He had to.

"I feel beautiful," she said softly. "You make me feel beautiful."

He touched her hair, the red-gold strands sliding along his fingers. She'd worn it up, but their run through the woods had sent her coiffure tumbling around her shoulders. "How does it know how to do this?" he murmured.

"Do what?"

He lifted a lock, watching the curl bounce gently in the air, then slid his finger inside the hollow core. "How do all the strands know how to gather together to make a curl?"

She looked as if she might laugh. "I have very intelligent hair."

"Just your hair?"

"My toes are quite clever."

Alec was suddenly consumed by a desire to see her feet. "This grows interesting."

"What about you?"

"Me?" He pretended to give the question serious thought. "I have very knowledgeable hands."

She took one and brought it to her mouth. "I like your hands."

He didn't say anything, did not trust himself to speak. He could barely draw breath, barely remember his name as she kissed each knuckle in turn.

"They are kind hands," she said softly. "And very capable."

"Oh my God," he moaned. "Gwen."

But she did not stop. She turned it over and looked at his palm. "Do you see this?" she said, touching the sensitive ridge just below the base of his fingers. "Calluses. How does a pampered earl get calluses?"

"I like working with my hands," he said hoarsely.

She nodded. "I do, too."

"I like taking long walks," he said.

She kissed his palm. "I do, too."

And then, because it seemed to fit the moment, he blurted out, "I like green."

She looked up at him, with those amazing green eyes. He hadn't even been thinking of her eyes when he'd spoken. Or had he?

"Is it your favorite color?" she asked.

He nodded.

And she smiled. "It is mine, too."

He watched her, wondering when it had become so fascinating simply to see another human being blink. But on her, on Gwen, it was a ballet. He could have stood there all afternoon, watching her lashes sweep up and down. The precise color of them against her cheek, the way she seemed to smile every time her eyes closed . . .

He was growing fanciful.

He was growing foolish.

He didn't care.

"My second favorite color is purple," she said, smiling up at him.

He almost said, "Mine, too," except it wasn't. And so he grinned back, and said, "I like orange."

"I like orang*es*."

He leaned down, letting his forehead rest on hers. "I like plums."

Her lips found his, but only fleetingly. "I like strawberries," she said.

He paused. "What has that to do with anything?"

She shrugged helplessly and let out a little laugh. "I don't know."

He touched her chin, then let his fingers trail along the edge of her jaw to her neck. "Do you have any idea how much I want to kiss you right now?"

"Some," she whispered.

"I have never felt like this before," he told her. Because he had to. She had to know that he was not inexperienced. He'd been with women. He'd rarely been without women. But he needed her to know that with her it was all new.

"Neither have I," she said, then admitted, "I don't understand it."

He kissed her again, nipping lightly on her lower lip. "I don't think you have to understand it." He moved to her throat, growling with desire as she let her head fall back, allowing him unfettered access to her warm, soft skin.

He turned her until her back was against a tree, and then he leaned her against the trunk, his mouth finding the base of her throat again, moving down, down the hollow above her collarbone, down to the swell of her breast, peeking above the edge of her frock.

"Alec," she moaned, but he heard nothing in her voice that wanted him to stop, and so he moved even lower, daringly so, running his tongue under the frilly lace edge. His hands were on her shoulders, and before he knew it, he was nudging one side of her bodice down.

He kissed her shoulder, then the soft flesh of her arm, then her breast, and then slowly, achingly, he took the tip in his mouth and gently nipped at it, growling with pleasure when he heard her soft moan of surprise.

Somewhere in the recesses of his mind he knew he had to stop. She was innocent, for God's sake, and he was making love to her against a tree. In the midst of a game of hide-and-seek. But he couldn't bring himself to pull away. Not just yet, not when she was sweet and passionate in his arms. Not when she was making those sounds, indescribable and endlessly seductive, from the back of her throat.

"That thing I said before," he gasped, pressing his arousal against her even though he knew it would only make him feel more frustrated, "about if I were your husband . . ."

She made a noise. He thought it might have been, "Yes?"

"It was a proposal." He pulled away, just far enough so that he might actually breathe. "Clumsy, I know, but—" He tried to sink to one knee but found he hadn't the balance, so instead he just kind of leaned funny. "Will you marry me?"

She did not say anything right away, which might have worried him except that she was so clearly trying to catch her breath. Finally, she looked up, and said, "Really?"

He nodded.

She nodded.

And thus Alec Darlington, the seventh Earl of Charters, and Miss Gwendolyn Passmore, daughter of Lord and Lady Stillworth, became engaged.

It was not the story they would share with their children. That version had rose petals, a diamond engagement ring, and (this was a last-minute addition to the narrative) a catapult.

They would have got away with it, too, if Aunt Octavia (as she would eventually be known) had not decided to tell her side of the story.

* * *

"OH MY GOD!"

It was what Gwen was thinking. *Oh my God oh my God oh my God.* Really, what else would she be thinking? She had (she was pretty sure) just got herself engaged to the Earl of Charters, who was (she was quite sure) doing very wicked things to her left breast, which (she was definitely sure) she was enjoying very much.

"OH MY GOD!"

Gwen's thoughts, however, rarely took the form of a shriek.

"ALEC!"

She froze. Or rather, Alec froze, his large hand still covering her. And his face took on an expression of dread.

"Alec Darlington, don't you ignore me!"

Gwen heard Alec curse, but still, he did not move. With great trepidation, she peeked out from behind him.

"What are you doing?" yelled Octavia Darlington. Her arms were up in the air, waving madly about, and Gwen could not help but think that it should be quite obvious what they were doing. She ducked her head back behind Alec, mortified beyond belief.

"Alec!" Octavia yelled again, and this time she actually whacked her brother on the back. "What are you doing? Oh my God, Alec, when I asked you to get rid of Miss Passmore, I didn't mean this!"

"Octavia," he growled. "Shut up."

But Octavia Darlington, once on her high horse, refused to dismount. "Don't you tell—"

"Quiet!" he snapped. He twisted into what looked like an extremely uncomfortable position. But he was keeping Gwen covered while he turned to face his sister, so she was grateful for that.

"Good Lord, Octavia, you sound like a fishwife."

"How could you do this to me?" she yelled.

"I assure you," he bit off, "it has nothing to do with you."

But then Gwen started thinking. "What did she mean . . ." she began.

"You were kissing her!" Octavia shrieked. "Kissing her!"

"For the love of—"

"What did she mean," Gwen said, with greater volume, "about getting rid of me?"

"Nothing," Alec said quickly, then: "Octavia, turn your back."

"I will do no such thing."

"Turn your back or, as God is my witness, I will strip you of your dowry."

Octavia gasped in outrage, but she turned. Gwen stepped away from Alec and righted her dress. "What did she *mean*," she said firmly, "about getting rid of me?"

"She is an idiot," Alec snarled.

"I heard that!" Octavia snarled right back.

"You were meant to!"

"Oh!" She planted her hands on her hips. "May I turn?"

"Er, yes," Gwen answered, since Alec was too busy glowering.

Octavia turned around, and Gwen only barely resisted the urge to take a step back. She looked furious. Her color was high, her ringlets (which Gwen did not think were natural) were bouncing, and her eyes were positively venomous.

"You are the worst brother in the world," she said to Alec.

"No!" Gwen cut in furiously. "Don't say that. You are not allowed to say that."

"You can't speak to me that way."

Gwen stepped forward, jabbing her finger in Octavia's direction. "Don't you ever say that about him again. Do you have any idea what I would give to have one more minute with my brother? One chance to tell him how much I love him?"

Octavia's mouth clamped into a firm line. Gwen couldn't tell if she was angry or embarrassed, and at that moment, she didn't care. "My brother was my best friend, and he looked out for me, and if he were still alive, he'd be here at this house party with me, just like yours is here with you, so don't you *dare* say that your brother is—"

"Gwen," Alec said gently, placing a hand on her arm.

But she would not let him comfort her. She shook him off, taking another step toward Octavia. "Why do you hate me?" she demanded.

"I'm not talking to her," Octavia said, turning pointedly to her brother.

"No," Gwen shot back. "You can't ignore me."

"Alec," Octavia said, "I want you to escort me back to the house."

"You can't ignore me," Gwen said again. All through the season, Octavia Darlington had been just horrid. She never invited Gwen anywhere. Her little groups of friends always seemed to close ranks when Gwen was near. And when the two were forced into contact, she was sour and curt.

Unless there were witnesses.

And Gwen, quite simply, had had enough. "Why do you hate me?"

"I don't hate you," Octavia sniffed.

"Oh, yes you do." Gwen turned to Alec and planted her own hands on her hips. "She does."

"I know," he said with a sigh.

Octavia let out a gasp, then pointed an angry finger at Gwen. "*She* is the one who is rude and standoffish. *She* is the one who steals every available gentleman from the rest of us. She is always surrounded, and does she make any attempt to send some our way? No!"

Gwen could only gape. If Octavia only knew how desperately she hated the season. She'd have happily sent over *all* of the gentlemen if she'd had any idea how to do so.

"Well, you won't have to worry about that any longer," Alec said to Octavia. "I have asked Miss Passmore to be my wife, and she has consented." With a sharp, sudden movement he turned back to Gwen. "You have, haven't you?"

Gwen started to say yes, but then she narrowed her eyes. "You didn't tell me what she meant about getting rid of me."

"It was nothing," Alec ground out. "She asked me to distract you so that the other gentlemen would not seek you out. A request with which, I might add, I was happy to comply."

"You didn't tell me you were interested in her," Octavia muttered.

"Would it have made a difference? Good Lord, Octavia, and don't you say yes!" He held up a hand, warding off whatever it was his sister had been about to say. "If you say yes, I will not be able to forgive you. I promise you that."

"But—"

"Don't!" he said sharply. "If you say yes, that means you care more about hurting Miss Passmore than you do about your own happiness, and if that is true, I can't bear to think that I might have had any part in your upbringing."

Finally, Octavia was silenced.

Alec turned back to Gwen, taking both of her hands in his. "Gwen," he said. "*The* Gwen."

She felt herself smile. She couldn't hold it in.

"I love you. I have no idea how such a thing happens in so short a time, but I know myself, and I know that it is true."

Gwen swallowed, trying to hold back tears. She didn't know, either, wouldn't have thought it possible, except . . .

She felt the exact same way.

"I adore you."

She nodded, hoping he would correctly interpret that as, "Me, too."

"I want to spend my life with you."

"I draw bunnies," she blurted out.

He blinked.

"What?" Octavia asked.

"In my sketchbook," Gwen said. She had no idea why she was saying this, and in fact, was already coming to regret it, but now that she'd started, she could not stop. "You asked to see my drawings. I draw bunnies. And squirrels."

"That's n—"

"With fangs."

"Fangs?" Octavia sounded curious, and perhaps a bit delighted as well.

Gwen ignored her, keeping her attention on

Alec. "Some of them look like people I know."

He started to smile. "Do any resemble me?"

She almost lied. Almost. "There was one squirrel," she admitted. "From this morning."

Alec's grin grew wider. "Is he handsome?"

"Not very, no."

He started to laugh.

"But I did draw him before I saw you at the lake. If I were to draw it now . . ."

"If you were to draw it now . . ." he prodded.

"I don't know," she said, frowning as she considered the question. "I suppose it might look a bit like Lord Briarly."

Alec let out a loud bark of laughter at that. "What has Hugh done to you?"

"Nothing," she admitted, "but there is no one else to consider. And he did write that horrid list."

"What list?" Octavia asked.

"Maybe you could give him horsy teeth," Alec suggested, tugging her a little closer, "instead of fangs."

"I could do that."

"What list?" Octavia asked again.

Gwen smiled at her new fiancé, letting herself sway into his arms. "I could draw him as a horse," she said, starting to lose her focus on the conversation. Alec was looking at her in that way again, and—

"Don't you kiss her again!" Octavia yelled. "Don't you kiss her in front of me."

Too late.

He kissed her.

And she loved it.

Almost as much as she loved him.

Chapter 9

Carolyn didn't think that it would be boasting to say that her plans generally went exactly as she intended them. One couldn't run the three assorted households attached to the Marquessate of Finchley and not become an expert at organizing people and things. But just now she was finding herself in the grip of a new and rather frustrating emotion.

The Duke of Bretton was still leaning against the tree and counting, trying to get to one thousand and obviously hoping that she wasn't noticing when he skipped numbers. Or hundreds of numbers.

"This is hide-and-seek, Duke," she told him. "Please try to keep your mind on those numbers."

Bretton groaned and kept going.

"Darling," she said to her husband, who had

just ambled up, "did you see who Gwendolyn Passmore walked off with?"

Her husband squinted around, looking about as uninterested as a man frankly bored by the mating practices of the *ton* could look. "Last time I saw, she had Charters gaping after her like a trout on a hook."

"She's not supposed to be with Charters," Carolyn hissed. "I marked her out for Hugh. And if she didn't want Hugh, it was supposed to be because she was in love with *him*—" she waved her hand at the duke—"but now that it turns out he can't even count properly, I'll have to forgive her for that."

"Nothing wrong with Charters," her husband said. "Good old family, an earl, nice fellow."

"I had her marked for Hugh," Carolyn said, feeling a little tearful. "Now my brother may never get married. I'm not sure that Miss Peyton is suitable."

"Why not? I had an interesting chat with her yesterday about drainage."

"That's just it," Carolyn said. "I like Kate, I really do. But I'm not sure that Hugh will appreciate all her knowledge. And she's so blunt!"

"Men like that," her husband said, bluntly. "Plus she's got a sweet little mouth. Though not," he said, leaning over and dropping a kiss on her lips, "as sweet as yours."

The duke straightened up from the tree. "One

thousand," he said triumphantly. "I say, where is everyone?"

"That's for you to find out," Carolyn said, almost waspishly, except she was never waspish. Well, hardly ever. "They're *hiding*, since this is hide-and-seek. Miss Darlington made it to a thousand at least two minutes ago, and she already ran off to find people."

Her husband grabbed her by the hand. "We need to hide," he said.

"Hide? I can't hide. I'm supposed to delegate. I have to stay—"

He pulled her away. "Go find everyone who's hiding," she called to the duke over her shoulder. And then, because His Grace had the look of a man about to take a nap or chase after that glass of brandy he had been talking about, "Go on, find them!"

Her husband pulled her straight into the house, up the stairs, and into her bedchamber. Luckily, her maid was nowhere to be seen. "What on earth are you doing, Finchley?" she asked, panting.

He pushed the door behind them. "We're alone."

"Well?"

"Then I'm not *Finchley*, am I?"

Despite herself, a small smile caught the edge of Carolyn's lips. "I suppose not."

He backed her against the door, his big warm

body crowding her against the wood. "So what's my name, then?" He bent his head and started doing something delicious to her neck.

"Hugh calls you Finchbird," she said teasingly. She found herself untying his cravat without quite knowing how it happened.

"My name," her husband growled, "is Piers."

"Yes, but you don't like being called Piers in public," she whispered. She had to whisper because he had managed to wrench down the bodice of her gown and . . . She gasped.

"We're not in public," he said, swinging her into his arms.

She put her hand on the curve of his cheek. "I shouldn't be doing this. I'm supposed to be organizing games for my guests. They'll wonder where I am."

"Games," he said with scorn. "Leave them alone, Carolyn. In only a few days, I've witnessed more games than I ever played in the nursery. They're grown men and women." He dropped her on the bed.

She lay back and wondered whether she should let him continue. "Games are useful," she said, loving the little wrinkles by Piers's eyes and the way he was unbuttoning her gown, faster than her maid could on a good day.

"Nonsense," he said, easing her gown down over her arms and starting on her corset.

"They force people to be together," she explained, kicking off her slippers. "It's part of my master plan to ensure that Hugh finds someone appropriate to marry."

"Maybe Hugh doesn't want to marry yet," Piers said.

"He does! He's the one who asked *me* for the list. But I'm afraid that Charters has stolen away Gwendolyn Passmore. I'll just have to focus on Kate now."

"Just as well," Piers said, wrestling with a recalcitrant corset tie. "Oops, snapped that. Gwendolyn wouldn't have kept Hugh on his toes."

"Do I keep you on your toes?" She stared at him, feeling a little qualm.

He pulled off her corset. Carolyn looked down. Somehow, he'd managed to strip her down to her chemise, and he was still dressed. She reached out and started unbuttoning his waistcoat. "Piers?" she asked. "Do I?"

Her husband was utterly absorbed in stroking the curve of her breast, and though she appreciated the thought, she persisted. "Do I keep you on your toes?"

"No," he said thirstily, stripping off his coat and throwing it to the side.

She blinked at him. "No?"

His shirt flew across the room, and his boots thumped onto the floor. "I don't?" She felt absurdly disappointed. Of course Piers loved her. He—

A big male body landed on top of hers. "You don't want me *on my toes*," he growled in her ear, pressing down in a way that . . . well . . . made Carolyn feel a sudden wave of heat. She wound her arms around his neck.

"I'm much better company when I'm off my feet altogether," her husband continued. He pulled up her chemise, and his mouth descended on her breast.

"I don't know . . . we should be out there playing hide-and-seek," she whispered, nipping his ear.

She felt his shiver right down the length of his body.

"I am now going to play hide-and-seek," he said a few minutes later, grinning down at her.

By then Carolyn had forgotten the conversation. She reached up to him. "Please, I need—"

"First *hide*," he said, a positively wicked spark in his eye, "and we'll worry about *seek* later."

The marchioness gasped, and then—well, gasped again.

By the time the marquess and his marchioness went downstairs again, the game of hide-and-seek was over. Rather reluctantly, Carolyn slipped her hand out from her husband's. There was a group of young ladies clustered around Miss Octavia Darlington, who looked, to her experienced eye, as if they were getting into a tizzy about something.

Piers pulled her back for just a second, and whispered in her ear, "How long until bedtime?"

She looked back at him, feeling a little blush in her cheeks. She shook her head. "Hush!" And then she moved away from him, feeling as if she'd like nothing more than to go back upstairs and take a long nap.

"Hello, dear ones," she said, nimbly inserting herself into the circle. "Do share the story with me, Octavia."

Octavia had her hand thrown over her face and was moaning "My eyes! My eyes!" but at the sound of Carolyn's voice, her hand fell down.

"It's nothing, Lady Finchley," she said. Two other girls nodded. "Nothing at all."

Carolyn sighed. She knew that *nothing*. "Now, I insist," she said gently. "What has happened to your eyes, Octavia? Are you getting a sty? Or a case of pinkeye?"

"No!" Octavia exclaimed. "It's just that my brother—"

Carolyn kept her smile bright. She'd bet one hundred pounds that Gwendolyn Passmore wouldn't be joining her extended family. Poor Hugh. "Let me guess," she said. "Your brother has fallen in love."

"Well, you *could* call it that," Octavia said disapprovingly.

Carolyn took the young lady by the arm. "We

could call it that because it would be the truth, wouldn't it?"

Octavia was silent for a moment, so Carolyn gave her a little pinch. "Because I'm just guessing, but I've noticed that your brother seemed enamored with Gwendolyn Passmore."

"He—in the woods—"

"He asked Gwendolyn to marry him in the woods," Carolyn said, adroitly cutting off whatever indiscretion Octavia was about to blurt out. "Isn't that romantic?" She fixed the other girls with a minatory glance, and they all nodded obediently. "I think we can all agree that darling Gwendolyn was the most beautiful girl of the season, and we can also agree that it's quite nice to see her so happily matched."

They all nodded like little puppets.

"Plus," she added, "all her suitors are now free to look elsewhere."

The girls' faces brightened. She couldn't remember ever being such a silly little cluck, but one had to assume she had been. She lowered her voice. "Have any of you met Captain Neill Oakes yet?"

They all shook their heads.

"A war hero," she told them. "I was there when he was presented to the queen."

The girls smiled politely. No, she was never this silly. "Of course, he had a terrible reputation before he left for the Continent," she added. "Quite the rake! A man that handsome is a danger to young ladies. Your mothers should be very wary, unless the tiger's changed his stripes." The polite disinterest fell from their faces, and their eyes sparkled.

She pulled Octavia's arm closer to her own. "Let's go for a little walk, dearest. I'd like to show you the view from the west window."

But she didn't bother with the view when she got there. "Gwendolyn is going to be your sister-in-law," she said to Octavia. "And unless I miss my guess, you were about to say something very indiscreet about a future member of your family."

Octavia's jaw set with an audible click of her teeth. "You should have seen—"

"Your brother is *in love*," Carolyn said, feeling a bit sorry for Miss Darlington. Clearly, she was so jealous that she couldn't see past her own nose.

Octavia nodded. "I know."

"And Gwendolyn as a family member might be very different from Gwendolyn as a rival," Carolyn pointed out. "She's a lovely person, and I would quite like to have her as my sister. I was hoping she would fall in love with my brother Hugh."

"I suppose I'm lucky," Octavia said. To Carolyn's dismay, her eyes welled with tears. "I get to stand next to her for the rest of my life, so that everyone can compare my figure to hers, and comment on how nice she is, and how sweet she is, and then they can have fun talking about how unpleasant I am!"

"Octavia!" Carolyn cried. "It won't be like that!"

Octavia dashed away a tear falling down her cheek. "She made me out to be just horrible in front of my brother," she said, gulping a little. "She—she said that she'd give anything to have just one more minute with her deceased brother, as if—as if I didn't love *my* brother, and I do."

"I'm sure that wasn't what she meant," Carolyn said, winding an arm around Octavia's shoulder. "I'd guess you had said something to Alec, didn't you? Something Gwendolyn didn't like?"

Octavia nodded.

"And she defended him. Do you know what, Octavia? From now on, your brother is going to have someone who loves him so much that she will *always* defend him. He's found someone who will be with him, and beside him, for life. Who will stand at his shoulder, and give him babies, and generally love him that much."

Octavia smiled mistily. "That sounds so . . . nice. Do you—do you love the marquess that much?"

Carolyn looked over her shoulder and met Piers's eyes. Her heart panged at the very look of him. "Yes," she said without hesitation. "Yes, I do. And you'll find someone like that too, Octavia.

But meanwhile, you simply must be happy for your brother, and for Gwendolyn."

"I will," Octavia said, taking a deep breath. "I've been rather a beast and—and I will."

Piers touched Carolyn's shoulder. "Thought you wanted me," he said. "You had that look in your eye."

Octavia dropped a curtsy. "I'll go find my brother," she said. "I believe I forgot to congratulate him on his betrothal."

Piers wrapped an arm around Carolyn. "Meddling, weren't you?"

She looked up at him and grinned. "Only a little."

Chapter 10

Four years earlier . . .

*M*iss Katherine Peyton watched the tall, broad-shouldered young man stride away down her family manor's drive and saw an opportunity for a private interview with him that she'd been seeking for days.

Had Miss Peyton been older, or wiser, or less riveted by her own intentions, she might have discerned the rigidity in the young Neill Oakes's bearing, the swift anger of his stride, or noted that though he'd forgotten his hat and his thick ebony hair was wind-whipped and his face red with the chill of the blustery November day, he seemed oblivious to it. And she might have wondered why.

But she was not older or wiser, and being absorbed with her own confused and riotous emotions, she did not wonder why. She was just sixteen, newly conscious of her budding femininity and eager to test its effect—especially on the young man heading down the drive. It never occurred to her to ask herself what he'd been doing at Bing Hall in the first place. Neill Oakes treated Bing Hall as his own and had since she could remember, behavior from which neither her mother—when she'd been alive—nor her father to this day had ever dissuaded him.

Perhaps Mr. Peyton felt sorry for Neill because he had no siblings and his mother had died but a few years back and he had resisted the importation of a new stepmother, *very* soon afterward, and the arrival of twin half brothers soon after that, twin brothers everyone in Burnewhinney County agreed were interestingly well developed for being said to be so premature.

Or perhaps Mr. Peyton appreciated Neill's having interceded at Eton for Tom, Mr. Peyton's heir and two years Neill's junior, delivering him from the servitude most junior lads endured there. Or, perhaps Mr. Peyton simply liked the lad, for Neill Oakes did have a devilish quick wit and a winning way and not only with the local lasses. He was just the sort of neck-or-nothing young blood that older country gentlemen liked to think they themselves had been at such an age.

But none of these things crossed Miss Peyton's mind as she grabbed her bonnet from her dresser and dashed down the stairway and through the back hall into the kitchen, where she plucked the housekeeper's shawl from a hook by the outside door and made her escape, hurrying after Neill.

Because she was intent on a kiss.

Gunmetal gray clouds scuttled low above the rustling gold and russet leaves of the poplar-lined avenue. A curt wind, heavy with the promise of storm, nipped at her nose and whipped the long satin sashes of Kate's bonnet, sending them streaming behind her like derby pennants. Neill was a hundred yards ahead of her by the time she made the avenue. She called out, but her voice was drowned in the rattle of leaves, so she lifted her light muslin skirts and ran, heedless of decorum.

She had loved Neill Oakes for as long as she could remember, and though she had never mistaken her emotions for sisterly affection, it had never occurred to her until lately that what she felt was more than friendship. But over the last year she'd found herself looking forward to his visits, eager to engage in verbal swordplay with him, and growing oddly breathless at the sight of his shirt-sleeves rolled up over his extremely masculine fore-arms. She caught herself studying the shape of his lips and wondering about their texture and realized that over the last months she'd become captivated by the hint of an Irish brogue he'd learned from his mother. She found herself eager to enter any conversation that included him as a subject, and as he was a hell bent babe, this was most conversations.

His reputation as a budding blackguard did not worry her; she knew him well. Better than anyone else.

She'd been with him when the groom's son had fallen into the river, and he'd dived right in to save the lad, never saying a word to anyone afterward lest the boy be punished for his carelessness. And she'd witnessed the tender way he held his infant half brothers and the civility with which he responded to his stepmother's ceaseless criticisms. And she knew, too, how deep was the sense of honor in this man whose name was a byword for rakehell.

Once he gave his word, nothing could induce him to renege upon it. Her brother Tom had told her how Neill had labored in Bucky Buckstone's field, hauling rocks the size of melons for five days straight when his father, angry over some imagined irregularity in a bill, had refused to pay an outstanding debt to the man. Neill had assumed the debt himself, offering his back and brawn in payment.

Oh, not that she mistook Neill for a saint. Far from it. He gambled often, his recklessness putting others—including her brothers—at risk as well as himself, and while he might listen civilly to his stepmother's complaints, they did not influence his behavior. Not one bit. He loved nothing better than a good brawl—Tom and he had blacked each other's eyes innumerable times—and he drank too much and too often.

And she was *fully* aware of his reputation with the local girls. She'd have had to be deaf not to, for her brothers—who considered Neill a paragon of all things masculine—were constantly discussing his conquests, and they made little beyond a cursory effort to exclude themselves from her hearing. Indeed, sometimes she overheard Neill himself extolling some girl's—well, *virtue* would hardly be the word for it.

But lately Neill's love life, which she had once sniffed at in disgust, now provoked . . . well, jealousy. He was ever toasting some country beauty at the Black Lion, but never her. He never danced with her at all at any of the local balls and fetes except for the sillier country dances that even children were invited to join in.

He should have. She was very pretty. She had only to look in the mirror to see that her skin was snowy and fine, her hair mirrored the color and sheen of milkweed floss, and her eyes, rather than the pale orbs that generally went with light coloring, were darkest blue, almost black, and therefore remarkable. Of course, she would never have much of a figure. She was simply too short and too reedy. But Harry Fentmorgan, the curate's nephew and a viscount, had told her at this year's harvest ball that she was as delicate as a faerie princess.

When she had informed Neill of this, he'd laughed.

But three nights ago, Billy Eggs, the smithy's apprentice, had raised his pint at the Black Lion and toasted her. She had it firsthand from her maid, Nell, who was second cousin to Nance Hightower, one of the tavern's maids. She'd told Nell, who'd told her, that Billy Eggs had lifted his pint at quarter past ten on Friday evening last, and declared loudly, "To Miss Kate Peyton, the prettiest girl in Burnewhinney County."

Some of the other men present had shouted "To Miss Peyton"—in and of itself, most gratifying—but Neill Oakes had jumped up from his seat "like a bull who'd been stung on the arse" and knocked the pint from Billy's hand, saying, "You won't be toasting Miss Peyton as though she was a common wench. Not in my presence," and everyone had gaped because Neill Oakes was the last man in the county to stand on ceremony, and to hear him upbraid Billy Eggs, with whom he'd shared many an untoward adventure, in so rough a fashion was amazing.

And then Billy had hit Neill, and the whole place had dissolved into a drunken brawl . . .

147

But that wasn't the part that interested Kate—evenings at taverns often dissolved into drunken brawls—what interested Kate was why Neill Oakes had taken such exception to her name being toasted in a tavern. Could it be, she wondered, because he had an especial regard for her good name? And if so, as what? A family friend *or* something more . . . ?

The question, once planted, had grown in significance with each passing hour, plaguing her as sorely as the hives she'd developed after eating mussels last spring. And with just as little relief. For from being ever underfoot, Neill had suddenly and unaccountably disappeared from their home, robbing her of the opportunity to gauge what, if any, tender regard lurked in his jetty eyes.

And if she discerned none? Well, then there was nothing for it but that she ask him flat out why he'd struck Billy Eggs, and if his actions were prompted not by romantic feelings but by a few pints, then it was time—past time—that Neill Oakes started seeing her as a woman.

Either way, by the time she left Neill's company this afternoon, she intended to learn firsthand the texture of Neill Oakes's lips.

She caught up with him on the banks of the river that separated their properties just as he was about to cross the footbridge that led to his family's estate.

"Neill!" she cried out, clutching her bonnet tight to her head against the blustering wind as long tresses of her hair whipped her cheeks pink.

He wheeled around, his thunderous expression smoothing when he saw that it was she, though no welcoming smile encouraged her nearer. But Kate had never needed an invitation to do what she wanted, so she hastened to his side, startled when he bowed as though she was a lady and he a gentleman and they were meeting on the streets of London and not by a muddy river. His good manners lasted exactly as long as it took him to incline his head, for as soon as he raised his eyes, he scowled again.

"What are you doing here, Kate?"

"Following you," she said, searching his eyes for a telltale sign of ardor. The only emotion she saw was exasperation, the same emotion she'd seen in him when she'd painted his father's prize broodmare pink at the county fair when she was ten. She wrapped her shawl close against her, one hand on her bonnet to keep it from blowing off.

He combed his thick dark curls back with his hand. "Well, what do you want?"

"Where have you been? It's been nearly a week since we saw you and you were just at the house but you left without seeing Tom and he was there. It seems most odd. I can only surmise that you have been banned from the premises." She said it lightly, in jest, and therefore did not see the slight jerk that her words invoked. "Have you finally done something that challenges even Father's seemingly limitless ability to find excuses for you?"

"Has no one ever taught you it is rude to pry?" he countered.

"They've tried," she replied, "but how will I find out that which I want to know if no one will volunteer to tell me? Would you rather I sneaked about, ferreting things out? Of course not. 'Twould be most distasteful. All in all, I'd rather be thought rude than artful."

He shook his head, his frown becoming a rueful smile, then a laugh. "Out of the mouths of babes . . ." he said.

"I am not all a babe anymore, Neill," she said, just as the first drops of icy rain began to fall, lightly pelting her upturned face. She shivered. "I am sixteen."

He smiled again. "Yes, I seem to recall you pestering me for a present a few weeks back," he said, shrugging out of his greatcoat and draping it about her shoulders. The big garment swallowed her in its folds, the hem pooling on the damp ground, covering her toes. At once, the scent of him surrounded her, and the heat trapped in the wool warmed her. But she longed for a more intimate knowledge of his scent and warmth from his arms, not his coat.

"Many young ladies have come out by the time they are my age and are even engaged."

He'd taken hold of the lapels on either side of her neck and was busily buttoning the closure but at her words his hands froze and his expression closed up. "Yes."

"I daresay I shall have my share of suitors."

"I have no doubt of it."

This was not going at all as Kate had imagined. So, she abandoned her attempts to subtly tease some sign of jealousy from him in favor of her usual modus operandi—bluntness.

"I doubtless shall be kissed, too," she said.

"Be damned you will!" The words broke from him with such unexpected force she blinked. He flushed angrily.

"What is the meaning of this, Kate? Why are you plaguing me with your plans for a disreputable future?"

Her eyes went wide. "Disrep—Neill Oakes, I should think you would be satisfied with your current stable of faults without adding hypocrisy to the lot. If a kiss makes a girl—a *woman* disreputable, then there is not a young lady over seventeen in Burnewhinney who can claim respectability, except for Nigella Lumley, and her unkissed status is certainly not due to a lack of effort in the matter."

"I am certain you exaggerate."

"I do not," she told him truthfully, and in her earnestness, leaned forward and placed her two small hands flat upon his chest. His heart beat thickly against her palms. "And I should think you of all people should realize it seeing how in all likelihood 'tis you who are responsible for many of those despoiled lips."

"You shouldn't say such things, Kate. You shouldn't know such things," he said, quite hotly, but flushing even more deeply than before.

"Why ever not?" she asked, quite sincerely flummoxed.

"Because it . . . it ain't nice, that's why," he said.

She laughed at this strange incarnation of Neill Oakes, the county's foremost scoundrel. "That's not what Mary Grant said. Or Beatrice Lumley."

"God help me," Neill choked out.

Kate raised a brow. "From what exactly is the Almighty to be saving you?"

"You."

"Me?" she asked, her wide-eyed surprise turning swiftly to fascination. "Why me?"

He looked down into her upturned face for a long minute before unhappily lifting his hand to sweep a strand of hair from the corner of her mouth. "You are a plague to me, Kate Peyton."

"Of course I am. Or so you have claimed for years. What of it? You are acting most oddly, Neill." Because finally, she realized that he was, indeed, acting oddly. His manner was agitated and angry, his gaze accusatory and fierce, and . . . unhappy. She moved closer, searching his dark visage for some clue as to what ailed him.

"What is it, Neill? Have you . . . have you *really* done something awful this time?" she asked worriedly.

"Yes. No!" he said. "Blast and damnation. What do you want of me, Kate?"

She blinked up at him. "Why, a kiss."

He stared down at her, and she noted absently the way the icy rain had caught like crystals in his black curls and how the shoulders of his jacket were growing dark with dampness and how firm his mouth was and how long and thick his eyelashes.

"I thought it was perfectly clear," she said softly.

"No," he whispered like a man condemned and hopeless, which had the extraordinary effect of making her feel intoxicatingly feminine, a woman in a way she never felt before, a woman who was both seductive and powerful. And it gave her the courage and the inspiration to do something she had never before done with Neill Oakes: flirt.

"No, it wasn't perfectly clear or no, you will not kiss me?" she asked, all coyness and feminine wiles.

In answer, he made an odd, half-strangled groan, which she took as a very encouraging sign.

"Well, I think you should," she said, smiling up at him through the misting rain.

In answer, he reached between them and seized the lapels of his greatcoat, inadvertently dragging her closer. "You're being absurd," he growled.

She wasn't afraid. She was riveted. She loved him, as much as a sixteen-year-old can love, and she trusted him. And she wanted him in a nebulous but nonetheless powerful way. "Not at all. I am being most practical. I have foreseen the inevitability of being kissed and after some deliberation have decided that I want my first experience to be an enjoyable one, a *most* enjoyable one, and as you are well-known to have some expertise in the area, it only makes sense that I should want you to be my first kiss."

She smiled up at him, cocking her brow, fully anticipating that he would now bend his head and kiss her. He didn't. He glowered. But he didn't release the chokehold he had on the poor material at her throat and he did not step back and so Kate stood on the very tips of her toes, stretching up as high as she could and . . . and . . .

Kissed him.

His lips were cool and damp with rain and quite, quite unresponsive. He hadn't wanted to kiss her after all. She might have lost her nerve then, dropped to her feet and fled in embarrassment, except that as her lips began their retreat, his head dipped, and his lips clung to hers, molding against them. His lips lingered, parting slightly, his breath hot on her mouth, his tongue slipping along the seam of her mouth and sending a jolt through her. She shivered as his kiss grew more urgent and demanding, his mouth yearning against hers, denying the paralysis that seemed to have gripped the rest of him. In no other way did he touch her, and though he did not release his hold of her coat, he did not move one inch closer.

Without volition, she melted against him, her hands splayed over his broad chest, bracing herself as his heartbeat thickened and his body tensed. Only when she'd wrapped her arms around his neck and pressed herself full against him did his statuelike stillness break. With a sound half growl half groan, he clasped her upper arms and physically lifted her away from him.

"I will not risk that which I value most for a moment's pleasure." His voice was so low she barely heard him.

She stared up at him, her thoughts reeling and her senses tingling with unsatisfied pricks of need.

"What do you mean?" she asked.

"I'm buying a commission in the cavalry," he said, breathing hard. "I am going away."

"What?" she asked, stunned. He had never spoken of joining the cavalry, never expressed any desire to wear a uniform. Never. And yet this was the thing he wanted most in the world? And he feared kissing her would jeopardize it because . . . ? Dear God, he did not for a moment think she would insist he had compromised her? He couldn't think so poorly of her! And yet— A sob broke from her.

"Kate, please. I cannot stay here."

"Fine. Go!" she choked out amidst her humiliation and pain.

"Kate, you cannot always have what you want. Not this time. In a few years, when you are not so young—"

"I am not a child!" she cried out, tears spilling down her cheeks and mingling with the rain. She wrenched herself free of his clasp and yanked off his greatcoat, flinging it at him. He caught it in one hand and took a step toward her, his other hand outstretched, his face pale.

"Kate—"

"Go to hell, Neill Oakes," she said and, wheeling around, fled.

ou are adorable, Miss Peyton," Hugh, Earl of Briarly murmured, stopping before a late-flowering rosebush in his sister, the Marchioness of Finchley's, garden. It was late afternoon, and the other houseguests were resting before dinner. But Lord Briarly had suggested that Kate might like to visit the garden, and as this fell in nicely with Kate's plans—Kate being a self-acknowledged master planner—she'd agreed.

Lord Briarly tipped Kate's chin up between his thumb and forefinger, angling her face with unexpected gentleness. Kate was no longer a green debutante. She understood perfectly well his intentions. Indeed, she anticipated it. She held her breath, preparing to be kissed and preparing to like it.

Hugh was very handsome and most manly. Indeed, he looked a great deal like her father's head groom, a large, muscular fellow with dark reddish brown hair and chocolate brown eyes. It would, of course, be nice had he trimmed his hair. It would lend him just that certain air of elegance he somehow, well, missed. He was also, truth be told, a trifle dusty, and having two seasons now firmly on her family's account ledger, Kate felt secure in opining that an earl oughtn't be dusty.

Still, he *was* an earl and he did have magnificent cattle and he did bathe. Which until recently was more than she could have said of her four brothers . . . She chided herself. She ought to have been attending more closely to what Briarly was about because as she'd been considering his lack of sartorial splendor, his head had been slowly descending toward hers, but now he'd paused, an odd, hesitant expression appearing on his face.

She knew that look. Having assumed the role of matriarch upon her mother's death six years ago, she was well versed in reading male expressions. The earl wanted encouragement. Males, young, old, servant, or earl, *always* wanted encouragement.

So when he smiled down into her eyes, Kate smiled back, lifting her chin even higher to make sure he understood that his kiss was welcome. Because it would be very pleasant to be pursued by an earl, especially now. Then she shut her eyes. And waited. And when nothing happened, experienced a twinge of rueful irritation. Must she do everything herself? She pursed her lips invitingly. Briarly swore.

Startled, Kate opened her eyes just in time to see Briarly spin around as a dark sleeve ending in a large hand shot out of nowhere and connected with his shoulder, pushing him forcefully away. The earl stumbled back, his muscular arms already notching into battle-readiness, but by now Kate, well used to ending masculine tussles, had already darted between Briarly and his assailant. She swung around to face the interloper and—

Neill.

She knew he had been invited; she'd expected him, but still . . . It had been four years.

She stared, her heart leaping in her throat, her breath rushing out between her parted lips as she took an involuntary step toward him. Her hands rose in an unconscious gesture of welcome as her gaze marked every detail of his countenance, every change and alteration: a sickle-shaped red scar on the hard chin, deep lines scoring cheeks now devoid of any boyish padding, black brows lowered over the large, Romanesque nose. He seemed taller, darker, broader. Everything about him was at once familiar and alien.

'Twas said his tenure in the army had matured him and that he was no longer the wild scapegrace whose name had been a byword for roguery in these parts. But since he'd just manhandled Briarly, an act much in keeping with his past, she questioned the veracity of those reports. And reports were all she had. Since his return from the wars, he'd been in London being presented to the queen.

"Move aside, Kate," Neill said, startling her with a voice both deeper and gruffer than she recalled.

Move aside, Kate? After being away at war for nearly four years and seeing her for the first time since his return, all he could say was, "*Move aside, Kate*"?

"I will do no such thing, Neill Oakes," she said, setting her hands on her hips. *Captain Oakes*, she reminded herself, though in truth she did not need reminding. Her brothers—one older and three younger—crowed about Neill's meteoric rise in the cavalry at every opportunity. From that and all the letters that passed between Neill and her family, one would think *he* was the son of the house instead of the son of the neighbor's house. And why not? He'd had the run of Bing Hall since she could remember.

"You *struck* His Lordship," she said, tapping her foot.

"I did not strike him. I removed him. He was

about to compromise you," Neill replied, turning his black gaze on her.

" 'Compromise'?" she sputtered. "Oh, for heaven's sake, Neill. Only an old grandmother could think so trivial . . ." She caught Briarly's astounded expression and blushed, starting over. "Nothing that has happened or that might have happened can be thought to compromise me. And I might add," she said, eying Neill darkly, "that were every kiss to lead to the altar, you would currently be heading a veritable harem!"

Neill's lean cheeks darkened, but his eyes did not unlock from hers. "As your chaperone, I am obliged to see to your welfare, both physical and social."

"My chaperone?" Kate echoed incredulously.

"Be damned if you are Miss Peyton's chaperone," Briarly said, speaking for the first time.

Kate moved to his side, visually aligning herself with him, feeling guilty that she'd nearly forgotten him. He had, after all, been about to kiss her. One would think such a thing would be noteworthy.

"Then damned you are, Your Lordship," Neill replied evenly. "Because I am Miss Peyton's chaperone. Guardian. Whatever the name of the role that assigns the safety of her virtue to another."

She eyed him closely. "Have you taken up unsavory practices, Captain?"

He looked mildly taken aback. "No . . . I would . . . I . . . What the devil do you mean?"

"I have heard that some officers posted in exotic locales developed the habit of smoking a weed that they say makes one prone to delusions, and as this is the only way I can account for your preposterous claim, it seemed probable you might have added a new vice to your already extensive repertoire."

Briarly made a noise that sounded greatly like stifled laughter.

"No, Kate," Neill ground out. "I am not delusional. If you doubt me, you need only ask His Lordship's sister. She will inform you that soon after I arrived this afternoon, your idiot brother Tom bolted from the premises, only *after* naming me as his stand-in."

Unfortunately, she didn't think Neill was lying. Tom had been none too happy about being thrust into the role of guardian and had only done so at their father's insistence. On their arrival at Finchley Manor, the flock of pretty would-be brides waiting to make her big, brawny, and handsome brother's acquaintance (she had no illusion of their having any interest in meeting her) had provoked an expression of hunted desperation on Tom's face. That look had grown more pronounced over the last few days as it dawned on him that the parson's mousetrap might be sprung not only on "poor old

Briarly," as he called the earl, but on himself. Since then, he'd been badgering her to leave the house party as soon as politeness allowed.

To simply fly the coop would be like Tom. He was hardly a font of conscientious behavior, a deficit in great part due to the unfortunate example held out by his paragon, the same black-headed Irishman who stood regarding her with such unreadable aplomb—and just when the devil had Neill developed aplomb? It was most unsettling.

Still, she supposed there was a certain irony to be enjoyed in the fact that the same rakehell who had led her brothers in countless disreputable japes had been press-ganged into playing toothless nanny to his friends' baby sister. Except right now she was not in the mood to appreciate it. Tom's defection played havoc with her plans, and she would have to reconsider, regroup, and reevaluate. Drat Tom, anyway.

She had come to Finchley Manor with the specific aim of securing a husband, and she intended to do so. The Peyton Hall household had gone to sixes and sevens during her two London seasons. The servants apparently declared holiday as soon as she passed out of the front door, the famous cheese their dairy produced had failed to take grand prize at the county fair during both her absences, and the orchard was plagued by aphids one year and spider mites the second. And as for the fracases got into by the two brothers too young to accompany her to town . . . She shuddered.

"Don't think for an instant that this is any more comfortable for me than you, Kate. I assure you, it is not," Neill said, breaking into her thoughts.

She didn't doubt him. His face was grim with annoyance. Where was the old laughter, the bravado, the damn-your-eyes attitude?

"I did not come here expecting to have to play doyen to you," he continued. "But the alternative, for you to remain here unescorted, unaccompanied, and unprotected"—here he shot a glare in Briarly's direction—"is intolerable."

"I am hardly unprotected, Neill. Lady Finchley—"

"Is most gracious in her assurances that she would be delighted to look after you," Neill broke in. "But it is not she Tom named to take his place, and she has more than enough to occupy her."

Ah, he was doing his duty. She felt like stomping her foot in irritation. She did not want his dutiful attention.

"See here—" Briarly had started to say, then abruptly broke off. "Just who the bloody blazes *are* you, anyway?"

"Neill Oakes," Kate answered. "Our neighbor's son. Captain Oakes."

Neill tipped his head. "At your service . . . er, . . ."

"The Earl of Briarly," Kate grudgingly introduced the two men. She swung to face Neill. "Now apologize," she whispered, trying to sound authoritative but fearing she only sounded desperate.

She needed to be here. And if Neill got himself kicked out of the house, all her plans would fall into ruin.

Neill studied her a moment before turning in Briarly's direction. "Excuse me, milord. I overstepped myself in a desire to comply with the duty with which I am charged."

Kate released a breath she hadn't even realized she was holding, oddly disconcerted. The Neill of old would never have apologized for something he did not regret, and he did not regret anything, and so never apologized. More than anything else, his apology brought home to her that he was no longer the brazen, brash youth of her childhood. And what of his *shoving* the earl? The Neill of old would have struck him. He'd struck lots of people. Mostly in brawls.

"I see," Briarly said, for some reason looking more irritated than he had a moment ago. "I believe I have heard of your war record, Captain Oakes. My sister is effusive. Apology accepted. 'Spect I owe you one myself, Miss Peyton. I hope you will not think unkindly of me?"

"No!" she assured him. "I don't. I won't."

She didn't know what else to say, not with Neill hovering within arm's reach, stonily dividing his gaze between Briarly and her. For an awkward moment, the threesome avoided meeting one another's eyes.

"So, how is it you are here?" Kate finally asked Neill. "Since you did not come intending to 'play doyen.'"

"I suspect because Lady Finchley felt it an appropriate patriotic gesture," he replied.

"Patriotic?" Kate said.

"Yes. Seeing how I was lately in a war." His smooth demeanor splintered just a shade. "Where did you think I was, Kate? What did you think I'd been doing?"

Of course, she knew he'd been in a war. The thought of him in harm's way had ruined many a good night's sleep, and even now was wont to play havoc with her peace of mind.

"I don't know," she replied quellingly. "You never wrote *me*. I thought you were wasting your life in the fetid corners of . . . wherever they have fetid corners," she lied, unwilling to have him guess how often and long she'd thought of him. "You always seemed to me destined to lead a low life."

He refused to be quelled. "I *did* write you. You never wrote back. "

It was the truth, but as Kate had no intention of offering him an explanation, she kept mute.

"Certainly one of that mob of brothers of yours

must have informed you of what I was doing," he went on. "We exchanged many letters."

"Of course they did, " she snapped back. "According to them, you single-handedly won a dozen battles, restored the Spanish throne, and infiltrated Napoleon's inner circle, after which you rode an elephant, wrestled a crocodile, and swam the Straits of Gibraltar."

For the first time since his unfortunate arrival, Neill smiled, and Kate recognized anew how devastating his smile could be, how rakish and irresistible. And hard on the heels of this realization came another: Rogue and scoundrel though he'd been—and still might be—the love she'd once borne him had never faded, it had only grown and ripened. She loved him still. She always had.

"Well, I did swim in the Straits of Gibraltar," he allowed disingenuously. "But only because I fell off a pier while half-foxed."

She laughed, she could not help it, and something ignited in his eyes.

"Did you miss me, Kate?" he asked, his head tilted slightly, his expression inscrutable. How could she answer that when she didn't know what he meant? She, too, had changed in the intervening four years. She had developed subtlety and sophistication. She was no longer a child but a woman. "Of course, I did. I was used to your being about.

I missed that nasty gelding of Tom's once we sold him, too."

He frowned.

"This is all very interesting," Briarly said. "But, perhaps you can reacquaint yourself with Miss Peyton at a more appropriate time, Captain Oakes. Though you may be my sister's guest, here you are very much *de trop*."

"Am I?" Neill asked. "Allow me to rectify the situation." He turned to Kate. "I believe I saw you limping just now."

She blinked in confusion. She wasn't limping—

Before she knew what he was about, he'd taken hold of her hand, pulled her forward, and was scooping her up into his arms as neatly and carelessly as a laundress collects bedding. Briarly's face darkened, and Kate realized that she had only to say a word, and he would intervene. But while she didn't *think* the new Neill would engage in fisti-cuffs with an earl, she was not sure.

So rather than object, Kate said, "How astute of you to notice, Captain."

Neill grinned. "Sir." He inclined his head toward Briarly and, without waiting for a response, strode off with her.

Chapter 12

*M*iss Peyton!" Lady Finchley exclaimed on seeing Captain Oakes emerge around the side of the house carrying her young neighbor. Carolyn left the front door open and hurried down the front steps of the manor, where she'd been seeing off the Singleworths, their eligible daughter having announced at luncheon that she was pregnant and intended to marry her baby's father, thus making any continuation of their visit beside the point.

Whatever was going on? Was Miss Peyton hurt? And why was Captain Oakes, and not Hugh, carrying her? Earlier, she had seen Hugh disappear into the garden with Miss Peyton, and she'd hoped that he was furthering his acquaintance with the delicate-looking heiress. But apparently not, since the wrong man was carrying her.

She'd only met the captain a handful of times, when she had first come as a bride to Finchley Manor. He hadn't been Captain Oakes then, of course, but simply the wild son of an Irish beauty and an immensely wealthy baronet, whose name was almost as ancient as the Dales and whose estate was almost as vast.

She recalled how surprised the local gentry had been when Neill Oakes had bought a commission and hied off to war, expressing doubt as to whether a young man of such undisciplined habits could ever bow to authority. But she'd been at court at the end of the season a few weeks ago when he, along with several other heroic soldiers, had been presented to the queen. He had looked worn, his eyes haunted and grave, but he'd carried his tall, broad-shouldered physique with a dignity she'd admired, and spoken to Finchley and her afterwards with humility and sobriety. Clearly, the reckless boy had become a thoughtful man.

He was just the sort of man whom Georgina could love, she felt sure of that. The annoying part of it was that no sooner had the captain arrived than Miss Peyton's rapscallion of a brother had cried off the party, but only after first abdicating his sister's care to the unhappy, but dutifully obliging, Captain Oakes.

Though, she thought eying Captain Oakes doubtfully, she couldn't detect any unhappiness in his current expression. He seemed quite content to be holding Kate in his arms. He was just the sort of man who looked dashing with a woman in his arms. Too dashing? she wondered, rethinking her decision to invite someone of his wealth and good looks to a gathering whose sole purpose was to find Hugh a wife. Though she wanted her darling Georgina to fall in love, it was even more important that she match up her brother.

At least, Miss Peyton seemed wholly immune to Captain Oakes's attractiveness. She looked just as chill as her delicate blond beauty would allow, which was icy indeed. Unlike her big, brawny brothers, Miss Peyton was tiny and finely made.

Really, Carolyn thought, God must have been snickering when he fashioned Kate Peyton, for Carolyn could not imagine another instance where the package so unsatisfactorily advertised the contents. She was not in the least delicate or fragile, and whatever air of etherealness her very petite feminine figure and bone-china-fine features conveyed vanished as soon as one engaged her in conversation.

It was not that she was bold or forward, she was simply, stunningly direct. Carolyn, whom marriage had already taught that any subtle form of communication is lost on the male psyche, suspected it was the result of Kate's being the only female in her household.

Carolyn had met Kate Peyton several times in London the past season and had found the diminutive beauty refreshing, if a little frightening. She didn't seem in the least eager to encourage suitors, and though she owned her own coterie of devoted followers, most gentlemen found her assertiveness off-putting.

"Is everything all right?" Carolyn called out as soon as the pair came within hailing distance.

"Everything is fine," Captain Oakes said, mounting the steps to the front terrace.

"Are you injured, Miss Peyton?" she asked.

Miss Peyton did not appear to be in any physical pain though the pupils of her dark blue eyes had dilated to black pools, and her expression could only be termed strained.

"My ankle," she said. "I turned it and Ne— Captain Oakes insisted on transporting me." She looked up at her rescuer. "Thank you for your aid, Captain Oakes, but you can put me down. I am confident my ankle can bear my weight now. It was only a trifling thing."

"You mustn't risk further injury," Captain Oakes said, jouncing the girl higher in his arms.

A black curl fell across his eyes, and Kate glared at the lock as though it personally offended her before sweeping it from his forehead. Captain Oakes stilled, and though not a muscle moved in his rugged countenance, his expression sharpened.

Carolyn stared, transfixed, confused, and completely at a loss as to how to go on. Primarily because she wasn't exactly sure what *was* going on.

"Pray, you mustn't think me overly familiar, Lady Finchley," Captain Oakes said. "The Peyton children and I were wont to treat each other's homes as interchangeable when we were growing up. At least until my mother died. Miss Peyton quite played havoc with the family's peace, too, I might add," he said. "Always hanging from chandeliers, hurling down the banisters, and terrorizing the stable hands. Not to mention the poor horses."

"Miss Peyton terrorized your horses?" Carolyn's smile froze. *Oh, dear.* Hugh would not like that. Not at all.

"She painted my father's prize broodmare pink for the county fair," he said, lowering his voice confidingly.

"I was but ten years old," Miss Peyton burst out. "And one can hardly count one horse as 'terrorizing the cattle.'"

Carolyn relaxed. Hugh could overlook a youthful folly.

"No, you did that when you taught your collie to ride bareback, and he proceeded to race around our pasture jumping atop unsuspecting horses."

Caught in her equivocation, an impish glint appeared in Miss Peyton's eyes, and her mouth curved in an irrepressible smile. Captain Oakes's

173

eyes danced in response. My, he really was a handsome man.

With an effort, Miss Peyton seemed to recall her annoyance. "Captain. *Please*. Put me down," she said, leaving Captain Oakes no choice but to oblige. Carefully, he set her on her feet.

"Thank you." Her skirts snapped as she turned away from him. Behind her, unseen, Captain Oakes grinned broadly.

"Miss Peyton always was a quick healer," he said.

Abruptly, Miss Peyton began favoring her left leg.

"Ah! As I suspected," the captain told Carolyn sotto voce. "Only Miss Peyton's concern that we worry over her injury has given her the courage to pretend it does not hurt. But, brave creature though she is, she cannot mask such agony for long."

An odd sound came from Miss Peyton's vicinity. Was she *laughing*? Or sniffling . . . ?

"Most brave," said Carolyn. She raised her voice to make sure Miss Peyton heard her approbation. "Most considerate of you, Miss Peyton."

"Exactly," said Captain Oakes. "She is the soul of consideration. The very epitome of a lady."

Miss Peyton turned back around. She *was* laughing. A rosy hue infused her porcelain skin, and her eyes gleamed.

"You've outdone yourself, Neill," she said before looking past him to Carolyn. "It's his Irish blood, you see; he can't resist making up stories. I am not brave. Nor am I as fine a lady as Gwendolyn Pass-more. But I assure you, Lord Briarly needn't lock his stable doors in fear that I might indulge a whim to ride a lavender horse."

"Of course not," Carolyn said. "I never thought a thing, and I am sure you're every bit as much a lady as—"

"Please, Lady Finchley," Kate broke in, her smile in no way reproachful. "I know who I am and con-fess to being unattractively satisfied with myself"—here she cast a glance so fleeting at Captain Oakes that Carolyn was not sure she'd seen it—"as, hap-pily, are Certain Others. Certain Others whose good opinion is guided by your own."

Oh . . . ? Oh! Carolyn realized. She must mean Hugh. Miss Peyton was concerned that she might not like her and that her dislike would influence Hugh. Well, she needn't have worried on either count. She liked Miss Peyton very much, but that was neither here nor there, as Hugh wasn't likely to be guided by anyone.

"I *am* standing here, Kate," Captain Oakes said, and the sound of his voice, almost a purr, sent a little thrill of trepidation through Carolyn. "Are you sure you want to have this conversation with Her Ladyship now, in front of me?"

"I am hardly likely forget your presence with you looming over me as you are, Captain. So, yes. I am very sure," Kate answered.

Carolyn couldn't see that Captain Oakes was looming over anyone, but he did seem to find something gratifying in the accusation, for he smiled once again.

"Forgive me," he said, bowing and taking a step back, which put him a good ten feet away from the girl, who suddenly seemed to realize the unfairness of her accusation, for she blushed hotly—the first time Carolyn had seen her fall victim to such a feminine reaction. She caught Carolyn's surprised scrutiny and blushed even more deeply. "I . . . I, er, I had best go and rest my ankle."

"Of course," Carolyn said.

"Allow me to escort you." Captain Oakes held out his hand, and Kate shied away from it like one of Hugh's unbroken fillies.

"No! No, I . . . I think it will do it good to stretch it out a bit," she explained, and hastily suited action to word as she limped away through the open front doorway.

"I thought Miss Peyton had injured the other ankle," Carolyn murmured, looking up at Captain Oakes.

At once, all thoughts of which leg Miss Peyton had injured vanished at the sight of his face. It was as though Miss Peyton had taken with her all the fire and passion that had animated the young man. The lights died in his black eyes, and a shadow fell across his face, blighting his dashing good looks, making him appear weary and sober.

Perhaps he regretted his offer to stand in for Miss Peyton's brother Tom? Clearly it was not a natural or easy role for a young man—despite his assurances that no one else was better qualified than he to supervise Kate Peyton and that, indeed, he very much considered it his . . . what was the word he'd used? Not obligation or duty . . . She'd thought it a strange term to use at the time . . . *atonement.* That's what he'd said; he considered it his atonement.

She hoped he didn't take the role too seriously. He must know that she would watch over Kate. She should remind him, so that he could relax and enjoy himself.

"You really mustn't take it so seriously," she said gently.

He turned to her, his thick black brows rising questioningly. "Ma'am?"

"I will be happy to act as Miss Peyton's chaperone. Young Mr. Thomas Peyton's role as such was more show than reality. In truth, he was meant to flesh out a dearth of gentleman," she admitted. "So you really needn't take to heart your kind offer to see to Miss Peyton's welfare."

"I am not sure Miss Peyton would agree that my offer was kind."

"Ah, but she is very young."

"Only in years," he said in a distracted tone. "She shouldered far too many responsibilities when her mother died. There were no painted horses after that."

Carolyn nodded her understanding.

"A girl should have some merriment."

"So should you," Carolyn said quietly.

He winced. "I believe many would say I had more than my share of fun when I was young. I'm afraid I gathered a rather unpalatable reputation. She always saw me as a bad influence on her brothers, you know. Trying to lure them into my reprehensible ways."

He was speaking once more of Miss Peyton. Poor Georgie.

"I'm sure you will rectify whatever sins you once committed by behaving in a most exemplary fashion toward Miss Peyton."

"Will I?" he said quizzically, with another flash of brilliance in his ebony black eyes. His lips twisted ruefully. "Of course, you are right. She deserves only the best."

And inclining his head, he bid her good evening.

Carolyn was still staring after the tall, straight figure of Captain Oakes when her brother appeared. So he *had* been in the garden with Miss Peyton. Well, fat lot of good it had done him.

Whatever Miss Peyton's assurances that she considered Hugh and herself to have a great deal in common—that being primarily their lack of interest in the *haut ton,* which in retrospect didn't seem much of a basis for marriage—Captain Oakes obviously did not care a farthing for them. Carolyn had seen the expression on his face, a resolve he might have worn looking over a piece of ground he'd been ordered to take in battle, and she doubted anyone, least of all Miss Peyton, stood a chance against such resolve. Even Hugh.

Now she had only to figure some way to break to her brother that his list was being decimated and decide on the next young woman she should offer for his contemplation.

"Did you see a black-headed brute come by carrying Miss Peyton?" Hugh asked upon reaching her side. "Say you did; otherwise, I shall be forced to send out a search party. I don't trust that Irish blackguard, despite his claims that he's the girl's guardian. He isn't, is he?"

"Well, in a manner of speaking. Tom Peyton did clap him on the back and gasp that he needed to watch after his sister before bolting—*why* are some young men so averse to a little female company?"

"Because they know that company for an evening too often becomes companionship for life. Now about Miss Peyton—"

"Oh. Yes. Well, Captain Oakes did carry her to

the top of the steps, at which point he set her down and she hobbled inside. However did she twist her ankle, Hugh? You didn't—"

"Chase her?" Hugh asked sardonically. "For God's sake, Caro, she's a nice-looking little filly, but not so much so that I'd forget myself. As it is, you ought to be thanking me for showing restraint by not knocking that blackguard flat."

Carolyn stared at Hugh in horror. "What did you do?"

"Ah. There's the loving sister," Hugh said. "I am roughly used by one of her guests, and she asks what *I* have done? I did nothing untoward or even unexpected. You told me to court a potential wife, did you not? Well, I courted Miss Peyton. Or perhaps I might more exactly say that I was *about* to . . . er, court her when that Irishman appeared and shoved me aside."

Captain Oakes had shoved Hugh? Oh, dear. Luckily, Hugh didn't look angry, merely irritated. She really ought to thank him for resisting getting into a brawl and ruining her party, so she said very prettily, "It was very good of you not to retaliate, Hugh."

Hugh snorted. "No sense to it. The chit is mad in love with the fellow and he with her. Proper waste of time trying to get between the two of them."

Carolyn blinked. Though she had come to the same conclusion, it amazed her that Hugh had, too. She would never have mistaken him for a sensitive fellow. "Why would you say that? You don't know a thing about young ladies."

"I don't," he agreed. "But Miss Peyton reminds me of a little Arabian filly I put with Richelieu last spring: shying and dancing and nipping at—"

"Hugh!" Carolyn said, giving her brother a sharp tap on the shoulder so as to remind him that she wasn't one of his stablemen.

Recalled to a sense of decorum, Hugh had the grace to look somewhat abashed. "'Scuse me, Caro," he said. "Point is, Miss Peyton has been struck off the list, and even without the appearance of the captain, I think it's for the best. She's rather unnervingly businesslike, truth be told."

At this assessment, so near Carolyn's own, she couldn't help but smile. "Well, this poses a bit of a problem," she mused, adding, "I *am* sorry you don't like her, Hugh."

"On the contrary, I like her very well," Hugh disagreed. "I'd just rather hire her to manage my estate than wed her to fill my bed."

"Hugh!"

He shrugged. "I'd always be worrying that I might not be fulfilling my matrimonial duties sufficiently and require instruction, don't you see? 'Twould be too demoralizing."

She laughed outright. "You are incorrigible. My house is full of beautiful young ladies, so I'm not worried about your future. But I had rather hoped that Captain Oakes would find favor with Georgie. She always liked a man in uniform."

"Georgie?" Hugh exclaimed, looking far more put out than he had while relating the tussle with Oakes.

"Yes. I cannot agree with her decision never to marry again."

"You were really thinking of pairing her up with *Oakes*? Are you daft? The man has a reputation as a regular limb of Satan hereabouts. And war will only have made him more susceptible to those demons that drove him before he bought his commission."

"His bad reputation comes from when he was a mere lad, Hugh. And you had a similar reputation, I might add. And, like you, I daresay he has outgrown his demons."

Hugh looked unconvinced. "Different, that. No, won't have it. Besides, Georgie's far above his touch."

"I would never have taken you for a snob!" Carolyn exclaimed. "Captain Oakes is wealthy, comes from an extremely old and distinguished family, and is accounted by all who knew and served with him a true war hero."

"Still not good enough for Georgie," Hugh said. "Anyway, it doesn't matter. Yon war hero is besotted of Miss Peyton; so should Georgie even want him, she can't have him." There was a distinct tone of satisfaction in his voice.

"Well, I didn't say she wanted him," Carolyn said, trying not to sound too curious. "Though, of course, she may. You know, Hugh, Georgie didn't want to be on your list."

He looked up at her, and she saw just a shadow of something in his eyes. "She did not say that," he stated.

"Yes, she did."

"She said, and I'm quoting here, that she had a fancy never to marry again."

"Heavens," Carolyn said, highly entertained. "You certainly listened carefully to that part of the conversation, Hugh."

"Yes, I did."

Carolyn couldn't repress a huge smile.

"And I am not a snob," Hugh continued abruptly. "I only meant that it's just as well Captain Oakes is besotted of Miss Peyton. He and Georgie would never suit. Never."

And with this apparently the final say on the matter, he took himself off.

Chapter 13

At dinner that evening, Neill waited while Miss Emily Mottram and her great-aunt and chaperone, Lady Diane Nibbleherd, were seated before taking his place between them. Kate, who'd avoided Neill while the guests had gathered in the drawing room before dinner, had yet to make her entrance in the dining room. She was probably still lecturing poor Finchley on irrigation systems.

His first meeting with her had not gone as planned. He certainly hadn't expected to come upon her in the arms of another man, her head tilted invitingly for his kiss. Had she shown the slightest reluctance to be in the bastard's arms, things would not have gone nearly so civilly. But she hadn't, and so he had simply removed the fellow, dutifully conscious of the role damn Peyton had thrust him into but far more conscious of the surging jealousy coursing through him.

And after he'd dealt with the man—who'd turned out to be his hostess's brother—he'd looked down into her face and for one wondrous moment her eyes had widened, and her mouth had essayed the beginnings of a smile and he had felt that now, finally, after four years at war, he had come home. It had taken all of his self-restraint not to take her in his arms and kiss her.

But even as he gazed hungrily into her lovely, fey countenance, he had seen her recall the circumstance that had led to their estrangement, and her expression had grown masked and impenetrable. It was disconcerting. The Kate he'd left had never hid her emotions behind a polished façade; she hadn't owned one. But she did now, and highly polished it was. The slight girl had become a striking woman, her cheekbones seemed higher, her nose more delicately fashioned, her eyes larger and darker and mysterious.

When she did arrive at the table, she would be placed between Albert Hunt and Louis DuPreye. As the affair between Albert Hunt and Lady Fourveire—seated farther down the table—was an open secret, and Louis DuPreye was a married gentleman, this suited Neill very well. He would not do well having to watch eligible bachelors ogling his Kate.

And she was, and always had been, *his* Kate—despite how badly, nay, how disastrously he had mucked things up four years ago. He couldn't believe how stupid he'd been. But then again, thinking back, perhaps he could. He'd been an arrogant, brash young ass. He'd always assumed he'd marry Kate—though he'd never made mention of the fact to her, waiting for her to grow up as he had—but with her sixteenth birthday, he'd began noting the way the other lads watched her and deemed it time to claim her for himself.

He'd applauded himself on the noble deference he'd shown her. He hadn't even kissed her, let alone declared himself. He'd been a model of propriety. He had said and done nothing to her with which her father could take issue. Indeed, he'd been in a self-congratulatory mood the day he'd gone to see Mr. Peyton to ask his permission to court her. He certainly hadn't anticipated Marcus Peyton's refusing him. Why would he? Neill was intelligent, well made, healthy, and his family was old and noble and very rich.

He had been humiliatingly wrong.

Marcus Peyton had been blunt. He considered Neill "ramshackle," "loose in the haft," "irresponsible and reckless," and while he had "some hope" that time would "make a man" of Neill, he did not consider him there yet. But the charge that had stung most had been that he, Neill, "had, at best, no more than a passing acquaintance with the concept of personal honor." Neill had many sins to account for. He had never denied that. But his honor was possibly the only thing he had never hazarded.

His father's lack of personal honor, demonstrated by his public display of grief while mourning Neill's mother at the same time he was getting ready to install his mistress in her place, had instilled in Neill a deep sense of loathing for all such dishonesty.

But if Peyton considered him dishonorable, so, too, must all of Burnewhinney. It was eye-opening, to say the least. Moreover, Peyton did not think Kate had seen enough of the world to choose so "unpromising a young devil when she might have an earl or even a marquess."

Mr. Peyton had gone on to explain, quite pleasantly, that Kate deserved all those things her mother would have wanted for her had she lived, and that included gaiety, frivolity, a proper debut in society, a few seasons in London, and a wide choice of suitors. As her father, he intended that she get them.

Neill, shocked and embarrassed though he was, had still argued his case and argued it passionately. Eventually, he had gained one small concession: Peyton would not unequivocally say "no" to his suit if Neill promised not to pay court to Kate, or attempt in any way to engage her emotions—which he considered childishly susceptible—until after she had made her bow and reached her eighteenth year. He would give Neill a chance to prove he was indeed, an honorable man. And if Neill refused? Mr. Peyton vowed to ban Neill entirely from the premises.

Angry and humiliated, Neill left Bing Hall and promptly went off to get drunk. Except Kate had ambushed him on his way. He could still see her face, impish and flirtatious and wholly desirable. And as he'd stared at her, he'd realized that he not only wanted to marry her because he'd always assumed he would but that he truly loved her.

He hadn't any notion of what to say or how to say it or even what his own promise to her father left him *to* say. His honor, the one thing he had never risked in his short but brilliant career as a rakehell, insisted that he abide by Peyton's rules. So he had done exactly nothing.

Until she'd kissed him.

It had taken every ounce of will to keep from swooping her up and simply carrying her to his father's stable. But . . . This was Kate. If he took her in his arms, if he told her of his love, hell, if he even asked her to marry him, he would lose her. And he did not want her for a kiss or an hour's kisses or an afternoon, or a night, a week, or a year. He wanted her forever.

The war between willful youth, used to having his way, and emerging man, willing to sacrifice his immediate desire for a future goal, was never so silently or savagely fought. He shuddered under her innocent young kiss; he broke into a sweat at the feel of her hands splayed so carelessly over his chest; he ground his teeth in frustration, as for the first time in his young life he realized what his black reputation might cost him. He could not let that happen.

But he couldn't stay nearby for two years, either, always wanting and never having, unable to speak as boys, then men, clustered around her, always wondering if she was kissing someone else. There was only one thing for it: He must join the army. And that is what he'd blurted out, then made it worse by being unable to explain that he must leave because he loved her and could not yet court her. When he tried to hint at his reasoning, he'd only made it worse by calling her a child.

She'd told him to go to hell.

And in a sense he had; he'd bought a commission in the cavalry and gone to fight in France.

He hadn't meant to be gone so long but, as though to make up for taking so long to emerge, his sense of duty would not be gainsaid. He must see Napoleon defeated. It was his atonement. It was his obligation. It was who he had become. But each letter from one of Kate's brothers had set his hand trembling as he opened it, afraid to discover if she had become engaged.

Now, finally, the little Corsican had been well and truly trounced and he was free of obligations and responsibilities and he'd kept his word to her father and *finally* he could speak except . . . except that Fate and damn Tom Peyton had stuck him in the role of Kate's chaperone, and honor, that ever-exacting bitch, demanded he not importune her while she was under his protection. And by God, he *would* be honorable. He would not give her father any excuse to refuse his suit.

"Are you thinking of the war, Captain Oakes?" the pretty brunette beside him asked.

"Pardon me, Miss Mottram?"

"You looked quite grim for a moment, and I thought perhaps you were recalling some troubling experience on the battlefield."

"Ah," he said. Young ladies liked to hear tales of heroism and derring-do. He wished that was all there was to war. "I was, indeed, thinking of a battle."

"And did you win it?" she asked, wide eyes bright with hero worship.

"I did not," he answered.

"Oh," she said, looking disappointed.

"I was ordered to leave the field."

"Oh," Miss Mottram repeated, as Kate appeared on Mr. DuPreye's arm. Kate's color was high, and there was just a hint of disquiet in her manner that most people would have missed. But he was attuned to every aspect of Kate's countenance and the unspoken vocabulary in her gaze and gesture. He could only think that he was the cause of her ill ease and felt guilty for depriving her of her enjoyment in the party.

". . . unhappy. I suppose one must follow orders, however."

"Excuse me?" He'd forgotten his manners, so intent on Kate he'd only heard the last words spoken by Lady Nibbleherd, Miss Mottram's great-aunt.

"I said you looked none too happy at being ordered to withdraw from the field," the old tabby said.

"I was most unhappy at the time," he said slowly, fully aware that Kate, despite the fact that her head was turned toward her dining companion, was listening. "But I understand now that I was not ready. I was too young and too impetuous, quite full of myself. Indeed, had I taken the field, I might well have lost all."

"You mean your life and those of your men." Miss Mottram nodded wisely.

He did not answer her and caught a frown puckering Kate's pale brow.

She had always looked like some confectioner's fantasia, a wee thing created of spun sugar, gossamer light, pale and shimmering, so fragile she might melt away in the morning dew. The years had made her seem even more unearthly. Yet, she looked older, too, riper, no longer sprite but faerie queen. Regal, self-sufficient, a woman who knew what she wanted. Her white blond hair glowed with the same health that brushed a rosy hue across the delicate cheekbones and in her full lips. Everything about her was brighter, clearer, lighter. Everything but her eyes. They had darkened into something more complicated, deeper, more intense and intoxicating: pansies in shadow, the Cretan sea at midnight.

She cast a quick, annoyed glance at DuPreye. He was leaning too close to her and when her gaze moved from him, his own dropped to her cleavage. He caught Neill's glare and only shrugged, unembarrassed. Neill's jaw tightened, and DuPreye turned his attention to his other companion.

"I believe you know Miss Peyton," Lady Nibbleherd said, marking Neill's interest.

"Yes. Our families own adjoining land."

"Your father is Sir John Oakes, is he not?" Miss Mottram asked. "I heard he is doing poorly. I'm so sorry."

Neill's father was, in fact, doing very well, but had given out poor health as the reason he had removed his young wife and adolescent sons to more convivial Italian climes, leaving the farm in Neill's hands.

"Thank you, miss," he replied. "He is as well as circumstances allow."

"So, you have known Miss Peyton all her life?" Lady Diane continued.

"I have." *And loved her through half of it.*

"Tell me," Miss Mottram said, "was she always so . . . sensible?" Then hastened to add, "Not that she isn't absolutely charming, but she makes me feel most *jeune fille,* and I believe I am her elder."

"But by a few months," Lady Nibbleherd hastened to put in, and from the quick startled glance Miss Mottram cast her, Neill assumed the few months were more likely a few years.

"Really?" He cocked his head. "How does she do that?"

"Well, she doesn't talk about fashion," Miss Mottram said with evident relish. "Not much, anyway. She isn't intimate with any of the pinks of the ton or the very fashionable ladies. She hasn't been to the theater or the opera even though she's had two full seasons. And yet she is so confident and so . . . dry. She quite talks to the gentleman as if, well, she was a gentleman. One could almost forget she is a young lady."

At this, Neill nearly laughed. He doubted anyone could forget for an instant that Kate was a woman.

Certainly not if they'd ever seen her with her eyes flashing and her hair rippling in the wind, laughing as she had on the manor steps that afternoon.

"She *is* very young," Lady Nibbleherd said, pursing her lips knowingly. "Often the very young affect an air of certainty to cover up their uncertainty. But if she hopes to find a husband, she would be better served by admitting her vulnerabilities. Gentlemen do not like a strong-willed, exuberant woman."

"Do they not?" Neill asked, trying hard not to smile. He loved Kate exactly because she was headstrong and . . . exuberant.

"No," Lady Nibbleherd said. "I have been married four times, and I know what gentlemen like."

"I am sure you are most knowledgeable."

"Well, I am." She sniffed, mollified. "I will say that Miss Peyton conducts herself in a more genteel manner now than she did when she came out. I daresay she wouldn't have received any proposals that first year except for her father's wealth."

Neill's interest sharpened. "She received marriage proposals?"

"You didn't know?" Lady Diane asked.

"Of course, he didn't, Auntie," Miss Mottram cut in. "He was away fighting the Frogs."

"Hm," Lady Diane said. "Well, Miss Peyton did receive a few offers. And a few more this last season, which leads me to believe she might finally be developing a feminine comportment. If she hopes to snag a—become a countess, she will have to. Briarly might not be very exacting, but his sister advises him—or so I am told—and she is."

Neill frowned. Kate had been quite anxious for him to apologize to Briarly, and later she'd been very eager to promote herself to Lady Finchley. And through her to the earl? Would *his* Kate have worried so much over appearances? He did not think so. Perhaps, he realized, she had changed. Perhaps, his heart pounded dully in his chest, she was no longer *his* Kate.

"Well, I think Miss Peyton is formidable," Miss Mottram piped in, dragging his thoughts back to his present company. "Yes. That's what I think. She's a most *formidable* young lady, and I admire her tremendously even if she does frighten me a bit," she said, darting a quick glance at Kate, who was surreptitiously watching their exchange.

She could not know what was being said—the table was too wide and the conversation up and down its length too animated—but her interest was evident. DuPreye leaned closer and murmured something in her ear. Her cheeks abruptly flamed with color as Neill caught a brief glimpse of his sleeve brushing Kate.

The bastard had touched her.

Fury boiled up inside him. He wanted to lunge across the table, scattering crystal and china, take

DuPreye by the throat, and shake him senseless. He did not. Four years ago he might have given in to the impulse, but this was not about him or DuPreye, it was about Kate. She would be mortified to be made the subject of a scene.

So, instead, he carefully folded his napkin and placed it beside his plate, turned to his dining companions to excuse himself, then rose. He strolled down the length of the table and around to the opposite side. The dinner service had not yet started, and several people were still standing in conversation, so his movement was not remarkable. He made his way toward Kate, who turned her brightly colored cheek away from him, fearing no doubt he was about to haul DuPreye from his chair and hurl him across the room. He would have liked to.

But, he only smiled and set his hand on the back of DuPreye's chair. Leaning down and pitching his voice so only DuPreye could hear him, still smiling, he said, "If you cause Miss Peyton so much as one soupçon of discomfort, if the shade of her cheek changes by as much as a degree, if you touch her, any part of her with any part of your person, I promise you I shall break every bone in your hand. Do I make myself clear?"

He did not wait for DuPreye to answer. Instead, he straightened, clapped DuPreye on the back in an overt display of bonhomie, and returned to his seat.

Throughout the rest of the dinner, the creamy purity of Kate's complexion remained unchanged.

And DuPreye's remained white.

As the party finished their dessert and waited for their hostess to lead the ladies out, Kate glanced for the hundredth time at Neill. She was entirely too aware of him for her peace of mind, too aware of the changes time had wrought in him. His face, once so easy to read, was guarded by a smooth and somber expression. The animation that marked his movements had vanished, leaving him still. He was changed. Too changed?

She'd been trying not to look at him all evening, certain others would note it if she did. But then he'd become deeply engaged in conversation with Miss Mottram and she'd found herself staring and all of a sudden her mind's eye was filled with memories of their last meeting, of the taste of his lips, the rock hardness of his chest, the wild, hunted expression in his eyes. She'd fled back to her home from that purloined kiss and spent the next two days sobbing silently into her pillow, pleading illness rather than providing her family with explanations.

Neill had written; she'd torn the letters to shreds,

unopened. He'd appeared at the door, demanding an interview; she had him sent away, knowing that even Neill wasn't going to break into their home uninvited. Though part of her wished he had. Why would he? Only a man madly in love would do such a thing. Neill, had he been madly in love, certainly would have. He would have stormed the castle and breached the dragon's den. But Neill wasn't madly in love.

But he would be.

When she'd done crying and abusing him, when she'd given up trying not to love him, when it had become clear that her heart was profoundly loyal and that once given it could not be taken back, she had rallied and vowed that when Neill Oakes returned, he would return to a woman. Not a *child*. One with experience—which her two London seasons had garnered her—one who'd been kissed—which she had. In other words, a woman who was his match.

When she'd discovered that he'd been invited to the Finchley's house party, she'd accepted her own invitation. Once here, she'd commenced flirting with Briarly just enough to spark Neill's competitive drive. Since he must always win, she must represent herself as the prize. But when he had appeared, instead of entering the field as a contender for her hand, he'd done so in the guise of chaperone. Oh! The ignominy of it! And oh, how much changed he'd become. So distant and disciplined. So aloof . . .

DuPreye had muttered something in her ear, and she came to with a start to find Neill's gaze upon her. At once, heat flooded her face, betraying her. A moment later, Neill rose from his chair and came toward her. She waited, shivering with trepidation, but he hadn't spoken to her at all. He'd only smiled and clapped DuPreye on the back and told him something she couldn't hear.

Why hadn't he spoken to her? True, she'd not spoken to him either, but that was for a very good reason. She'd been trying to provoke him. *He* didn't have a good reason. Unless he was being circumspect. Neill? Circumspect? Her frown deepened.

"Come along, all of you," Lady Finchley said, disrupting Kate's thoughts as she stood up next to her husband. "There'll be no port for the gentlemen this evening. We'll play games instead, and I promise nothing *too* naughty."

Kate followed the other guests into the drawing room, noting as she entered that Chartres was handing the ravishing Lady Gwendolyn Passmore an iced punch, and Briarly was standing behind Lady Georgina, Lady Finchley's widowed friend. She saw Neill leaning against the far wall, arms crossed, having set himself apart from the rest of the company. Not that the ladies let him remain there. Within a few minutes, a clutch of giggling girls had surrounded him. She almost laughed at the beset expression on his face, and the tension that had been building in her relaxed. He may have changed, but not so much that she no longer knew him.

"One lady at a time will be blindfolded and seated here," Lady Finchley explained, pointing to a chair that had been brought to the center of the room. "As soon as she is seated, the gentleman will queue up to kiss her hand.

"If she chooses, the seated lady can try to guess the identity of the gentlemen at once, or she can choose to *briefly* touch the gentleman's face and identify him by his physiognomy. If she can identify the gentleman simply by his gallantries, she will be awarded two points. If she can identify him after touching his face, she gets one point. But if she cannot name her suitor or she is wrong, she is out of the game. She stays seated in the center for as long as she can name her swains. The lady with the most points wins.

"I shall go first," Lady Finchley said, taking the seat and affixing a soft satin handkerchief around her eyes. The gentlemen traded grins and pushed Finchley to the head of a fast-forming line. He stepped before his wife and gently secured her hand, then with evident ardor bent his head and pressed a kiss on her knuckles.

Her brilliant smile flashed beneath the blindfold. "I don't need to touch your face, sir. It is one I kiss every morning—"

Finchley straightened, grinning triumphantly at the other men.

"—*Grandfather.*"

The group burst into laughter and Finchley spun around, swooping down on his giggling wife and lifting her up from the seat while pulling the handkerchief from her eyes.

"Baggage!" he declared fondly. "See what your teasing has got you? You've lost already."

"On the contrary, sir," she said impishly, her eyes on his. "I believe I have won."

At which he kissed her soundly, to the applause of their friends.

She fussed and swatted at him and colored up as pretty as a maid and looked around breathlessly, spying Kate. "Here, Miss Peyton. I am convinced you will do better than I." She held out the handkerchief.

"Oh, I . . . I—"

"Come along, Miss Peyton," DuPreye said, a trace of a sneer in his voice. "It's a tame enough game. Tame enough even for the country. And the very young."

She could not decline. She must show herself to be a woman, not a girl, wide-awake on every suit and not some chit a worldly man would dismiss. "Of course," she said, taking the proffered hand-

201

kerchief and sitting down. She tied it close over her eyes and waited uncertainly.

"Hold out your hand, Miss Peyton," she heard Lady Sorrel say. "Your first suitor awaits."

A cool hand took hold of hers and raised it. A warm dry kiss brushed across her knuckles. She tilted her head. "I am afraid I must ask to read your face," she said. She held up her hand, and the unseen gentleman guided it to his face. Quickly, her fingertips skimmed over his visage: pinched, narrow nose, sparse brows, overly long side-whiskers . . . Only the vicar wore such old-fashioned whiskers. "'Tis the vicar," she announced.

Approving laughter greeted her answer, and Lady Finchley raised her voice, "One point for Miss Peyton. Next gentleman!"

This time Kate knew to lift her hand. A firm hand took hold of hers, the fingertips long and the tips a little damp . . . She frowned, searching her memory for a long time for a gentleman whose fingers had a reason to be so cold. The Earl of Chartres had procured Lady Gwendolyn a glass of iced punch. "Lord Darlington," she said.

"Ah! Well done!"

"I say, how did she know it was Charters?"

"Two points!" Lady Finchley called. "Bringing her total to three. Next gentleman, please."

Kate was relaxing now. It was actually a rather fun game.

"She shall be impossible to overtake at this rate," she heard Lady Nibbleherd grumble as she lifted her hand for her next challenger.

"Are you peeking, Miss Peyton?" Lord Finchley asked.

"Not I, sir. The earl was drinking iced punch, and the vicar is the only man here with side-whiskers."

"Ah! Then let's find a challenge for her. No fur or ice to give the next man away," Finchley said. "You, sir."

She knew him as soon as he took hold of her hand. Recognition, bone deep and certain, danced along her nerves and rippled over her skin. She felt a blush rise to her cheeks and prayed the handkerchief hid most of the telling stain.

She felt him bending nearer, the very air seemed charged with his presence, then his lips, warm, firm, and mobile, pressed against the backs of her fingers. Did they linger just a shade longer than decorum allowed? Her breath was too shallow to say. She hesitated, uncertain if she ought to reveal how well, in how visceral a sense, she knew him or feign ignorance.

"I'm afraid I must . . ." She felt her blush deepen. "May I touch your face, sir?"

A strong, callused hand clasped her wrist, guiding her fingers to his face. They feathered across his features: the bold nose, the wide mouth with its deeply curved lips, the hard square jaw shaved smooth prior to the evening's dinner. His skin was deliciously warm, taut but resilient. His hair was cool and silky and thick.

" 'Tisn't fair," she heard Miss Mottram complain. "She has been assessing his features far longer than 'briefly.' "

She snatched her hand away and cleared her throat, reminding herself that she was a seasoned veteran of such games, before saying lightly, "I wouldn't even hazard a guess. I am afraid I do not know you, sir."

A little murmur of disappointment met her announcement, and she took off her handkerchief.

"Why, Captain Oakes!" she said on seeing him. She pressed a hand to her heart. "I am astounded. One would hope I'd know *you*." She batted her eyes.

His narrowed, but he only said in a quite unaffected voice, "Yes. One would hope."

Did he not care? Had he changed so much that she no longer had the power to provoke him? The thought disturbed her. Whatever their relationship in the past, whatever she had been to him, it had been such that with a few well-aimed words, she could invoke emotion, fire, *some* sort of passionate reaction.

"Who will be next?" Lady Finchley asked. "Come, ladies. Who'll challenge Miss Peyton's record?"

At once, Lady Nibbleherd volunteered her niece,

and amongst titters and laughter, Miss Mottram exchanged places with Kate. The rest of the evening passed quickly, one game led to another, the merriment growing as the evening hours waned. Kate laughed and smiled, played every game and won many, flirted with Lord Briarly and teased the blond and bemused-looking Mr. Hammond-Betts. She would have enjoyed herself immensely were she not waiting on tenterhooks all evening for Neill Oakes to approach and say something outré or do something outré like . . . like pick her up and kiss her. Which, of course, he didn't.

Damn the man.

And so it went for the next five days and nights. He treated her with the utmost courtesy. His conversation was pleasant, serious, and formal. It was maddening. The only reason he gave her for joy was that he seemed utterly oblivious to the calves' eyes cast on him by the majority of unattached young females. They simpered and tittered and fawned, but he showed not the slightest sign of returning their obvious interest. Instead, he stood back, contenting himself with the company of the other young gentlemen like Kitlas, Lord Landry, and Geerken, which in itself Kate found surprising as none of these pinks of the ton seemed the sort of fellow Neill would once have given the time of day.

Otherwise, he was entirely attentive without hovering, always within circumspect range, diligent in offering her his arm should she lack for an escort, somberly complimentary, but never overly so, on her appearance. In other words, he was acting the consummate chaperone.

And it finally drove her to desperation . . .

Chapter 14

"You have been pressed into service by your hostess and must to take me to town," Kate announced the next morning.

Neill, breakfasting on the terrace as he read the morning posts from London, set down his cup, folded his newspaper, and looked up. Kate stood over him, a vision of elegance in a rouge-colored sarcenet spencer that fit closely over her lithe curves. A decidedly provocative little dark blue torque perched at a jaunty angle atop her white-blond curls, its fringed satin trim flirting with her pink cheek.

His heart catapulted in his chest, reacting in a way it never had four years ago. But four years ago her smile hadn't been filled with such female deviltry, nor had her eyes held so much amusement. Four years ago she hadn't been a woman, he realized. The casual, unconscious sway of her hips, the silvery laughter, the elegant brow that arched so ... archly, the way her eyes danced a second before her full lips formed a smile, the tilt of her head, the fleeting arabesque of her fingertips as she illustrated some point she was trying to make, all of it conspired to make her mysterious and fascinating and utterly captivating.

She really was not his Kate. Not as he remembered her. Not that it mattered in the least when it came to wanting her. If anything, he wanted her more. The last four days had been torturous. He begrudged every man there her most incidental touch, coveted every smile she offered another, whether it be boy or man, footman or duke. He prowled the perimeter of whatever room she occupied, covertly watching the men there for any hint of over-familiarity toward her, quick to caution against further transgressions.

He told himself it was his duty to do so, his obligation, a matter of honor. In truth, he knew it to be because he wanted to claim her for his own, and he couldn't. Until they left here, he couldn't even court her; he was her bloody chaperone.

It took all his effort to keep his expression bland now, but he managed to do so as he stood up and gestured for her to take a seat. She shook her head.

"No, we haven't time to dally. We have to go to town this morning," she said.

"We do?" he asked politely.

"Yes, in order that I can buy some ribbons and return in time to trim my bonnet for this afternoon's picnic."

He was torn. Part of him very much wanted the opportunity for a few private hours in her company. The other part resented being thrust into the role of doyen, like some toothless old uncle. Once again, he consigned Tom Peyton to perdition.

"I am sure Lady Finchley will lend you the use of her carriage and a footman to take you."

"Were you not listening, Neill?" She shook her head impatiently. "All the footmen are currently employed setting up the marquee for the picnic or going about other errands."

"Perhaps one of the other guests can drive you?" he suggested. "Lady Sorrell has her own carriage, and she—"

"Oh, for the love of all the saints, why cannot you ever do anything without an argument?" she broke in, tapping her foot. "If you want to refuse, pray lord, just do so rather than posing all sorts of alternatives and excuses."

"I don't want to refuse," he said sharply. He might be prohibited by the rules of etiquette to court her for now, but that didn't mean he was going to deprive himself of her company if that was what she wanted, which she clearly did. Though why he could not say. "I will be delighted to accompany you, Miss Peyton."

"Hm," she said, her expression somewhat mollified. "If this is what passes for delight in you, I should be interested to see your reluctance, *Captain Oakes*."

He smiled. She'd always had the knack of teasing him where others stood in terror.

"I shall call for a coach at once."

"Don't bother. One is already awaiting us at the front of the house."

He cocked a brow at her. "Very sure of yourself, aren't you?"

Her smile was enough to stop his breath. "When I want something. Oh, yes."

True to Kate's claim, a blue cabriolet awaited them on the front drive. A young groomsman held the head of a high-spirited gray gelding while Neill handed Kate into the carriage before climbing into the driver's seat.

"The gray be a bit fresh, sir," the groomsman said worriedly. "Would you like me to change him out for an easier-natured beast?"

Kate answered before Neill could reply. "I will

have you know, young man, that Captain Oakes was once the most bruising rider in the county." She gave a sniff. "Indeed, I am amazed you have not heard of him."

Neill glanced at her, surprised that she had leapt so readily to his defense. Perhaps she had forgiven him his early sins and was prepared to return to the camaraderie of their youth. And from there might not a more intimate future beckon? Hope made him impulsive, and impulsiveness had ever been his bête noire. He was determined to prove to her he was mature, thoughtful, worthy of her.

"Excuse my ignorance, miss," the boy said, flushing. "I'm not native to these parts."

"Oh," Kate said, her indignation disappearing. "Well, now you know. There was no steed in Burnewhinney beyond Captain Oakes's ability." She shot him an impish glance. "I trust that is still true?"

"I daresay I can manage. Thank you." With a flick of his wrists, he set the gray off at a brisk but controlled trot.

They had gone but a short distance in an uncomfortable silence when Kate finally spoke. "Did you enjoy being presented at court?"

He hadn't in particular. London society held few charms for him, and pageantry did more for the morale of the populace than those it honored, but it seemed churlish to say so. "Yes. It was a great compliment."

She glanced at him out of the side of her eyes, her expression oblique. "You have changed then. You never used to care much for compliments."

He gauged his response before replying. "If one is to successfully lead men into battle and, more importantly, successfully lead them out, one must have their good opinion in order that they trust you. So, yes, in that I have changed. I know the value of having the good opinion of others."

The mockery disappeared from her face, and she bent toward him, touching his hand lightly. "I am ashamed of myself. I should have realized you were not interested in flattery as a means of improving your opinion of yourself."

He gave a short laugh. "Well, as I recall, the only reason I didn't care for flattery when I was a lad was because my own opinion of myself was so exalted it never required bolstering by others. Quite the cocksure limb of Satan, I was."

"Yes. You were." She sounded wistful. "I daresay that stood you in good stead, too."

"How so?"

"I cannot imagine one could become a captain without confidence. Just as the good opinion of others enabled you to lead, so, too, must have your self-confidence. Uncertainty would be anathema in battle."

Her insight and the gravity with which she spoke impressed him, and he looked at her carefully. "You speak as if you had considered such matters before."

"Yes."

He smiled, a trifle baffled. "What would have led you to deliberate on such things?"

She turned, holding his gaze with hers, and said, quite simply, "Why, you, Neill."

His startled reaction caused the reins to bounce on the gray's haunches, and the gelding danced sideways, forcing Neill to concentrate long enough to bring him back under control. By the time he'd done so, Kate had turned away and was once more calmly regarding the road ahead.

"What do you mean?" he asked, trying with difficulty to sound nonchalant.

She answered at once. "I was worried about you, of course. We may not have parted on the best of terms, Neill, but that does not mean I did not care about your welfare. So I thought about it. About you. And I decided that being bold and self-assured"—she darted a teasing look at him—"would not be an altogether bad thing in an officer."

"I am humbled by your concern."

She gave a light chuckle. She thought he was teasing her. He was not.

"Yes. I cared what happened to you."

"Then why did you never write?"

"I did."

Once again, she'd startled him. "But I never received any letter."

Again she chuckled, but this time there was a mature and sardonic edge to it. "Come now, Neill. You of all people know my darling brothers' abilities and lack of abilities. Since when has any of my brothers been capable of parsing together more than the most rudimentary notes?"

He stared at her. "You wrote those letters?" he asked, though as soon as she'd said it, he'd recognized the truth. None of the Peyton lads were particularly articulate or sensitive, and especially early on he'd been impressed by the tenure of their missives. For good reason: They hadn't been theirs. The evocative descriptions of the countryside and the detailed passing of the seasons, the droll anecdotes about various people they knew and the detailed references to the history they shared . . . They had all been Kate's words that had transported him for those brief, essential respites from the battlefields of France to home in Burnewhinney.

"Not in their entirety," she answered lightly. "Just the interesting stuff."

This time he laughed, and the gray pranced in response. "Good Lord, Kate, why not simply write to me and sign your own name?"

"Pride," she said simply. "You may not have noticed, being occupied with a surplus of your own, but I am imbued with my own overlarge sense of self-worth."

"As a matter of fact, I do seem to recall a niggling sense that there might be another conceit as great as mine sharing the county. But I marked it down as delusion."

She laughed, and he joined her. It was so easy to laugh with her. There was no subtext to it, no fear of its being misunderstood, no reason it should be.

"Your turn," she said. "Why didn't you simply write to me?"

"I—"

"And one attempt is hardly worth mentioning."

"Well, then, I was afraid."

"Afraid?" she echoed, startled.

"Yes. I was afraid that if I wrote you again, you might write back and . . . and put a final end to our . . . friendship. Which I value." He smiled.

"Why?" She looked at him expectantly.

He wanted to tell her, but he couldn't. He had waited this long, and the house party was due to end in but a few days. Then he could complete the mission Tom had given him and present himself to her father and receive his permission to court her. He would do this properly, by God.

So when he spoke it was in a light, droll tone. "It would be deuced unpleasant being neighbors with a family where one of its members wouldn't speak to you. Besides, we are old friends, are we not? And one must keep one's old friends." He smiled. She did not. "So, I contented myself with asking your brother in each of the letters I wrote to share it with your family."

A shadow crossed her face. "I see. Well, thank heavens you never wrote me then and gave me a chance to dissolve our friendship, for where would I be now if I had?"

"Kate?"

"What with Tom haring off as he did and leaving me without a companion to countenance my stay? I suppose Lady Finchley would have filled the breach, but it isn't exactly nice, is it? And one must have a care for appearances." Her voice grew tighter and brighter as she continued.

"Of course, some would say that a young captain who has no blood connection whatsoever to a lady is hardly a proper chaperone for said young lady, but then one must take into account that the captain is, as you so *pointedly* pointed out, simply an old family friend. So thank you, *old friend,* for helping aid me in my spouse-acquiring endeavors."

The pleasure he'd been having in their conversation abruptly ended at this reminder of the position, the *only* position, he currently occupied in her life. One he did not want.

"I'm delighted to have your approval," he said, keeping his eye firmly on the gray's rump. "I shall strive to give satisfaction. Tell me, is there anyone in particular whom you favor?"

"Oh, yes," she said pertly.

"Might I ask whom?" *That I might make sure that he is suddenly compelled to leave the house party.*

She shook her head. "No, I don't think so. What if he doesn't return my regard? Indeed, I do not know how I would survive the mortification"—her voice abruptly faded to little more than a whisper— "or the anguish."

Anguish? Was her affection already fixed then? Not on Briarly, surely. He didn't know the earl, but he knew men, and Briarly's manner toward Kate had lacked any tenor of exclusivity or evidence of a deeper regard. If he hurt Kate . . .

Neill snapped the reins sharply, and the gray sprang into a lope, curtailing any further conversation by the jangle of the traces and the growl of the wheels. If only he could drive the rest of this damned house party to its end as quickly.

For the next quarter hour Neill's frustration kept pace with the growing coolness of Kate's expression. He wasn't sure exactly what he'd done to rouse her ire, only that it had something to do with their being old friends . . . dear God!

The chit couldn't actually seriously think he was calling her *old*? But then, at twenty, she was hardly in the first flush of youth. Perhaps she felt her unwed state made her somehow less desirable. The little fool. He could attest that she was far more desirable now than she had been at sixteen, and he had no doubt that with the passing of each season, she would simply grow even more beguiling.

And he had no intention of allowing any other man to be privy to such knowledge.

But . . . damn it. *Damn it!* What if this mysterious would-be suitor came up to scratch before he had the opportunity to speak? Had he not been there as her chaperone, he might have declared himself, or if he'd arrived already having secured her father's permission to speak, he would throw convention to the winds and declare himself. But he was, and he hadn't. He'd raced from London in a lather to get to Finchley Manor because he'd heard she would be there, thinking, with the shrewd canniness of the seasoned campaigner, to gauge the lay of the land before sallying forth onto the field. Well, more fool him. He'd only effectively put himself on the sidelines while others strove for her hand. *What* others?

"Oh!" Kate cried, as they crested the knoll that dropped into Parsley. "I'd forgotten the fair!"

He followed her gaze. The small hamlet of Parsley spread out before them like a broken Christmas cracker, spilling fairgoers and revelers, merchants and their wares across the roads and into the surrounding fields. Booths decorated with ribbons and rosettes lined the main streets, their sharp-eyed attendants swatting at lads dashing in and out, snatching an apple here, a meat pie there. Hawkers with baskets tied round their necks dodged donkey carts laden with jugs of fresh milk and cider. Musicians and puppeteers set up impromptu stages wherever space allowed, vying for custom as they entertained with ribald songs and pantomimes. A small dog walked on its forelegs in front of an old man in a multicolored coat while a monkey cheekily begged coins from the circle gathered round.

Kate's eyes shone with delight, and her lips were parted, like a child's. "Would you like to stay?" he asked.

She hesitated but then shook her head. "No. No. Lady Finchley will wonder what has become of us if we miss luncheon."

And would someone else miss her as well? And she him? he wondered.

"You recall where the draper's is located?" she asked.

"Yes." He expertly guided the flustered gray through the throngs crowding the street, heading down the main thoroughfare. At the bottom of the street, he turned the cabriolet onto an equally crowded side street, where the draper's stood across from the town's stable. This road, too, was choked with pedestrians, mostly men, laborers from the looks of them, and many whom Neill recognized.

He pulled the carriage to a stop in front of the draper's, jumped down, and went round to the other side. Kate was waiting for him, already standing. He did not bother with the steps; he simply held his arms up and as easily and naturally as breathing, she leaned forward, bracing her hands on his shoulders while he spanned her narrow waist and lifted her to the ground. He looked down into her upturned face. For a second he held her there.

"Kate . . ."

"Yes?"

No. "How long will you be?"

She pushed away from him. "As long as necessary," she snapped and, without looking back, sailed into the draper's shop, her color high and her chin higher.

He raked his hand though his hair, swearing viciously under his breath as he climbed back into the carriage. He was just about to sit down when from his vantage he spied two men enclosed by a rope in a small square of bare land in the stable's side yard across the street. It must be the annual boxing championship and, by the looks of things, nearly at an end. One man lay prone on the ground while the other, a strapping blond youngster, raised one fist above his head as his companions clapped him heartily on the back.

Neill's gaze sharpened. By God, it was Tom, Kate's brother.

Neill jumped down from the carriage. All his frustration and anger came boiling up as he crossed the street, shoving his way through the ring of cheering men toward Tom Peyton, bloody Tom Peyton, the author of his current misery. Tom looked up, as the mob, sensing a dangerous newcomer in their midst, backed away from Neill.

"Come to congratulate me, have you, Neill?" Tom said on spying Neill.

"No."

"No? Well, there's a bit of rot. I've just won the county title for the third year in a row, and me best friend can't say 'good oh'?" he said plaintively. "Then what are you here for, and looking as black-eyed as any scoundrel, too?"

"I'm here to take the title from you," Neill ground out.

"Damned you say!" Tom exploded.

"Too late!" one of the men beside Tom yelled. "He already won, fair and square." He'd probably already collected a tidy sum betting on Tom to win and now feared he'd lose his winnings.

"Ain't too late!" shouted another. "Anyone can challenge anyone as long as there's two men standing. Them's the rules."

A chorus of shouts and hollers broke out, some for and some against Neill's right to challenge Tom.

"Look you here!" Neill thundered above the din. "If I win, I don't want the purse, the title, or the bloody ribbon."

"Then what do you want?" Tom asked, already flexing his shoulder muscles.

Neill told him.

Chapter 15

Kate had heard the loud catcalls and shouts and yelps of boys behaving badly too often to confuse it for anything else. Males, somewhere, were up to no good. She paid for the ribbon she didn't want and hadn't needed, the entire mission simply a device to spend some time alone with Neill—and how very well that had *not* gone—and went in search of the source.

She found it right outside the door.

A brawl was in progress. Two men faced each other amidst the tight circle of onlookers, both panting heavily, shirts sweat-soaked and half-undone. Kate stared in stunned disbelief. She knew them both. One was her older brother Tom and the other Neill Oakes.

Of all the bloody— Her lips flattened to a tight line. She had had enough.

Jerking her skirts high above slender ankles, she stepped off the raised walk and into the dusty street. Whether it was the obvious quality of her dress or the even more obvious danger in her dark blue eyes, the company of men parted before her like the proverbial Red Sea, closing tight in her wake as she waded into the fracas. She didn't stop at the edge of the fight circle, either, but strode right up to the two men now grappling on the ground, seized her big blond brother by a hank of hair, and yanked. Hard.

"Ow!" he howled, letting go of Neill and rolling on his back. He glowered up at her. "Bloody hell, Kate! That hurt!"

"Good! You ought to be ashamed of yourself, brawling like a boy. And the rest of you, too." Her lethal gaze swung around to encompass the group of increasingly uncomfortable-looking men.

"Billy Eggs, does your wife know you're here and, I'll guess, betting on blood sports? I thought not. And Granger Tobey, you're too old for this nonsense, and yet here you are, sporting a bloody nose. I would hope my brother did not give it to you since he's a full two decades your junior, but I don't have that much faith in his judgment."

"You shouldn't be here, Kate," a low male voice said.

She swung around, expecting to find Neill still on the ground—he'd looked like he'd been getting the worst of Tom's fists. Instead, she found herself having to look up. He was standing close behind her, his eyes glittering like ebon coals.

"Neither should you, Neill Oakes."

"Go back into the shop and wait for me," he said and, by God, if it didn't sound like a command.

"I most certainly will not. Of all the japes—"

The rest of her words were cut off as, with a growl, Neill grabbed her wrist, jerked her forward, and slung her like a sack of potatoes over his shoulder.

"Oh! Put me down! Unhand me at once!" she yelped, as the crowd of men erupted from silence into cheers.

"That's the way, Captain!"

"Well done, Oakes m'lad!"

"Show no mercy!"

"Oh!" she squealed, kicking violently and battering his broad back with her fists, every vestige of hard-earned sophistication stripped away in a matter of seconds before this provocation. "Put me down, you blackguard!"

In answer, he strode through the crowd with her slung over his shoulder, making for the stables.

"I say, Neill," Tom called out, sounding a little worried. "You aren't going to—"

"Shut up, Tom," Neill spat out. "I'll be back to finish what we started in a minute."

And with that, he kicked open the stable-office door. Inside, he kept ignoring Kate's protests—and pummeling—as he made his way to the tack-room door. He stepped inside. The room was small, with only one small window high on the exterior wall allowing in a shaft of light. Dust motes danced woozily at their entrance, and a pigeon, roosting in the rafter overhead, fluttered away through the narrow window. Well-tended headsets and tack hung from hooks on the wall, and a single saddle, oiled and clean, rested on a hobbyhorse in the corner. On the far wall had been piled a stack of blankets.

A raffish smile cleaved his dark, handsome face as Neill spied the blankets and, for just an instant, Kate's heart pattered wildly in a combination of fear and anticipation. Then he tossed her on the blankets and, without a glance, turned and walked out, shutting the door behind her. Kate stared slack-jawed with disbelief as she heard the unmistakable sound of a bolt being driven home.

He'd locked her in.

Though only twenty minutes, it seemed to Kate hours before she heard one final swelling roar from the crowd outside and, a few minutes later, the sound of footsteps. She scrambled to her feet and set her hands on her hips, facing the door as she prepared to give whoever entered, Neill or Tom, the sharp side of her tongue.

The door swung open, and the sudden bright light dazzled her eyes. She blinked at the tall, broad-shouldered figure outlined in the door.

"Neill?" she whispered.

He stepped inside, and she inhaled sharply at the sight of him. His black curls were damp and dusty, his chest working like a bellows beneath his ripped and sweat-soaked shirt. A bruise was already darkening one cheek.

He didn't say a word.

The sight of him sent a ripple of trepidation running through her. But she was a brave girl and used to handling miscreant boys. She knew better than to show fear or hesitation.

She marshaled her indignation. "Well, what have you to say for yourself?" she demanded. "Locking me up in here while you go and pummel my brother. I hope you left him still conscious? Although many would say, myself included, that consciousness in Tom is barely discernible from insensibility, as he doesn't seem to *think* too often. But then neither do you, Neill Oakes. I thought you had changed, but you're still the black sheep of *my* family, and how did that happen I should like to know since we don't even share a single ancestor?"

She was babbling, and she knew it. She always babbled when she was nervous. She made herself stop. She had already ruined her new image as a sophisticated young lady by acting a dervishine. She took a deep breath and exhaled, composing herself.

"Well?" she said.

"Are you quite done?" he asked, as poised as if they were conversing in Lady Finchley's drawing room.

She strove to match his aplomb. "Yes. I believe so."

"Good," he said, and though he spoke quite pleasantly, Kate shivered. "Because I have a few things I would like to say, if I may?"

She nodded, watching him warily.

"Thank you. First off"—he took a step toward her—"I am not your brother."

"I know that. I—"

He held up his hand, forestalling her. "Apparently you do not; otherwise, you would not be attempting to ride roughshod over me as you do that pack of reprobates with whom you live. So, let me make perfectly clear, *I am not your brother.* I have never had any brotherly feelings for you and, despite what you just said, I do not think you have ever had any sisterly feelings toward me. Am I correct?"

He took another step forward. Kate held her ground. Barely.

"Am I correct?" he insisted.

He seemed to be holding his breath.

"Yes," she agreed.

He released his breath, his expression going even more intent as his gaze trapped hers. He moved closer, step by inexorable step. Her heart raced.

"And I am not your uncle." He was more than two-thirds of the way across the room now, and Kate's courage, which had hitherto held, began to erode. She trembled.

"Nor am I your trusty, musty old family friend." She backed up; he stepped forward. Her shoulder banged against the wall. He reached up, tilting her chin, angling her face into the light.

"And, praise God, I am *not* your chaperone."

"What?"

"Your brother has just recently decided to return to the house party as your chaperone." There was just a trace of a dark satisfaction in Neill's voice.

"He did?" Kate asked, amazed.

"Yes," Neill said. "So now I am free to follow my own agenda."

"I see," she said breathlessly. He looked quite dangerous, his dark head bent toward hers, and yet, she wasn't afraid. At least, not terribly.

"No. I don't think you do," Neill said. "Not yet. But I intend to remedy that."

And with that, he leaned down and touched his mouth to hers, a brief, shivering glide of his lips over hers that made her knees go weak; and then it was over too quickly. Far, far too quickly.

"I came here for you, Kate Peyton. I have waited

for four years to woo you and win you and make you my bride," he said in a low, fierce voice. "And I do not give a *damn* what your intentions are or whom you've decided you would like to marry, whether it be the local vicar or a landed earl, because no one, *no one,* will ever love you as deeply or passionately or *honorably* as I have and do and will love you. No one."

Her eyelids snapped open. *He* loved *her*? *He'd* waited four years to court *her*? And yet he'd stood by while she flirted and simpered and played asinine games and pretended to be a polished woman of the world when all the while all she'd ever hoped to accomplish had been to spark some emotion in him that wasn't appropriate and avuncular and dutiful! Oh!

"Then why didn't you say so at once?" she exclaimed, reaching out and shoving him so hard in the chest that he stumbled back a step.

He stared at her in astonishment.

"Why did you not simply"—she shoved him again—"tell me you loved me?" She pushed again, violently. This time he didn't move. It didn't matter. She was furious, and it felt good to shove someone!

She braced her hands against his broad, hard chest, preparing to heave him straight over, but he grabbed hold of her wrists, keeping her hands locked against him.

"Because it wouldn't have been respectable."

" 'Respectable'?" she mouthed, astonished.

"Yes. I would not have it thought that I abused the intimacy granted me by my position as your chaperone to pursue my own ends. It would be considered ignoble. *Dishonorable.*"

"Oh, that's rich, indeed!" she laughed bitterly. "Since when did Neill Oakes give a farthing for the opinion of others?"

And now the anger in her had finally set fire to the anger in him. "Since your father informed me that, until I'd developed a sense of purpose, values, and honor, I would not be allowed to pay you court."

"He did?"

"Yes. Four years ago, just before you caught up with me at the footbridge."

The tension seeped out of her, and her rigid fingers relaxed against his chest, yet still he held them in place. His own expression softened as he stared down at her, reading her recall of the scene as she discovered new meaning in the words he'd said so long ago.

"He made me swear, on my honor, that I would not court you until you were eighteen," he said more gently. "I intended to abide by his wishes, but that same day when you kissed me, I knew I did not, in fact, have the resolve or fortitude to stand silently by as each day you grew more lovely, more winning, more . . . Kate. And the thought of having to watch other men court you in the meantime, as I knew they must, ate at me like acid.

"I realized I was not the man I thought myself. And I determined then that I would be the better man, the man you deserved, and not some spoiled brat who insisted on his way. So I bought a commission." He gently moved her two hands together, encircling both wrists in one of his own large hands and freeing the other. He reached up, brushing her cheek with a featherlight touch. She could not tell if he shivered or if it was her.

"But I did not count on how much harder it would be to be away from you, to be unable to watch you turn from girl to woman, to hear only secondhand of your antics and scarps and virtues and demerits. I imagined Tom must have thought I was mad, I hounded him so for every detail of every incident that regarded you."

"I didn't intend to stay away so long. But duty once answered is a jealous mistress, and not until Napoleon was well and truly vanquished was I able to return here to you, free of obligation and responsibility, praying you had not found someone else in the interim." His expression abruptly grew grim. "But apparently I was away too long, for now you tell me you've set your cap at some poor fool. Well, Kate, I cannot let you do that."

"Why?" she asked, gazing up into his harsh face,

longing to hear him say the words she'd dreamed so long of hearing from him.

"Because no one else knows you like I do. No one else understands you like I do. You'd terrify any other poor bounder with your bullying and sharp tongue. He'd have white hair within a fortnight of making you his bride."

This was not what she'd expected to hear, and she stared at him, shocked speechless.

"It's true," he said, nodding sententiously. "You're a virago and a tyrant and an angel and a sylph and a faerie princess and a tempest."

"I am not!" she said indignantly, her hands balling into fists on his chest.

"You are!" he declared, and now, for some reason, he'd begun laughing, his strong white teeth flashing in his dark, dirt-smeared face. "Kicking me like the veriest shrew and screeching like a harridan. The earl would be appalled."

"The earl—" she sputtered to a stop. "I do not give a fig for the Earl of Briarly's opinion."

He snatched her close, half-lifting her in his embrace. "Then who is it? Who have you set your mind on, Kate? Tell me what poor wretch you've a mind to spend your life tormenting?" And though his tone was cajoling, there was a fierce earnestness at its core. He gave her a little shake. "Tell me, I say!"

"Why?" she demanded. "So you can go and warn him of how near he stands to a dire fate?"

"No. So I can know what sort of man finds favor with you. What is his name?"

He looked so raw and exposed that she could not taunt him further even though his damned nobility had set her on a rack of frustration and despair this past week. "Neill Oakes."

His dark brows dipped in consternation as his gaze roved over her face, searching for irony or worse, but all he saw were her eyes, deep and dark, shining with a soft earnest light and a wash of unshed tears.

"You. Neill Oakes. The same man I set my heart on when I was fourteen." She gave a little laugh. "We harpies and viragos are a fiercely loyal lot. Once we pick our victim, there is a no-more-faithful scourge. You are the only man I have ever loved or ever will."

She pulled her hands free of his and wrapped her arms around his shoulders as she had done four years ago and, as she had four years ago, she stood as tall and pulled his head down to meet her kiss. "And now, lest you dare leave me to wait for you another four years, Neil Oakes, I intend that you should compromise me."

"What?" he asked, startled.

"I have heard of other women who use this ploy to bind a man to them, and I find I am not above such machinations." She nibbled at the beard-roughened angle of his dark jaw, and he shuddered.

"Of course, such schemes and ruses only work on the men who value their honor."

"Dear Lord, Kate, be careful what you start—" he whispered hoarsely.

"This was started a long time ago, Captain Oakes. Four years ago. So here, now, once again and only once, I will ask you: Will you kiss me?"

This time he did not stand as if transfixed. With a low sound of hunger, he swept her high in his arms as his mouth descended greedily over hers. He moved to the pile of blankets and eased her down amongst them, his mouth still married to hers. She arched up against him, reveling in the delicious weight of him, the powerful musculature, the heated dense skin. He opened his mouth over hers, his tongue lining the seam of her closed lips until she instinctively opened for him and tasted his tongue.

She was a country miss. She knew the ways of male and female, and she had waited so long, so eagerly, so ardently for this. Her hands flowed up beneath his ruined shirt, following the bunching muscles in his back up to the wide shoulders, clutching him closer. His kiss slipped from the corner of her mouth, to the angle of her jaw, then along her neck, a slow, heated, wet kiss that dropped to her neckline.

He nuzzled aside the thin fabric, baring her breast, his lips exploring with excruciating thoroughness the plump womanly flesh until at last he found her nipple and drew it deep into his mouth. She bowed off the blanket, pleasure spearing through her, her head thrown back as she clutched at his hair, holding his dark head to her.

When he lifted his head, his eyes were as jetty as the night and his expression fierce and triumphant. "You will marry me."

"Yes," she panted.

She wrapped her arms around his flanks, but he held her down, feathering kisses over her neck and cheeks, nipping at her shoulders and sucking her earlobes. "Soon?" he murmured.

"In all possible haste."

"Swear it."

"I swear it!" she vowed. "Only now, please . . . do . . . oh, *please*."

And he did.

Chapter 16

A very glum-looking Tom Peyton presented himself at Lady Finchley's later that afternoon and gave a long and completely incomprehensible explanation as to how he had found himself suddenly able after all to perform his brotherly duties and once more act as his sister's chaperone.

Carolyn, standing outside on the front terrace beside her husband while she listened to the young man, could not help but wonder if the black eye the young Mr. Peyton was sporting might have had something to do with this turnabout, but was too polite a hostess to inquire. It did not keep her, however, from speculating later that evening to her husband. Nonetheless, she welcomed the young man back warmly; Tom Peyton was a handsome, robust-looking fellow, and now that he'd returned, it meant that Captain Oakes who, despite what Briarly believed, had not shown the least untoward attention to Kate Peyton all week, could consider himself free to mingle with the other young ladies, adding a sum total of two eligible bachelors to the mix. Which made things a great deal more interesting for the unattached young ladies in attendance although, to her disappointment, Georgina showed no particular interest in the man.

Several hours later, as Carolyn was reorganizing the teams for the croquet tournament that afternoon, a footman announced that visitors were arriving. Surprised, Carolyn gathered her husband and went out to the terrace to greet their new, unexpected arrivals, only to find they weren't unexpected after all, as it was only Captain Oakes in Briarly's blue cabriolet, attending Miss Peyton. But then she saw riding along behind them a handsome, whipcord-thin gentleman of middling years.

"By Jove," Finchley murmured. "If it ain't old Peyton himself. Invited him, of course, but I thought he wrote back declining. Wasn't surprised. I don't think the old fellow's been in society for a decade at least! Now what brings him here?"

"A fifteen-hand Arabian with the looks of the Byerley Turk, if I'd have my guess."

Carolyn looked around to find her brother Hugh had joined them on the terrace.

"I wonder if he's breeding horses up there on

that farm of his," he murmured. "Shouldn't have loaned Miss Peyton my carriage had I known her father was breeding horses of that quality up there. Oh, well, from the looks of things, it's too late for regrets now."

"Whatever are you talking about, Briarly?" Finchley demanded, as the footmen hurried forth to help Miss Peyton down and assist Mr. Peyton to alight.

"Miss Peyton. I offered her the use of my carriage and suggested she find herself a suitable escort—like her chaperone, Oakes—and go to Parsley. Pray don't look at me like that, Carolyn. I thought it about time she and the captain get on with their, er, romance."

Carolyn peered more closely at the handsome black-haired captain and the petite silvery blond woman at his side. Sure enough, Kate's color was high and her eyes bright as the captain bent with all solicitousness nearer her, his gaze tender.

"Good heavens, Briarly, I didn't know you were such a romantic," Carolyn said with a laugh.

"Not romantic. Practical. The poor blighter was chasing off every fellow who dared pass more than a pleasant minute with Miss Peyton, and I feared he might go from growling to more physical means of doing so and thereby ruin Caro's fete. Can't have that, can we?"

"Oh, no, no. Course not," both Carolyn and

Finchley hastened to assure him, though behind his back they traded amused looks.

"So, how did Mr. Peyton come to be involved?" Finchley asked.

"Don't know, expect we'll find out though soon enough."

And the trio essayed smiles as Mr. Peyton mounted the steps, Captain Oakes and Miss Peyton following at some little distance behind.

He stopped at the top and beamed at them. "Well now, I expect you wonder why I am here," he said without preamble. "I know I sent me son Tom to watch over Kate here, and in the usual way of things that would be all well and good. But things aren't as usual. Neill here"—he gestured casually at the tall young man behind him—"has asked for Kate's hand in marriage, and I gave him my consent to ask her and ask her he did and apparently she said yes because now they're all in a dither to get leg-shackled. And young people in a dither ain't to be trusted. And Tom, good lad though he be, ain't no match against a young couple in a dither and less of an obstacle if they intend to do anything they oughtn't. So that's why I'm here and thanking you kindly for your hospitality."

And as he shook Finchley's hand and traded greetings with Briarly, Carolyn couldn't help but notice the smile Captain Oakes bent on Kate

Peyton at Mr. Peyton's explanation or the pretty way she colored up in response and Carolyn wondered . . .

But then she decided it was not her place to wonder, and she tucked her hand into her husband's and led the way in to tea.

Chapter 17

That night before dinner, Carolyn drifted through her drawing room surveying all the unmarried women. Frankly, eligible spouses for Hugh were falling by the wayside, though her annoying brother didn't show any signs of realizing what he was missing. First he was too slow to catch Gwendolyn before Charters snapped her up. And then Oakes practically stole Kate out of his very arms, if Carolyn understood Hugh's reference to "courting" Kate correctly.

It was profoundly annoying.

It didn't help that her husband was so unruffled. "Leave Hugh be," Piers had told her earlier. "He'll find someone on his own."

Caroline had caught herself chewing a fingernail. "Hugh is just so irritating. He spends all his time out in the stables. He might as well have stayed on his own estate and trained that stupid horse there. He hardly ever appears for the afternoon games, and yesterday I could have sworn that he brought the stink of the stables into dinner with him on the bottom of his boot."

"If you ask me," Piers had said, "he's not interested in those women you've got on your list."

"Good thing," she had retorted. "Because both of them found spouses before he got around to doing more than kissing their hands."

"I think he wants Georgina," Piers had said.

And then he had waltzed out of the room before she could even tell him that she had a suspicion of the same thing herself, which was just like a man.

But was Georgina interested in Hugh?

That was the thought that made Carolyn's heart sink, even as she circulated amongst her party, listening to the chatter and smilingly throwing in a comment here and there. Georgie had never shown the slightest preference for Hugh that Carolyn could remember.

How could she? Carolyn wrinkled her nose and tried to remember that she had a little sister's point of view. She would be the first, the very first, to say that Hugh was a prince among men . . . sometimes. He was strong, and honorable, and true to the bone.

But if there was one thing Hugh wasn't, it was

elegant. And Georgina? Carolyn knew her best friend as well as she knew herself. Georgie could spend an hour absorbed by the sheen of a fabric or the weave of some gorgeous silk from India in a way that even Carolyn couldn't. And Carolyn considered herself extremely well turned out.

Whereas . . . Hugh?

She knew for a fact that he had a valet, but a casual bystander wouldn't, half the time. Not to mention the fact that he was currently causing a scandal among the matrons by throwing off his shirt while training that horse of his. It was beyond scandalous. Not only was he not elegant; half the time he wasn't even clothed. Several of the strictest mamas wouldn't let their daughters anywhere near the stables for fear they might catch sight of his chest.

She sighed, noticing that Georgina had not yet appeared in the drawing room. No, it would never work. Hugh was probably attracted to her just because she was so dainty and beautiful—but the opposite would never be true. Georgie wouldn't settle for a man who sometimes had manure on his heels and could rarely be found in the dining room, and never on time.

Carolyn paused for a moment next to Gwendolyn and Charters. Somewhat to her astonishment, they were smiling benevolently at Octavia Darlington—who was standing rather closer to Allen Glover than one might expect of casual acquaintances. But poor Allen wasn't the type to be able to pop the question without encouragement, which Octavia looked eager to give him.

"I know that look," a voice said in her ear.

It was Piers. "I was just thinking," she said in a hushed tone, "that a certain young couple merely need a little nudge—"

"Don't make me play any more of those damned games," Piers said with a groan. "I beg of you, Carolyn!"

"I've asked hardly anything of you," she said indignantly. "Here you've been running off every morning grouse hunting, and I merely request a little time in the afternoon. And just look how well it's working, Piers! I vow this house is a veritable Cupid's nest."

"Just don't make me play any more games," her husband growled again. But she could tell he wasn't truly aggravated.

"Perhaps something that would mix up the seating at dinner," she said musingly.

"You are a menace," Piers said, taking her arm. "Shall I signal for the bell?"

"Oh no, we can't go in yet," Carolyn said. "Hugh's not here, which is neither here nor there because he's often late for supper, but Georgie isn't down yet either. I'll give her a few more minutes."

Chapter 18

*L*ady Georgina Sorrell had grown accustomed to feeling lonely, ever since Richard died. Before that date too, if she were honest with herself. Poor Richard was ill the whole last year of their marriage, and even before that they seemed to have forgotten how to talk to each other.

But somehow the loneliness felt particularly acute after watching Captain Oakes kiss his Kate so passionately that they didn't even know they had an audience. That would make anyone feel a bit dour.

It certainly wasn't because Carolyn had originally suggested that *she* should marry the captain. True, Oakes was the type she liked: big, with that sort of brute manliness about him . . . She jerked her thoughts away.

Brutish maleness was a ridiculous quality for a lady to admire.

Richard had been utterly unlike that. He was always debonair. Polished. Clean-shaven, sweet-smelling.

Boring.

There it was: the truth about her marriage finally admitted. Richard had been boring, and then he got that horrible illness and declined for a year. And through all the misery of it, he never complained. He was angelic, really.

It was hard to live with the memory of an angel.

He never kissed her so hard that she bent backward, the way the captain kissed Kate, nor looked at her the way that the Earl of Charters looked at Gwendolyn, as if he wanted to lick her from her top to toes.

And now all those happy couples were gathering in the drawing room to stare into each other's eyes, and she just couldn't . . . she just couldn't.

Her evening gown was new, made of a gorgeous brandy yellow silk, so heavy that it had wonderful drape. It was cut with a daring scantiness around the bosom that no debutante could get away with.

Yet even a new gown with flirty little sleeves and sleek lines didn't make her feel desirable. Or happy.

She drifted down the stairs, fingers on the railings. After Richard died, she had made up her mind not to marry again. But even when she reminded herself of the pleasures of eating breakfast alone, of never receiving a knock on her bedchamber door from a man, of never fearing that someone she cared for would be dead by the next morning . . .

Still the only thing she felt was envy. Green, fierce envy. *She* wanted to be desired so passionately that a man's face looked almost mad with it. *She* wanted to be kissed until her lips were rosy and her eyes were shining.

That did it. She reached the bottom of the stairs and rather than move toward the swell of high-pitched voices in the drawing room, she walked straight ahead. A footman sprang forward, opening the front door, and she walked down the steps into the open air.

The butler scrambled after her with a wrap, but she sent him back into the house. It was only seven in the evening, and the air was warm. The sky was the deep pearly blue that promised twilight. She wandered into the rose gardens, met by the faint hum of bees catching last sips from roses warmed by the sun.

The stables were beyond the gardens, through a little stone archway and down a pebbled path. By all rights the man in question should be in the drawing room, chattering to debutantes.

He had lost the first lady on his list to his best friend and the second to Captain Oakes. He should be at his sister's side, imploring her for the name of a third candidate. But Hugh hadn't made it to the table earlier than five minutes after the gong any day in the past week.

The air changed as she left the garden; the earthy smell of warm dirt and manure made roses seem effeminate and cloying. She walked toward the large ring adjacent to the stables. Light poured through the stable window to the rear, but the rest of the ring was in deep shadow.

For a moment she thought he wasn't here, but then she saw Hugh with his back to her, riding Richelieu slowly around the ring. She leaned against the fence, listening to the deep rumble of his voice as he talked to his mount. The horse was listening intently, perking first one ear, then the other.

Richelieu was a rangy, powerful animal, his coat a color of rich brown so dark that it looked near black in this light. There was something of the devil about him, in the tilt of his eyes and the way he kept shaking his bridle as if answering Hugh.

But it wasn't Richelieu who caught Georgina's attention. It was Hugh. Hugh, who was practically her older brother. Hugh, who had picked her off gravel paths when she'd sprawled, wiped her tears, likely wiped her nose, if not her bottom.

He wasn't wearing a shirt. He was riding his

horse around the ring without a scrap of cloth on his upper body. Just like that, her heart sped up and started thudding in her chest.

Her memory presented her, willy-nilly, with a picture of her marriage, one that made her husband look like a faded image in a mirror. Richard had been as sleek and white-skinned as she was. He hadn't been frail, until he was ill, but his arms were wiry and his chest hairless. He was neat, and elegant, and resembled a well-groomed swallow.

But Hugh—nothing about Hugh could be described as wiry, or sleek. His chest was pure muscle, the kind that came from fighting thoroughbred horses for mastery, day after day. Even in the waning light, she could see that his shoulders were enormous, his arms rippled with muscles as he loosely held the reins. He was turned to the side, slightly away from her, so she could see how the muscles marched down his broad back.

Her fingers twitched as her imagination leapt straight from watching to touching, to running her hands down those muscles and feeling him live and strong in her arms. He was like a medieval champion, practicing to defend his lady, or to start a Crusade.

She forgot to breathe, willing him to turn so she could see his chest. Finally, they reached the curve of the stable yard, and Richelieu turned toward her. The horse began to prance a little, lifting his legs in a graceful, flirty dance.

Hugh laughed down at the stallion, still talking. His skin was a dark honey, so he had probably made a habit of throwing off his shirt when he got too hot. His chest was shadowed with hair that darkened to an arrow just before disappearing into his breeches.

Wincing at her own foolishness, she discarded the idea of a medieval knight and turned him to a god . . . Apollo, training a new horse so that he could ride the skies to awake the sun.

Georgina swallowed. She should leave. Now. Before Hugh saw her, before she acted on the promptings of her overheated imagination.

He raised his eyes and saw her. It was a moment she never forgot, in the whole of her life: the great bronzed man astride a perfect horse, backed by sky the color of a dark sapphire. Hugh looked as remote and untouchable as any Greek deity—and yet the moment their eyes met, something flared to life in his face that she had never seen on a man's face before.

Something that was for her alone. Something that stole the breath from her chest and sent a shiver down her back.

And then it was gone, and Hugh was swinging down from his mount, giving her a cheerful hello.

"I suppose I'm late to supper again," he said, throwing Richelieu's reins over a post. He didn't seem to be aware that he wasn't properly clothed. The last rays of the sun caught on his shoulders and arms.

Georgina had an overwhelming urge to run. He was absurdly different from the men she had known. Too much, too male, too strong, too—too everything. "Yes, you should come to the meal now," she managed. "After you bathe, of course."

He reached out and pulled a linen shirt off the railing. "I had a bath after the training session this morning. You never come to watch." He pulled the shirt over his head.

"I didn't know you were admitting an audience for your ablutions," she said, laughing at him.

"I could make an exception for you," he replied, his eyes on hers. "But I was actually referring to my training sessions with Richelieu."

"No," she said. She refused to join goggling women who sighed over his shoulders and saved sugar for his horse.

Though to say that she wasn't sighing over his shoulders would be a lie.

"Why not?" he asked, sounding genuinely curious. "Don't you like horses anymore? You loved them as a girl. I still remember that little pony you had—"

"Sugarpie," she put in.

"That's right. Not a Shetland, but a Fell pony. She had a straight back, as I remember, and a temper."

Georgina smiled. "Do you remember how she would buck and carry on if she thought it was high time to return home? If I took her just a hair too far away from the stables, she would gallop me all the way home."

"I have a mind to take Richelieu into the country tomorrow," he said, pushing his shirt into his breeches. "Would you like to come with me?"

"I haven't a mount."

"Carolyn's mare is not as feisty as your Sugarpie, but she has nice manners. You'd be doing me a favor."

"Oh?" She raised an eyebrow.

"I've been working Richelieu too hard. I need to take him out for fun."

"Fun? I thought racehorses liked racing. Isn't that fun for him?"

"If training becomes too much like work, he'll lose heart. I'll let him eat some grass from a ditch, and steal an apple from an orchard, and just graze in a field, if I can find one without an irate farmer. I want to let him be a horse tomorrow, not a potential winner."

"Fun," she echoed.

He leaned over the railing and tipped up her chin with one finger. "Do you remember having fun, Georgie?"

"I often have a good time," she protested, her eyes caught by his lower lip. All those years when she thought of him as a surrogate older brother, why hadn't she noticed that his bottom lip was so deep? Because it wasn't an appropriate thought, that was why.

"You don't seem to be having a very good time this summer." He reached out and tapped her nose. "Droopy lips. Sad eyes."

This was the Hugh she remembered, the one who looked out for all of them, who picked up a trailing child, who dried tears and asked questions. "Well," she said, smiling a bit, "it is true that both of our prospective spouses were stolen away."

Something changed in his eyes. "I didn't know you had one."

"Captain Oakes?" she prompted. "Carolyn invited him to this party especially for me, and one of the women on your list snatched him up before I had more than a dance or two."

"But Bergeron is dancing attendance on you," he said, leaning on the fence as if he were prepared to talk all night. "And Geerken, though he's such a lame fool that I trust you aren't considering him. I was under the impression that you had sworn off matrimony, but if so, you clearly forgot to inform your devoted swains."

"I can't announce that. I would have nothing to do at balls. No one would dance with me."

"Yes, they would."

"No—"

He leaned a little closer. "You're a widow, Georgie. They would dance with you because you are utterly delicious, and they would love to bed you." His breath stirred the curls at her forehead. He smelled like clean sweat and faint spice, like straw and man.

"So you would leave me with no one to talk to but reprobates?"

"A rake's conversation is undoubtedly more interesting than Geerken's."

"You make it sound as if no true gentleman would wish to marry me, but I can assure you—"

"Oh, they want to marry you," he said. "Pembroke, Landry, and Kitlas. Especially Kitlas. He looks at you as if you're Venus herself. All except for Louis DuPreye, of course, and that's because he's already married."

"Then he should stop ogling me," Georgina said firmly.

"And touching you," he said. "You tell me if he goes too far, and I'll knock him into the next county."

Some dim part of her mind registered that Hugh seemed to have cataloged every man who had danced with her in the last week, every man who had paid her a compliment. Of course, he was probably just keeping an eye on her, the way a good brother ought.

"Unless you want him to touch you," he added.

"No," she said, hardly remembering what it was she wanted or didn't want, at least when it came to her suitors.

"You're so damned beautiful that you could tell every man in the house that you don't mean to marry, and they wouldn't give up hope."

"You're just being loyal because you've known me so long," she said, smiling at him.

"Hair like a flame." He ran a finger down one of her curls.

"Temper to match, that's what my mother always said."

"You must know about your eyes, so I'm not going to say anything about them," he said briskly (and disappointingly). "Perfect little chin, high cheekbones, gorgeous skin . . . Gods alive, Georgie, just who would you classify as beautiful if not yourself?"

She felt thrilled—and embarrassed. "I didn't mean that sort of beauty. I meant the kind of thing that Gwendolyn has."

"Gwendolyn?" He looked stunned. "Pale version of yourself, if you ask me. Like a faded portrait."

That was uncannily close to her comparison of Richard to him. "I didn't mean our physical looks," she said, trying to explain, though she felt like a vain fool begging for compliments. "It's the way Gwendolyn looks as if she stepped from the frame of a Raphael painting."

Hugh turned around and bellowed, "Fimble!"

A stable hand appeared in the doorway. Hugh gestured toward Richelieu and jumped over the fence. Georgina fell back a step. He towered over her. His hair had fallen over his brow, and his shirt billowed loose again.

"You're a fool," he said conversationally, taking her arm and walking back to the house.

"I know," she said. "Let's talk of something else."

"Right. Tomorrow. I'll see you at the stables at eight in the morning. We have to leave before people drift down to see Richelieu in training."

"I didn't say I would—"

They were just passing under the old stone arch leading to the rose gardens. He stopped and pulled her to a stop as well. She stumbled, and he caught her arm.

"You can't just rein me in like one of your horses, Hugh," she said, knowing she was trembling. And not from stumbling. It was the warmth of his hand on her bare arm.

"Damn it, Georgie." He stared down at her. "You know I'm no good at compliments."

"I was fishing for them," she confessed. "Just ignore me."

"That's just it. I can't ignore you. I never ignore you."

She opened her mouth, but no words came out.

"If I've learned one thing in this damned interminable week, it's that I feel happy when I see you. Whereas I don't feel a damned thing when I look at Gwendolyn. Other than relief that she took herself off my list," he added.

She could feel a shaky smile shaping on her lips. "Oh, Hugh."

He waited, just a moment. He was giving her a chance to start away, like a rabbit jumping from under a hedge. She could utter a careless laugh and scamper back to the house.

She didn't move, just stood there.

Hugh kissed the way he rode: ferociously, fiercely, with attention and control. Of course men had kissed her since she finished her mourning. But kissing Hugh didn't resemble those kisses.

Her fingers slid into his hair, and her whole self strained to grasp the sultry smell of him, the firmness of his lips, the strength of his arms around her, even the harsh feeling of the old bricks at her back.

"Georgie." There was something in the raw sound of his voice, the way her name lingered on his lips, that woke her up.

"I don't want to marry," she said, pulling back. "I'm not on your list, Hugh. You understand that, don't you?"

"The hell with the list," he said. And then he was kissing her again, and it was delicious and terrifying. That big body was up against hers, and even through the heavy silk of her gown she could feel the maleness of his demand.

That was Hugh. Whether he was taming a horse or kissing a woman, he wasn't afraid of his body. Even now his hands were running down her lower back in an utterly inappropriate way.

In a way that no man had ever touched her, now she thought of it.

"What do you mean, the hell with the list?" she said, as his lips slipped from hers and down her neck.

It felt so good . . . a temptation to stop thinking and simply revel in the way his lips caressed her skin. But Georgina *always* thought. She kept thinking throughout the intimacies she shared with Richard, back in the first year of their marriage, when they were still bothering with that sort of thing.

Richard would courteously inquire whether

something was acceptable to her, and she would think about it before deciding. Most of the time she agreed, though she had entirely rejected the idea of making love with the lamp lit.

She had the feeling that Hugh wouldn't be so courteous. Scandalously, he had his hand on her bottom now, shaping it, and that was something that Richard would definitely have asked about before he even thought of touching her. And she had a strong feeling that it never would have occurred to Richard to want to caress her there.

And yet it felt . . . It felt delicious.

"We shouldn't," she whispered, out of some fugitive sense of propriety.

Hugh straightened, glanced toward the house. "I have to dress for supper. Sit with me?"

"I can't sit with you," she protested. "You know that as well as I do. We are seated according to precedence, and as the Earl of Briarly, you are so far above me in that respect that I'm practically below the salt, as the old saying goes."

His hands tightened on her waist. "I'm not going to spend another damned meal watching Kitlas make cow eyes at you and DuPreye lick his lips and brush up against your shoulder. While I sit next to Gwendolyn, who has *no* conversation, by the way, grinding my teeth and hoping that DuPreye's hands aren't wandering toward your knee under the table."

Georgina felt such a surge of happiness that she could hardly stop from laughing. "But you must remain seated where Carolyn placed you!"

He looked down at her and growled. He actually growled, like some sort of dog. "I'll be in the seat next to you, Georgie."

"I—"

"Or I'll pluck you out of your seat and make you sit on my lap."

"Hugh, that's absurd," she protested. "You can't."

"I never take well to that word." The look in his eyes showed that he meant it. "You can tell Carolyn to switch the seating, so there's a place next to you, since it looks as if I'll be even later than usual . . . or I will compromise you."

Her mouth fell open. "And just how do you plan to do that in a crowded dining room?"

A gleam in his eye made color creep up her neck. "Darling," he said, rubbing his thumb along the line of her jaw, "I could—nay, I *would*—compromise you any place you give me permission."

"Well, I don't give permission," Georgina said weakly.

"Then I'd have to settle for pulling you into my arms and squealing. *Ach, Georgina, I can't get the feeling of your round bum out of my hand*."

She laughed. "You wouldn't dare. And if that's a Scottish accent you're trying for, you sound more like a drunken fisherman."

He was grinning, and his hands were sliding down her back, down . . . "But it's true. I believe you've ruined me for . . ."

"For what?" she asked, trying to calm her racing pulse. His hands were sliding delightfully, downward.

"That requires further investigation," he said, lowering his mouth to hers.

Chapter 19

$\mathcal{B}$y the time Georgina entered the drawing room, it was almost time to process to supper. She caught Carolyn by the hand, and whispered, "Your brother insists on sitting next to me at the meal." And, at the surprise in her friend's face, she added somewhat defensively: "After all, Gwendolyn is now betrothed."

"That's irrelevant," Carolyn said. "Hugh can't simply announce that he'd like to change his seat because his neighbor is betrothed. I've seated everyone on the basis of precedence precisely so that I needn't fuss over this sort of demand. I can't have the whole table peering at Lady Fourviere and Albert Hunt to see if they're really having an *affaire.*"

"I didn't know that!" Georgina said, somewhat diverted. "Isn't he the brother of a bishop?"

"Don't tell anyone, but I had to give them adjoining rooms. So why does Hugh want to sit next to you? Because he's tired of making small talk to Gwendolyn?"

"I believe so. He told me that he would create a scene unless he got his way."

"I suppose we could do something different tonight. I could make it into a game . . ." Her voice trailed off. "The more exacting mamas will *not* approve, Georgie."

"Please don't start anything until Hugh appears," Georgina said. "DuPreye will snatch me and embarrass his wife."

"Poor woman," Carolyn said. "Not to be cruel, but she must be used to it. I have to say, you look absolutely beautiful. Luscious, in fact." She narrowed her eyes. "What have you been up to?"

Georgina felt herself blushing a little. "Nothing!" And then: "Just having fun."

"And with whom have you been doing that?" Carolyn demanded. "I've been standing here making chatter for over an hour, and I didn't see you . . . were you in a corner somewhere? Oh, tell me you weren't with Geerken? I couldn't bear it if you marry him."

"I wasn't," Georgina said. "Don't be silly. If I marry again, and you know perfectly well that I don't intend to, I shall make it a prerequisite that the man can count to one hundred."

"Hmmm," Carolyn said, raising an eyebrow. "All right, I suppose I won't embarrass you by inquiring precisely where my brother comes into your . . . shall we say . . . nonmarital interests."

"Thank you," Georgina said, aware at that very moment that Hugh had appeared at her back. She felt it, she knew it, she even smelled him—a wonderful fresh, outdoors smell, like man and soap.

"Why, there you are!" Carolyn exclaimed. She was laughing up at her older brother, and Georgina could tell that her best friend was jumping to all sorts of rash conclusions.

"Hello, Caro," Hugh said, as casually as if he hadn't put a hand on the small of Georgina's back.

His touch burned through the silk of her gown as if he were touching her bare skin. With a quick twist, she moved away. She couldn't allow him to simply . . . well, act as if he *owned* her.

There was something in his eyes, but he bowed, gravely enough, and kissed her gloved hand. "Lady Georgina," he said amicably. But he held her hand a trifle too long, and she knew he was inwardly laughing.

"I'll just have a word with the butler," Carolyn said. "I have a wonderful idea." She trotted away.

Hugh's grin made Georgina's whole body warm and her heart start beating fast.

Across the room, Carolyn turned from the butler and clapped her hands. "Excuse me," she called. "I'd like to announce a very special surprise for this evening."

The room turned silent, matchmaking mamas regarding their hostess with a faint frown, gentlemen with a bored air, young girls with instant interest.

"We're going to play a game," Carolyn continued, "which will determine seating at supper tonight. The game is one of my favorites from the nursery. Surely you remember *Do you love your neighbor*?" She waved a hand at the five footmen bustling around the room. "As you can see, the servants are creating two large circles of chairs. Everyone with a January through June birthday shall retire to that part of the room, and those born from July to December shall stay in this part of the room."

"I say," her husband called, "you've separated the two of us, love!"

Carolyn blew Finchley a kiss. "I dine next to you daily," she said, dimpling. "Does everyone remember the game? Please sit down, alternating by sex. One person shall stand in the middle of the circle. I will begin in that position here, and my brother can take the other group."

"Wasn't it well done of her to remember that

our birthdays are in the same month?" Hugh murmured into Georgina's ear.

"Hush," she said, feeling herself turn pink. Hugh was being so obvious, standing next to her, as if—as if—

She couldn't follow the thought. Besides, Carolyn was explaining the game.

"I shall choose a lady and ask, 'Do you love your neighbor?' If that person says 'No,' I may claim one of the rejected neighbors as my dinner partner. On the other hand, if she *does* love her neighbor, then he may escort her to supper. The couple retires from the circle, and I shall ask again. The circle will grow ever smaller until we are all paired off. Does that make sense, everyone?"

There was a hum of excitement and explosions of giggles from the younger girls.

"I like it," Hugh said. "Prepare to be claimed, Georgie."

She tapped his hand with her fan. "Just because you begin in the middle doesn't mean that you will necessarily win me. What if I am sitting next to Lord Geerken? He appears to be born in the appropriate time period to join our circle."

"I fancy I can manage to win. Now come along like a good girl."

"I am not a good girl," Georgina said, laughing a bit.

"I can't tell you how glad I am to learn that," Hugh said, pausing to look down at her. That look in his eyes . . . it was indecent! Georgina felt her face growing pink.

A moment later, Hugh had taken charge of his circle and was ruthlessly shepherding people into seats. Georgina found herself sitting between Captain Oakes and the Earl of Charters. She couldn't help smiling. Hugh had deliberately placed her between men who had absolutely no interest in her company at the supper table.

"Now," Hugh said, looking around the circle. "Is everyone comfortable? Lady Passmore?"

"I think I should be seated next to my daughter," Lady Passmore said a bit fretfully.

"Ah, but dinner seating is *so* rigid," Hugh said sweetly. "First one sex, then another. Now if your son were here, I would be able to please you. Time to begin." He turned to Captain Oakes. "Oakes, old man, do you love your neighbors?"

Captain Oakes looked deliberately at Georgina, to his left, and then Lady Fourviere, to his right, and shook his head dolefully. "As a man of honor," he said, "I must admit that I do not love my neighbors."

Hugh swooped on Georgina before she even took a breath. And he didn't take her hand, either. He *grabbed* her—picked her up, and carried her straight out of the circle, to the squeals of scandalized matrons.

"Remove her chair and Oakes's," he said to a footman and, putting Georgina on her feet, turned back to the circle. "Captain, since you displayed yourself to be most unloving, you shall stand in the middle of the circle and ask the question of whomever you please."

Georgina watched Oakes turn around slowly, then play the game exactly as Hugh had, asking the gentleman to the right of Lady Kate if he loved his neighbors. There was a moment of hesitation as Lord Geerken apparently considered claiming Kate, but her charming scowl took care of that, and Oakes scooped her up and carried her out of the circle.

"I trust that no one is planning to pick me up," the Dowager Countess of Pemsbiddle said in a wry voice.

"This is not proper," Lady Nibbleherd said, sending her charge, Emily Mottram, a frown that indicated she should not allow herself to be hoisted in the air by a gentleman.

"In my case, less scandalous than impossible," the countess said cheerfully. "My corsets weigh more than Miss Emily does."

The conversation at dinner that night was far more boisterous than it had been on previous nights. Who had declared love for whom was, of course, foremost on every mind. Perhaps the most fascinating moment had occurred when there were only a few players left, and Mrs. DuPreye, finding herself next to her husband, announced that she didn't love her neighbors and pranced off with the curate.

Georgina was having a wonderful time. Whenever she met Hugh's eyes, her heart skipped a beat. And each time his leg casually brushed hers under the table, her pulse raced. Especially after it occurred to her that his leg seemed to be jostling hers a good bit of the time. She tried reminding herself that she was a staid widow, but she found herself smiling like a giddy, green girl.

They talked of this and that and nothing . . . She found herself telling him about the dolls she made for orphans.

"So you sew the clothing?" he asked quizzically. "But not the dolls' bodies."

"Exactly. I use rag dolls. At first I tried using dolls with porcelain heads, but we discovered that the dolls were being taken away from the children and sold. So now I begin with a rag doll, but I give each one a really exquisite gown with scraps of silk and lace, real gauze and spangles. It's so much fun!"

"Where do you get the fabrics?"

"Modistes are quite good about saving bits and pieces. I send a servant around to the studios every week or so. Of course, I pay for the scraps; otherwise, they would be sold to a bonnet-maker."

He smiled, a lazy sort of smile that warmed her to the bottom of her toes. "One of my clearest memories of you as a child was your attachment to that raggedy doll of yours."

"Esmerta," Georgina said. "I loved Esmerta. I was far more interested in making clothing for her than in sewing samplers."

"Do you suppose that you would be a modiste yourself, if you weren't born a gentlewoman?"

"Oh, yes. I would have my own studio. I used to dream of it when I was a young girl, before I really understood that ladies—well, that ladies marry."

"And did you marry Sorrell because he was so well dressed?" Hugh asked, fiddling with his fork.

"No." But she couldn't make herself say more.

"You were obviously in love with him. I still remember how your face shone on your wedding day."

She smiled faintly. "That's one reason why I shall not marry again. One can love a person easily enough and still not have the faintest idea who he is." And then, at his sudden movement, "I don't mean poor Richard was a monster or anything of the sort!"

"So what was he, then?" Hugh's voice was very deep and steady. Georgina felt as if they were in a little shell of their own, as if the chattering voices around them were miles away.

"He had a wicked sense of humor." Georgina

leaned to the side slightly to allow a footman to take her plate. Her shoulder brushed Hugh's. "We used to laugh . . ."

"That sounds very pleasant."

"Yes. Except that I finally noticed that we were always laughing *at* people. At the way one was dressed, or the ungainly shape of another's limbs, or the squeal of someone's laugh."

Hugh didn't say anything, and Georgina didn't look at him. She just kept going, telling him what she had told no one. "Richard liked to poke fun at people."

"Did he poke fun at you?"

"Yes," she admitted. "But never unkindly. I was—I was an extension of *him,* you see. He was kind enough to overlook my imperfections unless he was quite cross."

Hugh picked up her hand. She had taken off her gloves to eat, so his fingers were strong and warm around hers. "You could never be just a reflection of someone else, Georgie. And I can't see a single imperfection. Were you happy together?"

"Yes," she said, "Of course we were." But inside, she wasn't sure, and it showed in her voice. His fingers tightened. "Did you like Richard?" she asked.

"No," Hugh said bluntly. "But there's nothing unexpected in that. I'm the sort of man he loathed. And I . . ." He hesitated and obviously chose his words carefully. "Sorrell was far more of the gentleman than I am. You would have been a modiste if you hadn't been born to supposedly better things; I spend my time breaking horses, no matter my birth. There's many a gentleman who thinks I oughtn't to be doing it."

"You're not proper," she agreed. Every time she met his eyes, a little shock went down her spine and weakened her knees. It was the most peculiar thing. She was only talking to *Hugh,* after all. Hugh, her best friend's brother. Hugh, who'd been around most of her life.

Hugh—was just Hugh. Except that his hair kept catching the candlelight and glowing like a brand-new ha'penny. He had the same hair as Carolyn: thick, luscious, brandy-colored hair that fell almost to his shoulders. And his eyes were a beautiful color, brown with dark green, like the thick glass at the bottom of a wine bottle.

Of course she'd always known that Hugh was handsome. But he wasn't for her. She'd never even considered someone like him. Instead, her eyes roamed the ballrooms in her debutante year, looking for men who . . .

"Perhaps I did look for a gentleman who would understand my interest in clothing," she admitted. "But what an appallingly foolish reason to fall in love."

"Sorrell was remarkably elegant." Hugh had put her hand down and started peeling a small pear. The long curls fell gently from his fingers.

"The first time I saw him, he was wearing a black velvet waistcoat studded with pearls." She looked from Hugh's fingers to his face and saw that he was trying to control a grin. "I know. He was in a somewhat ostentatious mood, perhaps. But he had exquisite clothing. He had another waistcoat, of sky-blue satin, and he'd wear it with gossamer silk stockings of the same color."

"Exquisite," Hugh said. He had his mouth under control now, and he handed her the pear with a perfectly serious expression. "Are you as fashionable as he?" He peered at her gown. "That's a quite nice thing you've got on."

"Thing?" She started to giggle. "*Thing?*"

"Gown," he amended. "I like it."

"The sleeves are a little too belled," she told him. "And see this?" She pointed at the edging of lace around her bodice. "I would have used pearl embroidery instead of lace. Lace looks a trifle too flimsy with heavy silk."

"I like the bodice," he said, a thread of wolfish amusement running through his voice.

She followed his gaze and found herself turning pink. The edging of lace did little to cover her breasts, of course. "Really?" she said, throwing him a look from under her lashes. "What do you like about it?"

He leaned closer, and his leg pressed against hers. "You're fishing for compliments again."

"Yes," she said shamelessly, and just waited.

"The way it dips in front. I don't know the right words, but that gown is made for a man's admiration." His voice was a smoky whisper.

It was a dangerous game. She shouldn't play it; she shouldn't even think of such things. But Georgina felt a bit mad, so she gave him a little smile. "It's *such* an annoying bodice . . . so low that I can't wear a corset."

"Ah," he said. The little sound burned to the bottom of her spine. There was something in his murmur that made her suspect he made just that sound when he was making love to a woman.

It wasn't a sound she'd ever heard . . . but she could imagine it.

Even the way Hugh looked at her was more intimate than she and Richard had managed to be.

"What's the matter?" Hugh asked, dropping his hand under the table where no one could see and twining his fingers through hers.

She tried for a smile but knew it was bleak, at best. So she returned to clothing. "Richard had marvelous dressing gowns. He liked figured silk, the kind that was too bold to wear in a waistcoat."

"Tell me he didn't enter your chamber merely so that the two of you could sit about and admire his dressing gown."

The faint scorn in his voice made her sad, and she pulled her hand from his. "Richard was a good person. He never deliberately hurt anyone. He loved clothing the way—well, the way you love horses."

At the head of the table, Carolyn rose. "If the ladies would please join me in the drawing room."

Hugh stood as well, putting a hand under Georgina's elbow to draw her to her feet.

"The gentlemen will join the ladies in the drawing room," their host announced.

"I chose well for her, didn't I?" Hugh said into Georgina's ear. "Finchbird is just right."

"You didn't choose Carolyn's husband; she did!"

Everyone was flooding out of the dining room, but Hugh held her back, allowing others to go before them. "Of course I did," he said. "I turned down three or four proposals before Finchley got around to proposing. He could easily have lost her."

"Oh."

"Don't you remember how much she liked Lord Surtout's profile? She probably would have accepted his proposal on the basis of his chin, and then he would have dragged her off to explore the Nile. Or left her behind to wither at home. She was furious at me when I refused him. Luckily, Finchley returned from the country the next week and literally tripped over her at a ball."

"I'd forgotten Carolyn's infatuation with Surtout," Georgina said slowly. Her own mother had said yes to the very first proposal her daughter received.

The room was empty. With one smooth movement, Hugh backed Georgina against the wall.

"You seem to have a propensity for pushing me about," she whispered.

"I'm discovering all sorts of propensities when it comes to you, Georgina." His voice slid like rough honey over her skin, and then his lips were on hers. She sank into his kiss, and all the worries in her mind just fell away. He kissed her as if he knew her.

"You *know* me," she said, not thinking, just saying it.

"Mmmm," he said, a deep rumbling sound that spoke of pleasure. "Not as well as I want to." He pulled back and looked into her face, running a finger along her eyebrow. "You're like Richelieu. You need to have some fun."

"Fun?"

His smile was slow and easy. "Exactly." He lowered his head and bit her lip.

"Hugh!"

He nipped her again, and then started kissing

her. She kept trying to think about having fun, or not having fun, but she fell into the pleasure that was exploding between them.

His kisses made her feel crazily, dangerously young. But she wasn't young. She was twenty-five years old, and even older than that in her heart.

Hugh was older than she, but he was carefree and—

He gave her a little shake. "Stop thinking," he commanded.

"I—"

"You think too much. And you worry too much."

"*You* don't worry at all," she pointed out.

"It's better that way," he murmured, and his hands tightened on her hips, pulling her closer, up against—

He didn't feel like Richard.

Her body sizzled, and a part of Georgina, a wanton, forgotten part, made her push back against him. Made her curl her fingers into his hair and kiss him fiercely.

Made her thrill to hear his little groan and see his eyes go dark with desire. He didn't look at her as if she were a girl he'd known his whole life, or his sister's closest friend, or a widow—

But as if she were the drink he wanted more than life itself.

She didn't break free until there was a noise in

the doorway, and even then she didn't turn around to see who was there.

"Georgie," Carolyn said from the doorway.

She turned slowly. Carolyn was laughing and holding out her hand. "Unless there's to be a positive firestorm of gossip, you need to come with me now."

Georgina moved away, but she couldn't help looking back just as they left the room.

Hugh was leaning against the wall, head back, watching her go. It was the most erotic thing she'd ever seen in her life: this huge, beautiful man, his hair tousled by her hands, his eyes dark with desire, looking at her. Looking for her.

And that smile!

It was sensuous, it was wicked, it was inviting.

She turned her back on it with an effort.

"Don't forget we're going riding tomorrow morning," he called after her.

Carolyn giggled. "You're offering to escort me on a ride, dear brother?"

He growled at her, and then, when Georgina peeked over her shoulder again, "Tomorrow, Georgie."

He was ordering her . . . she should assert herself. She should—

She nodded.

Chapter 20

The entryway was full of gentlemen when Georgina came down the stairs the next morning. Apparently the party, at least the male part, intended to hunt for grouse again.

She was clad in her best riding costume, an apple green jacket with black braided fastenings and trim, and was happy to see its immediate effect on a number of men who looked up the stairs. This particular riding habit hugged her bust and hips in an entirely satisfactory manner. The only thing better than her habit was her darling little hat (green with a cunning feather) and her riding crop. Not that she would ever use a riding crop, but when one comes adorned with a glorious tassel in green and black, it certainly warranted carrying.

"How splendid that you will come hunting with us," the Marquess of Finchley said, moving to the bottom of the stairs and looking up at her with a wide smile of welcome. "We have so many indolent ladies in this party, my wife among them, that we are undesirably male."

"Nonsense," Georgina told him, smiling as she descended the last stair. "If I were to accompany you, you wouldn't be able to spit and swear and tell bawdy jokes."

"Did you hear the one about the widow and the preacher?" DuPreye asked, moving forward to take her arm.

"Luckily, no," she replied, pulling away from him.

His hand snaked out again and caught her elbow. "You're dressed for riding, Lady Georgina. I'd be more than happy to join you, rather than tramp around the meadows in search of a bird or two."

Finchley had known Georgina for all the years of his marriage to Carolyn and clearly guessed from the look on her face just how much his wife's closest friend wanted to spend the morning with the lascivious Mr. DuPreye.

"Absolutely not," he said, slapping DuPreye on the back. "You swore you'd take down at least two birds today, don't you remember? That was after you missed every shot yesterday, not to mention nearly winging Oakes."

DuPreye cast him a sour look. "Perhaps the party would be better off without me since you make such a point of that unfortunate accident. It could have happened to anyone."

"I insist, I insist," Finchley said genially. "Lady Georgina will take herself on a gentle ride through the grounds, no doubt. Whereas we men must bring home the supper. One of the neighboring farmers, Mr. Bucky Buckstone, has been kind enough to grant us access to his woods, DuPreye. Even the most bungling hunter will have success there, not that I would describe *you* as such, of course."

"You mustn't miss the opportunity," Georgina said, giving DuPreye a cold glance that would have dissuaded any gentleman who deserved that label. "I rarely ride for more than ten minutes, so it would truly be a waste of your time."

"Another time," DuPreye said, giving in. "To-morrow morning, perhaps."

"If I might speak to you privately for a moment, Lady Georgina?" Finchley asked, rather unexpectedly. He led her into a small sitting room, and said without preface, "I'm in horrible trouble."

"Why?" she said, staring at her host in surprise. "Is something wrong with the hunting excursion?"

"It's nothing to do with that. It's Carolyn's birthday present." He ran his hands through his hair, destroying the exquisite style fashioned by his valet that morning.

"What is the matter?"

"I had an absolutely marvelous gift. I had booked the entire troupe of the Royal Court Theatre, and they were coming to do a special performance of *Twelfth Night* in the private theater here, tomorrow night."

"Oh, Carolyn will absolutely love that!" Georgina cried. "What a marvelous husband you are."

His jaw clenched. "The idea *was* a good one."

"What happened?"

"They're not coming. A messenger arrived last night to say that the better part of the troupe has been locked up by the magistrates in Bath. Apparently they put on a performance that mocked the Prince Regent, and part of the audience took umbrage. The idiots! Their patron *is* the Regent!"

"Surely you could try to bail them out," Georgina suggested.

"They're in *Bath*," he said miserably. "Bath. That's a good three days' ride from here. I promised Carolyn a special present, and the worst of it is that she knows that the theater is part of it."

"You have your own theater on the grounds?"

He nodded. "Carolyn found out that I'd had it prepared for a performance, though not that I promised a small fortune to that particular troupe to come up here to the Dales. She's expecting a performance for tomorrow night, for her birthday, and I have nothing."

"I've never acted a day in my life," Georgina said. "I'm so sorry."

"I didn't mean that you had to act. I just wondered if you wouldn't mind looking in on the local fair while you're out riding this morning? My butler heard there might be a group of players traveling with the fair. The village is only a mile or so down the road."

"Of course," Georgina said. "If I discover players of any kind, I shall bid them come to the manor tomorrow by eight."

"Even if they're just jugglers," he said, looking a great deal happier. "I'll send two groomsmen with you."

"There's no need."

"No, I must insist. There's no danger if you stay on my grounds, but I wouldn't want you to ride unaccompanied into the village. You don't seem to have a maid with you this morning."

"I won't be unaccompanied," she said, knowing that a foolish little smile was playing around her lips.

The marquess raised an eyebrow. "Dear me. Every gentleman but one is present for my grouse-hunting party. Don't tell me that you found your name on a certain list?"

"Certainly not!" She raised her chin. "We are childhood friends, after all. I belong on no man's list."

He smiled down at her, and Georgina thought,

not for the first time, how very lucky her friend Carolyn was. "I concur. You are far too original to belong in a list of names, Lady Georgina. I wish you a pleasant morning. And knowing with whom you are spending time, I rather think you shall have one."

Hugh was just starting to contemplate the idea of returning to the manor and pulling Georgina out of her bed when the lady in question sauntered up to the stables.

She looked like an exquisite, outrageously expensive box of sweets, ribbons, tassels, and feathers flying. Her beautiful curls were piled on top of her head, and atop that sat an absurd little hat. She had a riding crop tucked under her arm, and had the smallest waist he'd ever seen.

For a good moment after she arrived at the railing, he couldn't even think of an adequate greeting.

Just when her jaunty smile was fading, he found his tongue, and said, "Georgie, you put me to shame."

Just like that, her cheeky grin popped out again. "My modiste is French," she said, with a marked lack of modesty. "Do you like it?" She spun in a circle.

In the past ten years, his sisters had spun in front of him any number of times. He'd learned a great deal from those encounters. One never, ever, indicated that a bodice might be a little too tight, or skirts a little too short. One never pointed out that crimson made a red nose redder, or that horizontal stripes were not always entirely flattering.

Praise was the ticket. Praise and more praise.

So he opened his mouth—and nothing came out. Georgina's waist was so small that he felt as if he could span it with one hand. She had a froth of white at her neck that he wanted to snatch off so that he could see her beautiful throat. He caught just a glimpse of her ankles, and they were the slimmest, most delicate ankles he could have imagined.

In short, her riding habit made him want one thing, and one thing only: to pick her up in his arms, stride into the stables, and toss her onto a bed of straw.

Preferably straw, but he'd be happy to employ a nice sturdy wall.

"Hugh?" she asked. "Don't you like my new habit?" She didn't look disturbed, though, and he had a fair sense that she could measure the effect on him.

"Yes." He turned away before she could realize that that effect was all too evident in his breeches. "Carolyn's mare, Elsbeth, is saddled and waiting for you."

She walked over to the horse with a little saucy wiggle in her step. So he tossed her into the sidesaddle and threw his leg over Richelieu without even looking at her.

He was occupied for the first few minutes in letting Richelieu understand precisely what the rules were. He had Richelieu's measure by now. A more mischievous, lighthearted horse he'd rarely known. There wasn't a mean bone in him, but on the other hand, he loved to flirt with disobedience.

Sure enough, the pleasures of riding down the avenue leading from Finchley Manor were enough to encourage Richelieu to shy at a passing insect, pretend that he was frightened of a swallow startled from an oak, and generally behave like the high-strung, happy animal he was.

Hugh's hands and voice were occupied for some time with reminding Richelieu that he was not the lord of the manor and that shying and bucking were not good manners.

He didn't even look at Georgina until they had turned into a country lane. He had just brought Richelieu back down to the ground after a frolicsome attempt to touch a cloud with his front hooves when he realized that Georgina was white as a sheet.

"What's the matter?" he asked, stopping in the lane.

Sure enough, Richelieu knew that his voice was serious and stopped playing about, flicking his ears to show that he was listening carefully and waiting for instructions.

"Nothing," she said, forcing a smile. "What a lively mount he is."

"He's just playing," Hugh said. "I allowed him to show off because I don't want to break his spirit. But see what a good lad he is? He is entirely obedient when my voice calls for it. All that bucking can't have bothered you, did it?"

"Of course not," she said. But she was looking straight ahead. He couldn't even see her profile because of her cunning little hat and its foolish curling feather.

He moved Richelieu over just a hair, enough so he could lean over and snatch off the hat. It came with a *ping* as a hairpin flew down onto the dirt road.

"What are you doing?" she demanded, rosy color returning along with indignation to her cheeks.

He grinned at her. "I can't see you when you're wearing this thing."

"It's not a *thing*," she replied hotly. "It's a riding hat, the most fashionable of its kind in all London."

"Kiss me?"

"What?"

He leaned closer. "Kiss me," he commanded, just to see whether she responded to the urgency in his voice as sweetly as Richelieu did.

"Absolutely not," she said, sounding as scandalized as a fifty-year-old matron. "We're in an open lane. And besides, there's no reason for the two of us to kiss each other."

"There, you're wrong," Hugh said. "I was just thinking that if you kissed me, I wouldn't send this ridiculous hat spinning over that wall."

She turned her beautiful little nose up in the air. "I am not a woman to be bribed." And then she added, "If you throw away my hat, I'll tell your sister."

In normal times, that would have been a stumper. He hated being scolded by his sisters, particularly by Carolyn. But he didn't want Georgie wearing a hat like that, a hat so fashionable that she looked like—like a duchess. He threw it.

She stopped her horse. "I seem to have lost one of my accessories."

"Really?" he asked, enjoying himself enormously.

"I must beg you to retrieve it for me," she said. Her chin was as firm as a general's. She turned those eyes of hers on him, and for a moment he was lost. In the morning sunshine, they were dusky violet, fringed by long, curling eyelashes.

"Georgie," he said throatily, reaching out for her.

But, of course, she was a consummate horse-woman, and her mare backed neatly out of his arm's reach. "My hat, *if* you please."

Two could play at this game, so he jumped down and made sure to tie Richelieu to a post, where he could enjoy the grass growing in the verge. Then he leapt over the low stone wall, in the direction of the hat, and flung himself to the ground.

He was lying in a clover field. Above him the sky was the faded blue color of skimmed milk. Bees danced from clover to clover. He pulled off his neckcloth and stuffed it into the pocket of his jacket.

Chapter 21

It was at least five minutes before Hugh heard a thrashing noise, and Georgie's head appeared over the top of the wall. "I see you have fallen." Her voice had a wry note that he remembered, even from when she was only seven or eight. She always had a tendency to comment on life rather than throw herself into the fray.

"Join me," he said lazily, not getting up, as any gentleman should in the presence of a lady.

"Are you suggesting that I climb the stile and fling myself on the ground?"

"Yes," he said with heartfelt emphasis.

"And then kiss you in a field, I suppose?"

He was rather hoping that they would make love in a field, but he judged it prudent not to say so. "I would love to kiss you in this very field. May I lift you over the wall?" He got up, the better to help her.

"Hugh, what on earth do you want from me?" Her eyes were bewildered.

He came closer, smiled at her. "A kiss."

"After last night, I know that—I know you want to kiss me. But why now? Why do you suddenly feel so? I've been around you for years. We spent last Twelfth Night together, and I doubt you did more than give me greetings of the season."

"I had a mare foaling," he protested. "I don't think I even came in the house for a few days. I lived in the barn."

"I wouldn't know," she said flatly. "You hardly made a point of speaking to me when we were in the same room."

"I hadn't realized," he said, discovering that they had strayed onto dangerous ground. "I didn't see you."

"Of course you saw me," she said. "Just as clearly as I can see my hat on that twig over there. So will you please pick it up, give it to me, and stop this absurd behavior so that we can continue into the village?"

"I feel absurd around you," he said, knowing it was true.

"Now that you've *noticed* me?" she asked. There was a tone in her voice that told him clear as day just what she thought of his behavior last year. And the year before. And likely the year before that.

"It wasn't just you," he said. "I didn't see anyone."

"What do you mean?"

"I mean that I only vaguely remember the Twelfth Night holiday. I was thinking about my stables. I know that my sisters were running about, and you were there, and Finchbird, of course. Oh, and my aunt Emma."

"Plus a good four or five other people," she pointed out.

"I didn't see them. I don't remember them. I had a mare with twin foals. I do remember looking at you and thinking how sad your eyes looked, but I didn't know what to say about that, or how to make you feel better, so I just went out to the stables."

She snorted. It was a ladylike snort, but a snort nonetheless.

"I'm seeing you now," he offered.

Georgina had snapped off a twig of hawthorn and was fiddling with it. Her delicate fingers made some sort of yawning hunger rage in his body, a hunger to strip off her gloves and press his mouth to her palms. "I don't think I want to be seen by you," she said, not looking at him.

"What do you mean?" He pushed up her chin with his hand so she had to meet his eyes.

"You don't know anything about life."

293

He had a very judicial answer to that. "What are my deficits? Tell me, and I'll improve."

Her eyes had turned dark lavender, grave and sad. "You don't see . . . you just don't understand."

"I see you now, Georgina. Believe me, I'll never be able to go back to entering a room and not know if you're there. And I wouldn't want to either," he added. "I will always look for you first." His voice was fierce, and even though the whole idea was new to him, he knew it was true, in his gut. He would never be the same.

"People *die*, Hugh. They die."

Her face was so white that he could have counted every one of her adorable freckles. "I know that. I almost died myself, just last month."

"That's just it! You *don't* know."

"Of course I do. I know there's a reasonable chance of it, and that's precisely why I asked Carolyn for the list. You don't think that I'd darken the door of a ballroom without a damned good reason, do you?"

The smile in her eyes was tinged with that sadness he hated. "No."

"Unless you were in the room," he said, knowing it was true.

She wrinkled her nose. "Very pretty."

"Very true. Now."

"My point is that you don't really think that death exists. But it does, Hugh. It does. People are there one day, and gone the next. And you could easily be one of those people, given the dangers of the work you do."

"You're not worried about Richelieu's bucking, are you? Not when your own pony used to excel at it? You know perfectly well that I'm not going to fall off in the middle of pranks such as those."

"I know it, and I was frightened anyway." He knew she was telling the truth. "I don't want to be afraid," she said, the same wrenching sense of truth in her voice that had been in his.

That was a bit of a facer. "I'm not sure what you're saying." He said it carefully.

"You're like a boy, Hugh. You don't understand how fragile life is. You don't realize that the thread breaks between one moment and the next."

"Georgie . . ."

"You're a boy," she said flatly, looking down at her gloves again.

So she thought he wasn't man enough for her. She really did want an older man, the way Carolyn had said. All this flame between them, which he knew damn well would never go away . . .

He had to be sure. He couldn't just let her go. "Are you saying that you don't want to marry me?"

"You haven't asked me, but yes." She met his eyes steadily, and he saw nothing but determination there.

"Because I'm not man enough for you."

"I don't mean it as an insult," she said earnestly. "It's—it's wonderful for you that you are able to take such joy in the moment, in the present. It's just that it's all different for me."

"Because your husband died. And if you did marry again, Georgie . . ." His voice was a little hard, so he gentled it. "What sort of man do you want?"

"I told you!" she cried. "I don't want to marry. Ever."

"But let's just say that you did. Describe a *man* to me."

"That's not the right word," she whispered.

"Then describe the kind of man who would understand what you're saying."

"I think it's important to realize that people really die," she said. "They do. You live your life as if you didn't believe it was a possibility. You're twenty-eight, and you just came out of a weeklong coma. And yet you'll never stop breaking horses, will you?"

He shook his head.

"You don't think death will come for you," she stated. "You think the rules don't apply in your case."

He could argue with her. But what was the point? If a woman didn't think you were a man, if she thought you were still a boy, then she didn't respect you. And if there was one thing he knew from working with animals—and people—it was that respect could not be demanded.

He'd encountered plenty of people who didn't respect him. Who thought he was coarse and foolish because he didn't care to dress in brocades and silk, who thought he was stupid to ignore his seat in Parliament, who didn't understand how he could enjoy getting sweaty and filthy working with horses.

Not a single one of them had thrust a dagger in his heart like this.

Georgina didn't respect him.

He nodded.

Then he went over and picked up her hat. Took a deep breath, put a smile on his face, and turned around. "Right," he said, drawing on years of putting on a cheerful face before his sisters. "Let's go on to the village, shall we?"

"Hugh," she said, when he was on her side of the wall again. He could tell from her voice that she was distressed.

He forced another smile but didn't quite meet her eyes. Instead, he put her up into her saddle and fetched Richelieu. His mount realized immediately that all the fun was over and paced down the road like the intelligent, well-bred horse that he was, and would be.

Hugh forced himself to think of that, not of the woman riding next to him. He'd get over this. Of course he would. It was like a firestorm that had blown over him, like a dream in the night, and with the same substantiality. A quick, bright thing that was meant to come to nothing.

Georgie tried to say a few things, so finally he took hold of the conversation and turned it firmly to horses. Since she had little to say about that, he told her about all the bloodlines in his stables, even those in Scotland.

The village of Parsley had one main cobbled street, and it was thronged from top to bottom with happy, shouting people. Carts lined the side of the street, selling everything from puppets to meat pies.

Hugh pulled up. "The fair is in full swing. Every farmer within two hours must be here."

"Where shall we find the players?"

"The pub," he said. "When players aren't acting, they're drinking. Besides, I didn't have breakfast, and I'd love a few rashers of bacon."

"Neither did I, actually," Georgie confessed.

"We'll have to lead our horses, given the crowd."

"Do you know where the inn is?"

He reached up to bring her down from her horse, dropping his hands from her waist instantly. "I've been here a few times with Finchbird. There are only two things in Parsley—the public house and the church. Church is over there. We'll go in the opposite direction."

He set off, leading the horses. He couldn't help

but notice as he walked along that women tended to smile at him, their bright eyes inviting. A black-haired wench with a saucy turn to her plump hips actually beckoned to him, and he laughed back at her.

"Are you having fun?" a voice said by his side.

He glanced down at her. Georgie had pinned her hat back on, and he couldn't see more than the tip of her annoyed nose. Good. It wouldn't hurt the grand Lady Georgina to learn that other women judged him man enough.

"Yes," he said, honestly enough. "You made me feel like a boy, Georgie. No more than a green-headed fool. So yes, I am enjoying myself." And he gave a big smile to a cherry-lipped Jezebel perched on the side of a cart, her legs swinging over the edge. She blew him a kiss and shouted something he couldn't hear.

"I'm walking next to you," Georgina said furiously. "As far as that lightskirt knows, I might be your wife!"

"Women are strange that way. They respond to men, not to women. If DuPreye were here, for instance, she wouldn't care about his marriage—and she would know immediately that he didn't either."

"So you are—"

"If I were truly your companion, of course I wouldn't smile at other women," he pointed out. "What was Richard like in that respect?"

"He *never* smiled at other women."

Hugh could believe that. Georgie's husband had looked as if milk ran his veins, rather than blood. And now he thought about it, that was probably the sort of man she was looking for this time around as well.

He sighed. Her absurd little feather was brushing his shoulder; he could just see a tumble of red curls; he would give anything to pull her closer and kiss her nose. It wasn't as if anyone would give a damn. The street was a jumble of people with no interest in a couple of gentry, walking their horses down the street.

"The Black Lion's up ahead," he said, nodding at the long, low building.

"What a peculiar emblem they have," Georgina said.

It looked like a large clothing pin to Hugh. The whole situation was making him feel achy. That wasn't something men felt, and even if Georgina judged him a stripling, he knew precisely what he was.

A man. A man in need of a foaming mug of ale.

Chapter 22

Georgina was completely confused—and sad. She felt as if a chasm yawned at her feet. It was the same sense of grief that beckoned after Richard died.

And yet she hadn't really mourned Richard, not the way she would . . . not the way she would Hugh, if Hugh died. The idea made her feel ill.

Even though she wasn't Hugh's wife.

And this fair wasn't making her feel any better. The screams of hawkers and children were competing. Everywhere Georgina looked there were flags, tents, and people selling everything from gingerbread to rocking chairs. But mostly women smiling at Hugh, she thought sourly.

Richelieu was unexpectedly behaving like one of the most perfectly trained horses she'd ever seen.

He picked his way toward the inn, watching the children darting from side to side with all the anxiety of a turtle. The horse who had shied violently at a blue fly a mere half hour earlier didn't even jump when fireworks exploded somewhere in the near vicinity.

Georgina felt an overwhelming desire to get Hugh to look at her. "Richelieu is acting like an angel," she called.

He glanced over at her, and his eyes were perfectly friendly, in a brotherly sort of way. "Isn't he?" he asked genially, giving Richelieu a pat. Her eyes followed the movement, and she realized that Hugh wore no gloves. Now she thought of it, she couldn't remember ever seeing him in gloves.

His hands were large, twice the span of Richard's fingers. And they were as strong as his shoulders, hands that had seen hard work and reached out for more. He had already turned away and was bending over, talking to a man lounging in front of the pub. But she couldn't take her eyes from his left hand, holding Richelieu's reins.

They were the hands of a man.

Not a boy.

Not those hands. A scar ran across the wrist; she could just see the thin white line in all that bronzed skin.

"What happened to your wrist?" she asked.

He heard her, but he didn't turn, just kept chatting, before he gave the man a coin and handed him the two horses' reins.

"Bit of an accident," he said easily.

It was all gone. All that lovely fire between them, the way he looked at her and made her feel desirable, truly desirable for the first time since her marriage, all that was gone as if it had never existed.

Trailing behind him into the crowded inn, Georgina felt as if she were the tail on a peacock. Every eye turned to glance at Hugh, then stare at her.

There were no other ladies in the pub. "Hugh," she said.

She hardly heard herself over the clamor in the room, but he turned instantly. "Yes?"

"Won't we take a private room?"

"Oh, they don't have that sort of thing here," he said. "You don't mind, do you?"

"No," she said, rather faintly. She had just time enough to realize that she was not only the only lady, but the only woman at all, before he led her over next to a low window, and they sat down.

The table was blackened with age and scratched with people's initials. It wasn't particularly clean either. Georgina couldn't look up because she kept meeting men's eyes, and that made her uncomfortable. They looked curious. And greedy. Almost as if they thought . . .

"I do believe they've decided you're my lady-bird," Hugh said cheerfully. "They're not used to your level of elegance."

Georgina swallowed.

"Not to worry. No one will address you while I'm here."

A tapster appeared and gave her the same glance as everyone else, as if she were expensive but available.

"Breakfast," Hugh said. "Whatever you've got. I'm hungry, and I'm sure Her Ladyship is as well. Even more importantly, we need to talk to any players that came along with the fair if they're on the premises."

"Drinking in the back," the tapster said, taking off without another word.

She dropped her eyes and found herself tracing with her finger the lines of a word cut into the table.

"Balls," Hugh said, leaning over and reading it.

Georgina pulled back her finger as if she were stung.

"Such a lady," Hugh said, amused.

He wore a plain black coat that strained over his shoulders. He'd taken off his neckcloth, and his throat was open, reminding her of all that golden skin underneath.

Her cunning little habit felt stupid and overtrimmed. She pulled off her hat and put it on the floor by her stool. She gave the tasseled riding crop to a boy riding a wooden broomstick. He shrieked.

She would have taken off the stupid jacket if she could. It was too tight for a matron, for a widow. It probably made her look like overdressed mutton, like an old woman trying too hard to be everything she could never be again.

Richard would have said that. Richard had very firm ideas about what women should and shouldn't wear. Their best conversations were about women's clothing, actually. They would go to the theater and whisper through the whole performance, discussing the costumes and the sets. Then they would go home and dissect the clothing worn by everyone in the audience.

Tears stung her eyes, thinking of it. Richard was fiercely scornful of women who tried too hard, who couldn't accept the fact they were getting older.

She could hear him in her mind's eye, excoriating some poor woman in her thirties with the temerity to wear a low-cut dress. Not that she was in her thirties, but she was a widow. She cringed, thinking what Richard would make of her tight riding habit and the reason she wore it. It was only when she heard Hugh's voice calling to her that she snapped back to the present.

The innkeeper returned with two plates heaped with eggs and bacon. He put them down before them, and said, "This here behind me's Mr. Lear, the Player. You'd best let him sit down or he might fall over, to tell the truth. He's been drinking out back since sunup."

"Lear?" Georgina echoed.

The man who walked in the innkeeper's wake hardly seemed, at first glance, to fit his Shakespearean name. He was wearing ragged leather with great boots turned over at his knee. But then . . . he wasn't one to be underestimated either. He smiled, and he gave the impression of being someone who could kill while smiling.

"Aye, Lear, as in the greatest of the great tragedians," the player said, taking the seat that Hugh gestured toward. "I thank you kindly for that, my lord. Now I'll tell you before you ask me, my lady, that I borrowed the name from a king though he was a king who mightily enjoyed acting, I might point out. As an actor, I have no real reason for a name of my own, as I spend most of my time being someone else, so why not choose a name of my own liking?"

He was drunk. Charmingly, probably habitually, drunk. His speech was just a trifle slurred, and he sat at the table with a kind of loose-limbed freedom that suggested he was three sheets to the wind. Still, he was beautiful, even at fifty-odd years, with high cheekbones and eyes like slumbering jewels.

It occurred to Georgina that this was probably what kings actually looked like: haunted, tipsy, and tired.

"Do you know what time Finchley wanted the performance?" Hugh asked her.

She put down her fork. The breakfast might not be elegant, but the bacon was excellent. "Eight o'clock. Would that be agreeable with you, Mr. Lear?"

"You catch us at the very point of decadence," Lear said, a lazy mock in his voice. "We grow rusty and forget our lines. But surely you can expect no better of a troupe whom you come across in a dog's bollocks like Parsley."

"Here now," the innkeeper said, appearing again suddenly, "you keep your manners about you when you're in Parsley, or we'll toss you out on your bollocky ear. Shall I bring you and the lady something to drink with that meal, then?" he asked Hugh.

"We can always improvise," the player said rather dreamily. "That's how I started out, you know. Back in London."

"Ale for myself and Mr. Lear, and a glass of lemonade for Her Ladyship," Hugh said. "What sort of things did you improvise? Are you always the King, or sometimes the Fool?"

"Always the Fool, and yet sometimes a King," Lear said sadly. He raised his mug of ale and drank.

"I wonder if you have a play that would be suitable for the Marchioness of Finchley's birthday?" Georgina asked. "The marquess mentioned that he had hoped to have Shakespeare's *Twelfth Night* performed."

"We can't do that one," Lear said flatly. "I can do you any selection of gory romances, complete with corpses and appropriate songs. Ghosts, battles, strangled women, ghosts of women; there is a difference, you know, between the male and the female ghost—"

"What is the difference?" Georgina asked.

"Oh, the male ghost is obsessed with vengeance, I find," Lear said, drinking again.

"And what are the females obsessed by?" Hugh asked.

"Prick songs," Lear said. "Snogging. Same as when they're alive, really. Hanging around singing 'Willow, willow' because somebody did her in a hedge."

"Willow?" Hugh asked dubiously.

"It's a song from a Shakespeare play," Georgina told him.

"Oh, Shakespeare," Hugh said, his face clearing. "If I came back as a ghost, I'm going for your sex's routine, minus the singing. Prick songs sound much better than vengeance."

"What is snogging?" Georgina whispered.

He laughed from behind his tankard of ale. "Just what you think it is, darling."

Darling! The word curled into her heart.

"We can do *A Battle of the Centaurs, Including the Love Story of a Eunuch,*" Lear stated, "or *The Merry Tragedy of Pyramus and Thisbe.* Either one."

"The love story of a eunuch?" she asked somewhat dubiously.

"*Pyramus and Thisbe,*" Hugh intervened. "A eunuch is demoralizing for a birthday, even if the man in question is lovestruck. Tomorrow at eight, Mr. Lear. The Finchley butler's name is Slack. He will be happy to show you the theater whenever you choose to arrive. I would just ask that you do not dress as players when approaching the manor, in case the marchioness should happen to glimpse you."

"We will be there with our royal velvets and glittering crowns safely hidden in trunks. My lady. My lord." Lear rose and ambled away without further farewell.

"Excellent," Hugh said dryly. "Well, I think we're done here." Before Georgina registered what was happening, he had swept her out of the tavern and thrown her up on Elsbeth again.

He seemed to be turning the horses' heads toward home, and she couldn't bear that idea. In fact, it made her feel wild with sadness not to mention anger at herself. Though she couldn't—didn't have time to—think that through. "Where shall we find an apple for Richelieu to eat?" she asked.

"There are apples in the stables," Hugh said, leading the way back out of town. He *was* intending to simply return home.

"Weren't you going to teach him to have fun?" she asked, telling Elsbeth with just a nudge that she would like to keep up with Richelieu.

"I think we've all had more than enough fun for the day, don't you?" His voice was wry, and he did look at her then.

His were the bland, cheerful eyes of a friend. It was as if the attraction that flared between them was already just a memory. The kind of memory she would take home, the way she took home the memory of her marriage. Take it out in the dark of night and wonder what went wrong and what she could have done differently.

The anger of it choked her throat for a second, and her knees tightened on Elsbeth, who misinterpreted and started forward, flying into a full gallop.

It was so unexpected that she almost lost her seat, except somehow she never really lost her seat on a horse, even riding sidesaddle. Not since she was eight years old or so.

And while she could have stopped Elsbeth by her second stride, she didn't. Instead, she just leaned forward, into the wind, and let the mare tear down the lane. They were running away. Away, away, away.

She heard the ragged end of Hugh's shout, then the pounding of Richelieu's hooves. He would catch them in a moment. Richelieu was bred for speed and the race. She didn't have to look to know that the horse's ears were flat back, and his limbs were eating up the ground, dust swelling behind them. In another second, Hugh would have a hand on her reins.

To the left there was an old stone wall. To the right, the hawthorn hedge wound its way all the way from Finchley manor to here. She and Elsbeth leapt the hedge because it was easier to fall off a sidesaddle when you swerved left. They cleared the hedge as lightly as a dragonfly skims the surface of a river and tore off through the field.

She heard Hugh swearing, but his words were torn away by the wind. Maybe he thought Elsbeth was running away with her. Who cared what he thought? The edge of the field approached, and they galloped straight into the next one, leapt a fallen-down stone wall, pounded down a country lane, just long enough so that she could hear Richelieu's hooves land on the dirt.

Then they were off over another hedge. She miscalculated slightly, and almost slid from the saddle, but managed to hang on. It was just as well that she had left her riding hat at the pub, because it would have been long gone. Fashionable hats were not designed for tearing across the countryside.

By now Elsbeth was starting to blow, and her neck was dark with sweat. Gallant, sweet thing that she was, her ears were flickering, waiting for the next command. She was still enjoying herself . . . but growing tired.

They jumped one last hedge, just because they could and because there was a pond on the other side. Then Georgina slid off Elsbeth, and before Richelieu had even cleared the previous hedge, she had unbuttoned the hateful jacket, turned it inside out, and used it to rub Elsbeth's neck.

"You're a sweet lass," she told her, catching her own breath.

Elsbeth blew into her palm and nickered a little, saying in horse language that she'd like to do that again. Just not at the moment. Then Georgina pulled off her bit and bridle and let her amble to the pond.

Richelieu sailed the hedge with a good three feet to spare. That horse *would* win the Ascot, Georgina thought. He had heart and verve, as well as astoundingly powerful legs.

Hugh was out of the saddle before Richelieu's hooves touched the ground, but instead of laughing at the fun of the chase, those large hands closed on her upper arms like a vise and he gave her a shake. A hard shake. "What in the bloody hell do you think you were doing, Georgie?" Another shake.

She pulled free, stepping backward, and his hands fell away. Fury swept down her back. "You have no right to—"

He wasn't listening, she could already tell. He just reached out and hauled her into his arms like a sack of grain, put his mouth over hers between one word and the next.

It was a Hugh kiss: like a firestorm, a kiss so fierce and possessive that she couldn't possibly fight it. Not that her body wanted to. Her mind went into a haze of pleasure the moment that hard body came against hers. Her knees went weak, and her arms wrapped around him . . . and she pretty much forgot to breathe.

"You can't do that sort of thing," he said fiercely a moment later.

Georgina hadn't even thought of it for this reason, but now she just grinned at him. "Why not?"

"You're not a good enough rider for that sort of frolicking about."

She narrowed her eyes at him. "Show me a hedge high enough for Elsbeth to clear, and I can take her over it. Just who do you think is a better rider than I?"

"Me," he said promptly.

"You? You fall off all the time," she said. "I don't. I *never* fall off."

"Well, you—"

"And what's more, *I* am riding a sidesaddle," she said, speaking over him because this was important.

He didn't look so angry anymore. "Are you saying that I should take lessons from you?"

"I don't fall off. I never take a hedge my steed can't manage."

"Neither do I," he said promptly.

"Then why did you give me a shake?" She didn't look at him, just brushed off a leaf that had landed on her white shirt. For some reason, she felt a bit vulnerable without her jacket. Her bodice was made of frail Irish linen. She could almost see the pink of her arms through its sleeves.

"Because you—" He stopped.

"I'm the best rider on a sidesaddle that you know." She just stated it, because it was true, and he knew it.

"You frightened the shit out of me," he said, giving her another little shake. But it was a gentle one this time. "I thought—"

"Fear," she said primly, "is a very unwelcome emotion, I have always thought."

He surprised her. He threw back his head and laughed, the kind of bellow that rolled right across the field and made Richelieu prick up his ears to listen before he went back to cropping grass. "You were trying to teach me a lesson?"

He was a big, beautiful, brute of a man, and she wanted him. She looked at him laughing in the sun, the strong column of his neck brown and powerful, and she allowed herself to know the truth.

She wanted him with a kind of raw, fierce desire that was the antithesis of anything she'd felt in her marriage. She wanted him with an ache that started in her chest but spread down her legs.

Still, she was nettled by the fact he was laughing at her, so she turned away from him and walked over to Elsbeth, who was peacefully cropping the dandelions that grew all around the edge of the pond.

He followed her. "Do you remember when we went swimming, years ago?" he said, into her ear.

She hadn't realized that he'd come so close to her and shivered. "Swimming?" she echoed. "I don't know how to swim."

"Don't tell me you've forgotten." There was something wicked in his voice.

"I've never been swimming," she stated, certain of that. Swimming was not an activity that proper young ladies even considered. And Lord knows, she'd always been proper.

"I was ten years old. It was the summer my mother died, so you and your mother were staying with us at the estate."

She slipped her hand into his. "I'm sorry. I was

only six. No, I must have been seven. I don't have very clear memories of that summer."

His smile was generous, joyful, even. "She was a wonderful mother, not at all as proper as a countess should be. I was mad for horses, from the moment I escaped from the nursery."

"That's not a surprise," Georgina commented, holding his hand tightly.

"She used to come to the nursery and take me down to the stables. Even that summer, I came to her chamber every day and she would draw pictures of horses for me. She always drew me on top of the horse, jumping over a hedge that was higher than the manor, winning a race . . . my favorite sketch shows me clinging to a horse whose hooves are just clearing the moon."

It wasn't enough to hold his hand, so Georgina did something she had never done before. She moved in front of a man, cupped his face in her hands, and kissed him. And then she wrapped her arms around his neck and hugged him as tightly as she could.

Being Hugh, he took a hug that was meant to be consoling and turned it into something quite different.

"Wait," she said, pulling back a few minutes later, the breath catching in her throat. "I want to—"

He took her face in his hands this time. "What?"

he said, meeting her eyes, fierce and intent. "What do you want to do, Georgiana Sorrell?"

It was too much. "I want to hear about your swimming excursion. The one where you think I joined you though I didn't."

The smile that curled on his lips told her that his question would return, but he didn't argue the point. Instead, he sat down on the grass and pulled her arm so that she lost her balance and fell into his lap.

"Hugh, you can't do that sort of thing!" she protested. "You can't pull me and trip me and generally act as if I were a mare with a bridle."

"I never think of you that way," he said, tucking her sideways. His fingers brushed her slippers, then slowly, scandalously, caressed her ankle.

"That either!" she said, sticking her legs out straight so that he didn't ruin her concentration with his games. "Now tell me where you went swimming."

"The horse pond," he said promptly. "You probably don't remember the estate—"

"Yes, I do," she interrupted. "I was there for a week at Twelfth Night, remember? The horse pond is behind the stables, and it isn't really a pond. It's more like a widening in that stream that runs through your property."

"It's still there," he said thoughtfully. "Though

317

I didn't know that you even came to the stables during Twelfth Night."

"We've already established that you didn't see me if I did," she said tartly. Because the truth of it was that she had come down to the stables a few times and watched him putting his horseflesh through their paces, and had even taken a peek at the twin foals, though she would bite her tongue before she admitted such a thing.

"So you prayed to the gods to avenge my blindness," he said, dropping a kiss on her ear.

"What?"

"And the gods avenged you," he continued. "Because now, for the rest of my life, I'll always know where you are, Georgina, or I won't feel comfortable. I'll always see you first, in any room I enter. And I'll always want to find you there."

She swallowed and bit her lip hard. His voice was so steady and calm, the voice she remembered from her childhood. He wasn't demanding anything of her, or even asking for a response. He was just—

Stating it.

Telling her.

"The swimming?" she demanded, since she didn't know how to respond.

He sighed and dropped another kiss in her hair. "I used to go down at dusk, all sweaty from riding, and fling myself into the pond. That summer . . . it was all different. Mother was dying, and the doctors came and went all the time. All the servants, the whole household, revolved around it."

"I know," she said, leaning against him. "I know just what you mean."

"I forgot about Richard's illness. Of course you do." He brushed the curls away from her forehead and kissed her there. "Well, so I had more freedom that summer. My sisters—and you—were penned up in the nursery with a phalanx of nursemaids, but I was old enough to escape. And escape I did."

"I don't remember that summer clearly," she said, frowning. "My mother was so close to your mother and father . . . we came every July, of course. In my memory, it's just summer after summer, time in which we could escape the nursemaids too, and take our dolls to the stream, and play with you, and build willow-huts."

"I would strip off my clothes and jump into that pond," he said.

"Well, I never did that," she said with a laugh. "So why do you think that I went swimming with you?"

"Because you did just that."

She was silent for a moment. Then: "No!"

"I don't know what Caro would have done without you that summer. You carried a handkerchief in your pinafore."

"I always carried a handkerchief," Georgina pointed out. "One of my mother's rules."

"You would hand it over if anyone started crying," he continued. "Not that I ever cried. I didn't believe in it."

"I suppose boys don't cry," Georgina said with a sigh. The only man she'd ever seen cry was Richard's valet, just after Richard died. She'd let him sit by Richard toward the end, because . . . just because.

It was only when his valet came out of Richard's room with his eyes swollen and tears still falling down his cheeks that she knew she was a widow.

"You didn't realize it yet," Hugh said, resting his chin on the top of her head. "You gave me that handkerchief a few times, as if you thought I needed it. I always pushed it back with disdain, but I appreciated the gesture."

"I don't remember," Georgina said. "How odd."

"Then my mother died. And we were all put into blacks, and my great-aunts arrived, and it was quite horrible." His arms tightened around her. "It was harder for me to get out of the nursery, but I managed it, a few days after. Before that . . . well, the girls needed me."

"You were the best big brother," she offered. "Even to me, and I'm not your sister."

"Thank God for that," he said with a thrum of heartfelt thanks in his voice that made the joy spring up in her heart again. "I went down to the pond, not because I was going to cry—"

"Since boys don't cry," she supplied.

"Because it was all watery down there, and no one would notice in case I made a mistake of that nature."

"Where do I come in?"

"You escaped as well, except I didn't know it. You must have followed me. You were—what?— seven years old, so I can't imagine how you managed it."

"Oh, I can," she said, loving the way his arms formed a warm cage around her. "I was so trained to be aware of protocol, and servants, and the right thing to do that I always knew exactly how to do the wrong thing. It was unavoidable. You are told not to kiss in dark corners long before you have an impulse to do it."

"Did Richard kiss you in dark corners?" He sounded curious, not jealous.

"No. So I escaped from the nursery?"

"The first I knew of it was when I looked up from splashing around the pond, which was deliciously warm, by the way. There you were."

"On the edge of the pond?"

"You had already taken off your pinafore and your dress, by the time I saw you. I was so caught by horror that I didn't do a thing. You had your shoes and stockings off within a moment, and then

321

you threw off your chemise and just pranced right into the water."

"No!"

He was laughing. "Yes. You did. You, the entirely proper Lady Georgina. You took off all your clothes without the help of a maid, and you went into the water as if you were born to swim."

"What did you *do?*"

"I couldn't get out," he explained. "Because I hadn't learned much about propriety but I knew for sure that young ladies weren't supposed to see a boy's pump-handle. So I backed up, deeper in the water, and you followed me. And then, before I knew it, you were splashing me."

"I can't believe I don't remember such a thing!"

"I've never forgotten. You were the most beautiful girl, Georgina. The most beautiful thing I'd ever seen. Your skin was as white as the inside of a flower. Your hair was usually all pinned up and neat-looking, but when you threw away your bonnet, it fell down your back."

"You didn't—"

"Feel desire? I thought of you as if you were one of my sisters. But at the same time . . . it was confusing. You were so different from me, and so pretty, and so—so feminine. All that hair, and the way you shrieked when I splashed you."

"You splashed me? That wasn't very gentlemanly."

"I didn't know what else to do. Of course I splashed you, and you shrieked and splashed me back, so I got water in my mouth because I was laughing so hard, and that's the way it was."

"But how did you ever get out of the pond? And how did I?"

"My father's stable master heard the rumpus and came out. He was no fool and knew he was looking at a disaster in the making. So he whisked you off somewhere, and ordered me out of the pool, and that was that.

"As far as I know, no one ever found out. I heard at supper that you had accidentally fallen into the horse trough, and after that your mother didn't allow you around the stables, and anyway the summer was over, and we were all moving back to London."

"I should never have said that you don't understand death, should I?" she asked quietly.

There was a moment of silence, and then he dropped a kiss on her nose. "I wish you were right," he offered. "I can't remember not living with the knowledge. I loved my mother with all my heart, and she died."

"Then why do you keep training these horses yourself?" she cried, frustrated. "Because you might well die too, you know."

"I don't know if you've noticed this, Georgie, but none of us are going to escape death."

She snorted.

"I can't live afraid."

"You're not thinking of the people who have to be afraid *for* you."

Without warning, he rolled backward, taking her with him, so he was lying in the clover, and she was lying beside him. Right beside him. She froze instantly, every inch of her body suddenly aware of his. That big, muscled, gorgeous body. Her fingers trembled, wanting to touch him.

"Georgie," he said. That was all. But she knew what he was saying. And she knew what her answer was, except that she was her mother's daughter, and nothing like that could be put in words.

Chapter 23

$\mathcal{I}$nstead of answering him, she simply rose to her feet.

A shadow crossed Hugh's eyes, and she knew that he was afraid that she was leaving. It felt good to tease him, so she turned with a little wiggle of her hips and walked a step to the edge of the stream. He couldn't see, but she was undoing the pearl buttons at her wrists.

A moment later she felt him at her shoulder, but she didn't turn to say anything.

"Georgie," he said again. This time his voice had darkened to velvet, and it rushed over her senses and stung every nerve into life.

She didn't turn around, just concentrated on slipping each little pearl button out of its button-hole. Then she pulled off her linen shirt and laid it primly to the side. He still hadn't said anything, or done anything, as far as she knew.

Her riding skirt took a moment or so. Her boots another moment. Her garters, stockings, corset . . . they all seemed to fly off her. Then she had on nothing but her chemise. She took a deep breath and pulled off her chemise.

Then she turned around to see what he was doing.

He was naked.

The rest of him was as beautiful as his chest. The muscles in his legs were huge, as befitted a man who could control a stallion with a nudge from his knees. They were shaded with dark hair.

"You didn't have hair back then," she said, managing to meet his eyes.

"You didn't have breasts." His voice was somewhere between sensual and downright dangerous. It made her feel as if she were looking at her body through his eyes—seeing herself as creamy, curved, and delicious.

Without a word, she raised her arms and started pulling pins out of her hair. There weren't that many left after her mad cross-country race, but somehow her ringlets had stayed up. Now they tumbled down her back, the color of dark roses.

Richard approved of her body, and had told her so in his considerate way. But he always thought her hair verged on the vulgar.

The memory made her raise a hand and pull a thick lock of hair forward over her breast.

Hugh groaned, a hoarse puff of air that startled her. "Do you like the color of my hair?" she asked.

"I've never liked anything but red hair. Not since I was ten."

She couldn't stop smiling. "You did say that when Caro suggested Gwendolyn Passmore for your list."

"Too pale," he said. "Her hair is like an imitation of yours."

If she stood here another moment, she would simply leap on him and start touching him in all the places and ways that a lady should never touch a man. Especially a man who wasn't her husband.

So she turned on her heel and marched into the pond instead.

Immediately she realized why ladies don't swim. Because it wasn't pleasant to feel muck under one's toes. And water was rather cold. And though it looked perfectly clear on the bank, now that she was in it, she couldn't see the bottom, which made her feel queasy. And . . .

There was a tidal wave of a splash, and a powerful body cut through the water. He stood up opposite her. "Bloody hell, but this is cold," Hugh said, shaking wet hair out of his eyes.

Georgina didn't need to be told. Her nipples had turned from raspberries to rocks. Her belly was protesting the little wavelets of cold water that welled out from the splash he made. She had absolutely no impulse to go any deeper.

"If you splash me," she said, "I'll have to kill you. Just so you know."

"We all have to die sometime." He grinned mockingly.

He deserved to be splashed, and the only thing that stopped her was the conviction that he would return the favor.

"Was the pool warmer when we were children?" she inquired. She couldn't stop looking at his shoulders. And his waist. And below. The water was just clear enough that she could see . . . him.

She hadn't looked earlier, of course. What she could see suggested that he and Richard were not alike. That was a polite way of putting it. She felt a pang of alarm, given the fact that she hadn't enjoyed Richard's invasions very much, although her husband had been considerably smaller.

Then she raised her eyes to find that Hugh was grinning broadly and watching her. "So how do I measure up?" he asked, laughter in his voice.

She turned up her nose. Far be it from her to criticize her dead husband. "You're a bit smaller," she said briskly, "but—"

The smile fell from his face, and he was beside her in one stride. "Georgina." He said it low and threatening, but she was too busy getting used to the cold water that he had sent lapping over her stomach.

"Do you want to rephrase that?"

"What?" she demanded, shivering.

He nipped her lower lip and nudged his hips forward.

She couldn't help looking down, and now they were close enough that the water was translucent. She could see everything. Her heart thumped, and when she looked up she was quite sure that her dismay was in her eyes. "This won't work," she said quietly.

Hugh looked stunned. "It won't?"

She bit her lip, feeling tears threaten. She shook her head.

"You're telling me that Richard Sorrell had such a big pump-handle that you can't even contemplate mine?" He took a step back and raked a hand through his hair. "Bloody *hell*!"

She couldn't even smile. "I'm sorry."

"For what?" His voice was steaming with frustration and anger, though who he was angry at she didn't know.

"You're too—"

"Don't even go there," he said tightly. "This has damn well never happened in my life, and I can't believe it's happening now."

"You're too large," she said desperately, to his back, since he was leaving the pool. "I'm sorry, Hugh, but it will never work. Never."

He froze. "What did you say?"

"If all you care about is some sort of contest over the size of your thistle," she said crossly, turning to splash out the other direction, "you can rest easy."

He was next to her in a moment and picked her straight out of the water into his arms. "Look at me, damn it."

"You needn't swear," she said tartly. But she met his eyes.

"Are you telling me that Richard wasn't some sort of giant amongst men?"

"I think you are," she said honestly. "And it's not going to work. It—" She gulped and decided that she might as well be honest. "It hardly worked for Richard and myself. He was very considerate about it, and even so, he could hardly fit."

The look in his eyes sent a dark thrill down her legs. "We can work on that, Georgie."

"Don't call me Georgie!" she snapped.

"I thought you liked it." He was walking steadily out of the water, and since only her toes were still trailing through cold water, she was happy.

"Not when . . ."

"When it's so necessary that you be a Georgina rather than a Georgie?" He put her on her feet, and she instantly missed the heat of his body. Then he started walking away, toward Richelieu, who had wandered a good distance away.

Was he leaving? She stared at his back, dumbstruck. True, she had said that it wouldn't work. But she hoped . . . well, she hoped he could work some miracle. Because somewhere along the way she had decided to do an utterly scandalous thing, something that could ruin her reputation forever.

Hugh pulled at a bundle rolled behind Richelieu's saddle, and then strode back toward her.

There was another difference with Richard. Hugh's thistle stood upright. All the time. Whereas her husband . . .

"What did you fetch?" she asked.

His smile had the smugness of a cat in the cream jug. "Blanket roll. I always have an extra." He threw it onto a bed of buttercups and plucked her off her feet, with the same lack of éclat that he always displayed. A moment later, she was lying on her back, stark naked, staring up at Hugh.

"Is that itchy?" he asked her, as casual as if they were on a picnic.

"Yes," she said, too dumbfounded to do more than answer.

He snatched her petticoats, tucked them under her, and threw himself down next to her. He didn't touch her. He didn't roll over on top of her. He just leaned in, delicately, and kissed her.

They didn't say anything for a while. Georgina

tried to formulate words when Hugh pulled away from her mouth and started doing something so delicious to her throat . . . kissing her, and nipping her so that she found herself whimpering and clutching his shoulders, hoping that he would keep going.

Lower.

To her breast.

That very thought was enough to break the haze in her mind a little, and she murmured, "Hugh, perhaps . . ."

He responded by taking her mouth again. It was a primal kiss, one that told her without words that he was in charge, and she should just stop thinking.

Georgina let him do it because, after all, she was the one benefiting from all that male enthusiasm. It was awkward, but something about the way Hugh held her, hard, and didn't let her break away, drove her wild with desire.

In fact . . . "Hugh," she said, hearing her own breathy voice with a shock of surprise. "We aren't going to . . ." She broke off in a moan.

"You undo me," he said. His voice was a dark growl. Then he put his mouth on her breast. Just like that. With no preparation, without asking permission.

And she yelled. That was the only word for it.

No, she was wrong. That hot, wet mouth suckled her, and she didn't yell: She screamed.

It didn't make him stop, either. He just suckled harder, until she arched her back to make it very clear that he was welcome to keep going.

It wasn't until a warm hand slid up her leg that Georgina regained even a modicum of conscious thought. She yelped and tried to sit up.

A big hand pushed her down again, but she couldn't summon the protest that she meant to because he nipped her, and that drove her body into a sweet, dark place again. So she closed her eyes, closed out the big, empty blue sky and all that air around them and just dropped into the frantic, tight feeling in her body, the way heat was coiling in her legs and building in her stomach.

She kept trying to arch up, but that big hand held her down. Then she found herself trying to pull him on top of her, and that was scandalous enough that her eyes flew open, and she squeaked, "No!"

"Yes," he said throatily, and there he was. Hugh. She was flat on her back like any hussy, and he was braced on his forearms, grinning down at her.

She was scandalized. Of course. But she was also so happy that she couldn't breathe. He was looking at her . . . *that* way. His eyes were—

And his hands—

"We shouldn't," she said feebly. "Not outside."

His eyes laughed down at her, and all that laughter was side by side with desire. For *her*.

That was what she never saw in all the days of her marriage. And what she saw in the eyes of other men, looking at the woman they desired.

"Why not?" he asked, and the husky sound of his voice thrummed down her legs like a musical note.

"Not proper," she said, with a little gasp because he had his hand on her breast again.

"I'm not married," Hugh said.

"I know that." Her fingers were clenched around his neck. What she really wanted to do was touch *him*.

But she wasn't sure that was allowed. Richard certainly would not have wanted to be touched. But then he hadn't wanted to kiss her neck, or her arm, or the side of her breast either.

"If you make love to me, Georgie, you're marrying me." His thumb rubbed harder, and she heard a little pant come out of her mouth and shut it firmly. "I love that sound you make," he said, conversationally.

"We can't do this . . . outside," she said, sidestepping the whole question of marriage.

"Why not?"

"Because—because we're outside. And it's not—"

He took the word *proper* from her lips and kissed her into that storm of heat and pleasure again, until she knew without words that propriety had nothing to do with this particular day. This particular moment.

With Hugh.

"Are you ever proper?" she murmured, when he was kissing his way across her throat again.

"Rarely." He had been braced above her, his body not really touching hers, and he rose back up on his knees. "It doesn't interest me."

Georgina couldn't help gurgling with laughter. "That doesn't surprise me."

"A proper young lady would never pant in the outdoors," he informed her, making her do just that with one rough pass of his hand.

"I—" she gasped.

"A proper gentleman would likely never say this."

"What?"

"For God's sake, Georgie, will you touch me? *Please?*"

She swallowed. "Is it . . . is that allowed?" It sounded so stupid that she closed her eyes for a moment. "I mean, would you like me to do that?"

He had a curious look in his eyes, almost like sympathy and a lot like regret, but then he gave her a grin, flopped on his back, and spread his arms. "I'm yours."

Georgina sat up so fast that her head swum. He was gorgeous. She carefully got on her knees next to him, and then paused. She didn't want to just touch.

She cleared her throat. She thought she knew the answer, but . . .

"Can I do more than touch you?"

His lazy smile would be outlawed in a Puritan county. "Georgie, darling, if you want to put that gorgeous mouth of yours anywhere on my body, you will make me the happiest man in England."

She took a deep breath and didn't even try to stop the delighted smile on her face. She probably looked like an idiot. Who cared?

This was Hugh, apparently the first man in her life who had seen her body, even if he was only ten at the time. And Hugh was the first man whose body *she* had ever seen in good light. So it was worth making an event of it.

So she inspected him. Closely, slowly, starting with his neck and slowly, slowly making her way down his body. Not touching him.

The interesting thing was that she seemed to be affecting him even without a touch. By the time she reached his waistline, he was holding on to the blanket like a drowning man, and his breathing was ragged.

"Georgie," he said, once.

"I'm thinking," she said, not listening to him. Because she'd reached the most interesting part of his body. Her whole life she'd called a man's instrument his *thistle*. But that word didn't seem to have any relation to what Hugh had. A thistle was soft and squishy and round. And Hugh was hard and long.

The very thought of it made her feel . . . she had her legs curled underneath her, but they suddenly felt uncomfortable.

Hugh made a strangled noise in his throat. "Georgie, please . . ."

"Mmmmm," she said.

And then she leaned over and did exactly what she wanted to do. She put her hands on his thighs, and those muscles jumped under her fingers. She stroked him softly, with a feather touch, then more firmly.

He groaned again, and the sound of it went straight between her legs. She was going to do something that she'd never even dreamed of, and yet the moment it came into her mind, she was consumed with the desire to do it.

Without looking at Hugh, because she was pretty sure that he never had *this* in mind, she bent over, letting her hair hide her face, and put her lips directly on top of him.

He shouted, and his hips jerked up. And just like

that, her lips slid around him. He tasted like the outdoors, like a lake and a spicy man, all mixed up together.

She liked it.

He was saying something, but she paid no attention, just dragged her hands slowly up his thighs, teasing him. And then brought them to the same place.

"No," he said hoarsely. "No."

She raised her head. "Don't you like it?"

He stared back at her, his eyes wild. "No one has ever kissed me there. Ever."

She grinned and turned back to him. He made a strangled noise before her lips even touched him. Joy sprang just from giving him pleasure, from the way the muscles in his thighs were knotted and fierce, from the way his hands clenched at his sides.

She played with him, bringing her hand in the mix, running a finger up his leg, listening to the sound of his groans, until he suddenly said through clenched teeth, "That's it—can't do any more." He put her away firmly.

"Oh!" she said, rather surprised. She had thought that he was enjoying it more and more.

His jaw was clenched, and his eyes were hot. "I have to ask you something, Georgie."

Her heart stilled, and her hand dropped from his thigh.

"Tell me that Richard didn't teach you that."

"Richard?" she said, her voice squeaking. And then pulled herself together. She cleared her throat, not even bothering to imagine how horrified her husband would have been if she had even touched him so intimately. "No, certainly not," she said, starting to scramble to her feet. Her body felt confused, hot and a little dizzy. "Of course not. It was—just a stupid thought. I—" She bit off the words and found herself standing.

Even thinking of Richard made her feel odd . . . cold. The very thought of Richard . . . what would Richard think—not of what she'd just done, but of her, in a field, without clothing? A shiver of distaste went up her spine.

Hugh had stood when she wasn't watching. She took a step back.

"I shouldn't have said that." His voice was dark, thrumming her nerves.

"Well, perhaps not," she said, wrapping her arms around herself and shivering again, just a little. "You know, this—this isn't really my—I'm not a person who—" She couldn't even think where to put her hands, on her breasts, or elsewhere?

"Forget Richard."

Her back stiffened. She couldn't forget Richard. What sort of wife—widow—would that make her? But then, what sort of woman was she? She turned in a blind panic and headed toward her clothing.

"I'm sorry," she said, over her shoulder. "I have to go."

She just managed to snatch her skirt before he reached her. A hand came around her waist; she gasped and clutched the cloth to her breasts. "I can't do this," she cried, her voice catching. "I don't know what I was thinking. Please let me go."

"I'm a jackass," Hugh said. "Georgie. Please. I didn't mean to mention—I didn't mean to bring it up. It was just that no woman has ever—"

"Don't say that again!" She could feel heat in her cheeks. "Richard would *not* have countenanced such a thing. Obviously, I'm—It's only me." She pulled free of his arms. "I need to go." Tears burned in the back of her throat. She should have known not to just do whatever came in her head. She wasn't any good at that sort of thing. Look how many times Richard had had to gently correct her, and she had never even—

She wrenched the skirt up her legs only to realize that Hugh was pulling the fabric away at the same moment.

"Leave me be!" she said fiercely.

He was the biggest idiot in the world. One moment Georgina was looking at him, sultry and hot and a little dazed, and the next her eyes were bleak and—what possessed him to ask such a thing?

It was because when she touched him, when she

even smiled at him, he felt a primitive wave of possession.

Her lips touched him, and he thought, *mine,* and she smiled and he thought, *mine,* and when she put her lips on him, he thought something that was absolutely idiotic.

"Forgive me," he said, dropping her skirt and grabbing her shoulders so that she couldn't escape.

"Of course I do," she said, pulling her skirt over her hips. "I think I must have gone mad for a moment. I—I embarrassed myself. I apologize."

"Apologize? For what?"

She shot him a furious look.

Still holding her shoulders, he suddenly understood. If looks could kill, hers would burn him where he stood. "You think I don't respect you," he said, pulling her closer.

Her mouth set mulishly.

He dragged her into his arms. She was all soft and warm where he was hard, and just like that his blood started pounding through his body again. He said it into her hair. "You think I don't respect you."

"This is a very uninteresting conversation," she said, pushing against him.

But he held on to her. "You think I am horrified by the kiss you just gave me."

"*I* am horrified," Georgie said, pushing his hand

away. "I can't imagine what came into my head. I'm—"

"It made me delirious," he said flatly. "Crazed, cracked, mad with pleasure."

"Wonderful." She managed to twist away from him and grab her chemise.

He went after her, because he would always, always go after her. He wrapped his arms around her from behind, so quickly that she squeaked like a mouse in the walls. "I love you."

Her body froze.

He kept talking, the happiness of it roaring through his blood. "I love you, Georgina. I think I've loved you always, even before you went swimming with me. Nothing you do could ever horrify me, or disappoint me, or make me lose respect for you. Nothing."

He waited a moment, but she didn't say anything. Her hair had fallen forward, all around her face, and he couldn't see her expression. So he started kissing her ear, still holding her so closely that she couldn't escape. "When you kissed me so intimately, I suddenly realized that if you had ever given pleasure to Richard of that sort, I would have to kill him."

"He's already dead," Georgie said. Her voice was a little muffled, but she didn't sound angry anymore.

"I know. I'm sorry he died. But I'm not sorry

that he died, because you're *mine*, Georgie. I think you always have been and I just didn't realize or I could never have let you marry the man. Never."

She took a deep breath, and then slowly turned in his arms to face him. Her beautiful eyes were painfully uncertain. "So you asked that because you were jealous?"

He kissed her so hard that she melted into his arms, letting her feel his ferocious desire, the desire that made him crazed at the very idea of Richard. The possessiveness too, and at the bottom of it all—the love. "You're mine," he said hoarsely, a moment later.

"Hugh," she whispered. The tremor in her voice was as intoxicating as brandy. It went to his head.

"Did you really think that I was disgusted by what you did?"

She hesitated. "Richard would have been."

He clenched his teeth for a moment and managed to keep back a curse. "I'm not Richard." He pushed his thigh in between her legs, letting her feel the strength of his leg against her most sensitive part. "Not. Richard," he said fiercely.

Georgie's eyes went a little unfocused, just the way he liked them. She shivered against his thigh.

"I want to lick you all over," he said. "I want you to lick me. I want to make love to you on top of the dining-room table, and in the water trough. I want you to lean over my library chair and smile at me. I want you to let me seduce you in the stables."

She gave a gasping little giggle.

He moved back and dropped to the blanket once more. His tool stood up proudly. "Please," he begged. "Please, will you do it again, Georgie, just for a moment, even for a second? I just want to feel it once more in my life. Please."

Chapter 24

$\mathcal{H}$ugh was almost babbling. Georgie looked hard at his face, just long enough to discover that there wasn't even a trace of horror or surprise in his eyes. There wasn't. There was lust and—and something else.

She knelt beside him rather primly and put a hand on his chest. It was muscled and hard under her fingertips. She was too embarrassed to meet his eyes, so she just concentrated on his body, finding what he liked, what gave him pleasure.

It was madness, making love like this, in a way that—

She had to stop thinking of Richard. Wrap up the memories and put them away somewhere. Because Richard, and his rather horrified experience of her body . . . that didn't have any part here, in the warm sun in a field of buttercups, making love to Hugh.

Hugh was . . . Hugh. He was stretched out like a boneless cat, his eyes gleaming with pleasure, his body trembling at her touch. She rubbed her thumb over his nipple, ran her fingers over his taut waist, wandered a little lower. The hoarse sound in the back of his throat was encouraging.

But she had barely touched him before he suddenly erupted under her, and she found herself flat on her back, six feet of hot aroused male on top of her.

"I can't do it," he said flatly, staring down into her eyes. "Not without making a possible ass of myself and losing control, and I'm not doing that with you."

Georgie had to admit, she loved the sound of that. "Losing control?" she said, feathering her hands down his back and giving an experimental wiggle. "What does that look like?"

He didn't answer, just lowered his head and began to nuzzle her breast. She lost track of her question and started to whimper, her hands curling instinctively, pulling him closer. For the first time in her life, she felt a melting emptiness, a hunger that could only be assuaged by another person.

"Hugh," she said, her voice coming out a mere whisper. "Please, I . . ."

He responded by dipping a finger between her

legs. Georgie arched straight up against his body with a faint scream. Two powerful strokes, and she broke, shaking and crying against him, clutching him hard.

"*Yes,*" Hugh said in a hoarse whisper. "I don't think this will hurt, sweet Georgie." Then he pulled back, and before she could register what he had said, he thrust.

Georgie's eyes flew wide open. It felt entirely different than what she had experienced before, when her body seemed to fight her husband's invasion. Instead, Hugh slid into her, hot and big and powerful—and rather than rebelling, her body ached for more.

"Does it hurt?" he whispered, withdrawing.

She wasn't listening. Instead, she was trying to pull him back, whimpering. "Hugh."

A slow grin spread over his face, and he gave her a hard, quick kiss. "I'll take that as a *no,*" he said. And slid back into her welcome. The grin fell from his face. "God, you feel so good. So small and wet and damned perfect." His voice was hardly more than a growl.

Georgie instinctively rose to meet him, clenching hard, trying to keep him with her. He pushed deep and steady, again, and again. Her first orgasm melted into another as she sobbed and cried, her body instinctively responding to his thrusts.

"I can't—" Hugh gasped.

But Georgie couldn't answer. She was caught in the moment, arching hard against him, reaching down to pull him even closer.

At the touch of her hand on his arse, he did lose control. She felt it in the way his body ground against hers, in the groan that tore from his throat.

He pulled back, braced on his forearms. "You are *mine*," he said between clenched teeth, his voice no more than a growl.

He was—Georgie squeezed her eyes shut, feeling the heat building again, shuddering helplessly.

"I love you." Hugh's voice broke, and he bent down to take her mouth, his body driving her straight into a firestorm of pleasure. But not enough to obscure his words. Or the joy in her heart.

Chapter 25

When people talked about fallen women, they never discussed how those women handled the embarrassing moments. The aftermath of the fall, so to speak. Everyone knows that the first thing Eve did was fashion herself a gown from some leaves, and Georgie could see exactly why.

It was embarrassing.

One moment you were so caught up in the pleasure of it that you were . . . well, grunting, and crying, and generally acting as if you were cracked. But then, when it was over, you found yourself lying in a field with clover stuck in the back of your knees, and likely other places as well.

And your hair is rumpled, and you aren't as clean as you would like, and your clothes are a good distance away.

"Damn it," Hugh groaned, throwing an arm over his eyes. "Richelieu took off."

Georgie sat up, happy to think about something else. Her breasts bobbled against her chest, and she wrapped her arms around them. She looked around, but while Elsbeth was still peacefully cropping grass, there was no sign of Hugh's pride and joy. "Where did he go? Do you suppose that he returned to his stable?"

She looked back at Hugh, but he didn't appear to be as anxious as a man should be who had just misplaced the future winner of the Ascot. Instead, he was looking at her breasts.

"God, you're so beautiful," he said, his voice hushed and almost reverent.

That made her feel a bit better. "So are you," she said shyly. "That is, you're very handsome."

He rolled over on his side. "I'm a bit brutish, and I always have been. But you, Georgie . . . you're all curves and your skin is so smooth and you taste so good. I feel as if I shouldn't even touch you." He reached out and ran a finger over the curve of her breast.

She loosened her arms, and her breasts plumped into his hand. In one smooth movement, Hugh came up on his knees, just before her, and pulled her to her knees as well.

Georgie was mortifyingly aware of her bare arse, the way her breasts were touching his chest, the tangled grass under her knees. But then she looked up into his eyes and forgot all about her discomfort.

"Lady Georgina Sorrell," Hugh said formally, taking her palm and putting it to his lips, "would you do me the great honor of becoming my wife?"

Tangled sentences went through Georgie's mind . . . She never meant to marry again. She never thought to . . .

An uncharacteristic touch of uncertainty flashed through Hugh's eyes. "Georgie?"

She had to ask. "I'm just—"

He kissed her palm again, his eyes on hers. "What is it, sweetheart?"

"You didn't even know I was in the room last year at Twelfth Night," she said in a rush. "I just . . ." Her voice trailed off.

"I'm an idiot, and I always have been," he said. "Carolyn would concur, wouldn't she?"

Georgie nodded.

"I don't dress like an earl. Hell, most of the time I don't even *smell* like an earl. But I know how I feel," he said fiercely. "I love you, Georgie, and you are mine. You're going to marry me because that's just the way it is."

The smile in Georgie's heart must have been in her eyes, because his grip on her hand loosed a bit. "You want me to marry you, even though you sometimes go off and practically live in the barn?"

"I have never put my horses ahead of my sisters, ahead of the people I love. And I will never, ever put my stables ahead of you."

Georgie's smile trembled. "I've never been first in anyone's life," she said before she could stop herself.

It was a few minutes before Hugh stopped kissing her, and by then she was convinced that in his mind, *she* was the first. "Will you?" he asked, once more.

Georgie's eyes were filled with tears. "I love you, Hugh," she whispered.

"But will you marry me, the way I am, with all the horses, and the stupidity, and the stink of the stables?"

"I wasn't going to marry again."

His fingers tightened on her shoulders. "Was it so awful with your first husband that you can't contemplate it again—or is it something about me?"

"I didn't mean to love you," she said, smiling through her tears.

"Then?"

"I thought perhaps that if I didn't marry I wouldn't . . ." But her words were tangled in her head, and her fears seemed paltry and foolish now. Still, there was one thing that had to be said. "I'm not sure I can have children."

The words seemed almost to echo in the air, so Georgina kept talking. "You made the list, or rather Carolyn made the list, and it was all about having children and making an heir." She swallowed hard. Still Hugh said nothing. "I just don't think that I—perhaps we could just have an *affaire*?"

"An *affaire*," he said. "With you? No."

"Oh, well—"

But he took the words away. "You are my life and my heart, Georgie. I feel as if I have been walking around the world blindly, at least until last week, when I looked up and there you were; it had been you all the time. I don't give a damn if we never have children."

This time tears rolled down her cheeks. He kissed them away.

"In fact, you are the only person I want in my life, so perhaps it would be better if there weren't any children," he said, sitting back and scooping her onto his lap.

"Richard and I tried and tried," Georgie told his chest. She couldn't bring herself to meet his eyes yet.

"I don't care," Hugh said. The words were a deep rumble in his chest, and she knew she heard the truth in them as if it were written on his skin.

So she looked up, and it was written in his eyes.

"Do you love me, Georgie?" he asked.

"So much," she said, her voice breaking.

"Then marry me. Because I love you as much. I promise to be more cautious while training horses.

I'll take care. And meanwhile, we'll love each other for as long as we can, and that's all that matters."

Mr. Bucky Buckstone, whose fields ran right around the pond, and who had discovered a great mud-colored horse cropping his wife's pansies, stopped short, his mouth falling open. There was no limit to what the gentry was up to these days. There they were, naked as the day they were born, right in his field.

He watched for a moment, but when the pair sank down into the grass, he turned the horse's head away and started back the direction he'd come.

"I know who *you* are," he told Richelieu. "You belong to that earl as is visiting the great house, and I'm guessing it's him who's back there in my field. Lucky for the earl that it's me who's found you and not some others around here."

His ears had turned a bit red, and he walked fast. As he told Mrs. Buckstone a few minutes later, there were no limits to some people's nerve. And even when she reminded him of a certain incident that happened twenty-three years ago, on a warm summer night when he came a-courting, he wouldn't budge.

"That was *us*," he said stubbornly. "Them's gentry."

Mrs. Buckstone laughed and picked up another sheet. It was washing day, and she was pinning clean linen to the line. "And why shouldn't the earl be doing some pole-work in a field, same as any other of God's creatures?"

Bucky had no clear answer for that, so he just shook his head again and took Richelieu round the side of the house for water.

Chapter 26

$\mathcal{L}$ady Georgina, soon to be Georgina Dunne, Countess of Briarly, was dreaming. A little boy with a headful of chestnut ringlets and eyes of pure mischief was running about her bedchamber, shrieking at the top of his lungs. He was riding a broom, and even as she watched, he swept a teacup from her dressing table.

She was calling to him, trying to get him to stop before he broke something—because he always broke things—and loving him so much that her heart ached with it, when she suddenly woke from the dream.

Waking tends to happen when very large male bodies land on one in the middle of the night. Especially when that male has a hand under one's night rail before one has even shaken off the dream.

And then the dream slipped away, because, well, Hugh was nuzzling her neck and making hungry sounds, and his hand . . .

That hand!

Of course one couldn't remember a dream, in the midst of all that.

"What are you doing here?" Georgie gasped. "Hugh, you shouldn't!"

"I should," he said, and his voice was not one to be argued with. "Everyone in this dratted place is finally asleep. I thought Finchbird would never retire." Then Hugh returned to what he was doing, and by then Georgie had lost the will to fight, as they say of beleaguered countries.

And she had forgotten her dream.

Which explains why the said Lady Briarly kept staring at her baby son, Gage Willet Dunne, some nine months later and saying, "I just can't explain it; I feel as if I've already met him, as if I've known him forever."

The babe's proud papa, who leaned over and kissed his son, then his wife again, shook his head. "I've never seen anyone with a look like that, Georgie. Just look at him. He looks as naughty as can be. Now *I* was an angel when I was a babe, but this one . . ."

But that would happen nine months later. On this particular September night, the earl had thrown his future wife's night rail clear across the

357

chamber before he remembered something that he really had to do. So he raised his head, and said, "Excuse me, darling."

Georgie looked down at him with a sound somewhere between a squeak and a gasp, and said, "Please don't stop what you were doing."

"I must. I have to give you something." He dropped a kiss on her thigh. Then he climbed out of bed and walked across the room.

"You're naked!" she exclaimed, apparently noticing this for the first time.

"Of course I am," Hugh said, lighting a lamp on her dressing table. "A gentleman never hops into a lady's bed with his boots on. Christ, it's cold tonight."

Georgie had rolled onto her side, and now she was propped on one elbow, watching him. Her gorgeous red hair fell in swirls over her breasts, and he was struck again with the sense that she was too beautiful for him. For someone like him.

But then he looked at her face, and the wanton, enchanting little pout on her lips that told him, clear as day, that no one had ever given her pleasure the way he did.

So he got back under the covers next to her and pulled the sheet over both their heads. There, in the warm cave created by their bodies, lit by a soft golden glow from the one lamp, he said firmly: "I love you."

Georgie smiled, and the joy in her eyes made his heart sing. "I love you too," she whispered. "Are we going to make love under the sheet? You're so romantic, Hugh."

They were under the covers because he thought certain important parts of his anatomy were in danger of freezing off, but he didn't see the point in disabusing her if she thought he was being romantic. "I'd make love to you anywhere," he promised, meaning it. "Even in a pile of snow."

Then, with a typical lack of finesse, he added, "I didn't have this with me in the morning." He picked up Georgie's hand and slid the ring over her finger.

"Oh," she breathed.

"I suppose it's old-fashioned," he said, realizing suddenly that his mother's ring might not be exactly *au courant*. It held a circle of diamonds surrounding a rose imperial topaz.

But Georgie's eyes shone. "It's beautiful, Hugh. It's the most beautiful ring I've ever seen. Was it your mother's?"

He nodded and dropped a kiss on her nose. "My father gave it to me after she died, and told me that I should give it to my wife."

A tear rolled down her cheek, and he kissed it away. "That's the most lovely thing that I ever heard," she said, her voice choking.

"She would be very happy," Hugh said. "She

would like you, Georgie." But then he wanted her to stop crying, so he just rolled on top of her and set about distracting her.

He was very good at that sort of thing.

So good that Georgie didn't really have a chance to examine her ring until the next morning, and she was still peeking glances at her hand as she strolled into the breakfast room. It was quite late, and most of the party had retired to the drawing room.

In fact, Caroline and Piers were the only people left at breakfast, and since Caroline leapt to her feet and cried, "There you are!" it was clear that they had been sitting in front of chilly toast and lukewarm tea, waiting for her.

Georgie couldn't stop her smile. "I slept a bit later than normal," she said, coming around the table to sit next to Caroline.

"I imagine—" Caroline cried, but then her voice broke off. "Oh, Piers, look, my brother—my mother—that's—oh, Georgie, I'm so happy for you!"

It wasn't until later that Caroline said something that Georgie never forgot as long as she wore that ring, which was the whole of her long and happy life. "This is just what my father would have wanted," Caroline said. "I do wish he was alive to see it. He was disappointed when you fell in love so quickly, and in your first season. And he wasn't happy when you married Richard though, of course, I never said as much to you."

"He wasn't?" Caroline said, rather startled.

"It had nothing to do with Richard, but he thought you were just the person who might be able to keep Hugh from retreating into the stables. He always felt that Hugh took our mother's death the hardest, and you helped somehow, during that awful time. Something happened that made him think the two of you would be perfect together."

She didn't say any more, and Georgie didn't enlighten her. But for the rest of her life, whenever anyone mentioned swimming, the Countess of Briarly always looked at her husband with a secret smile—the smile that kept him out of the stables.

Epilogue

Carolyn led the way into the old-fashioned theater, chattering as she went. "You see?" she
said, waving her champagne glass at the stage.
There had been a great many toasts in celebration
of her birthday at supper. "The first Finchley marquess built it specifically for one of Queen Elizabeth's progresses around the country. She loved
theater, you know. I can't say it's been used much
since then, but I hope that when we have children,
we'll use it more often."

Her husband looked down at her with the sort
of doting expression that Hugh used to hate and
now was pretty sure was settling permanently onto
his face as well. "I've put you in Queen Elizabeth's
spot, darling," the marquess said. "On the stage."

"Oh!" Carolyn exclaimed. "That's the chair from the blue parlor."

"The one that's in the portrait of Queen Elizabeth sitting on this very stage," Finchley said proudly. "You are going to sit in the place of honor. Because it's your birthday." And he leaned over and said something into Caro's ear that Hugh couldn't hear, but he had a fairly good idea what it was because Caro turned pink, and her husband dropped a kiss on her nose in a way that was absolutely forbidden in polite society.

It made him think about what he'd do for Georgina's twenty-fifth birthday, and her thirtieth, and her fiftieth, and her seventieth, for that matter. He looked down at her, and his smile must have said something, because her cheeks turned rosy, and she said, "Hugh! Stop that!"

Meanwhile, his sister was creating havoc, of course. "No, I don't want to be up there on the stage by myself, Piers," she was saying. "I want you with me. And I want Georgina as well, because she and Hugh are just engaged, so they should be celebrated."

"For that matter, Miss Passmore and Lord Charters are in the same situation," Hugh pointed out.

"And I am very happy to announce that Miss Peyton has accepted my hand in marriage," came the deep voice of Captain Neill Oakes.

"A veritable riot of Cupids must have infested the house," Hugh muttered to Georgina.

"Regrets?" she said, grinning up at him.

"Never," he said, unable to keep his voice light. "Never." And then he kissed her too, because if one's host is breaking societal rules, one might as well follow suit.

"All newly betrothed couples shall join me and Finchley on the stage," Caro announced, clapping her hands and gesturing to the footmen, who scurried from the sides, carrying seats.

Hugh flagged down a little sofa and snuggled Georgie next to him. Gwendolyn tried to hang back, shaking her head, but Alec managed to talk her into a chair to the side. And Kate was sitting on Captain Oakes's lap, which was distinctly improper—except they were all so used to seeing him toting her about that it seemed natural. Something wrong with her ankle, Hugh thought. In the end, they all sat in a semicircle ringing the stage, with their backs to the audience.

There was a hum of anticipation in the audience.

"You did tell Lord Finchley that we're not responsible for this performance, didn't you?" Georgie whispered.

"You'll have to call him Piers now. You're part of the family," Hugh said. The very idea brought him dangerously close to kissing her again. But since they were actually sitting on the stage, with a good twenty gentlefolk down below surveying them as if they were the performance itself, he restrained himself.

There was a series of pops to the side of the room, and footmen spread across the stage, and through the audience, offering brimming glasses of champagne.

The Marquess of Finchley rose. "May I offer a final toast to my wife, in whose honor we are all assembled?"

Hugh had already had rather more champagne than he cared for; he was fond of a good port rather than this airy, feminine stuff. But he drank anyway.

Plus, Georgina raised her glass silently—not to Carolyn, but to him.

"What?" he whispered, bending close.

"To you," she said.

Something thumped in the area of his chest, and he finished off his glass, thinking how lucky he was. A footman promptly filled all their glasses again.

At that moment, Mr. Lear walked onto the stage. He was wearing a suit of yellow velvet, with something that vaguely resembled a halo around his head. If halos tipped drunkenly to the side and hung over one ear.

"So these are the newly betrothed couples!" he said, giving a bawdy smile to the four couples seated on the edge of the stage.

"One of which is married," Carolyn said cheerfully.

"Ah, Lady Finchley." Lear bowed so low that his halo lurched dangerously. He straightened quickly, grabbing it with his right hand. "It is with the deepest respect that I offer you the condolences of everyone in my troupe."

There was a moment of silence. Piers seemed about to say something when Lear corrected himself. "Congratulations! Not condolences! Congratulations!" He continued. "We are most happy to present the merry tragedy of Pyramus and Thisbe, often played before royalty and always adored. The characters are myself, in the character of the Moon, a fierce lion, and the two gentle lovers, fair Thisbe and handsome Pyramus."

"Excellent," Carolyn cried, clapping her hands again. "I hope you don't mind if I say that aloud. It feels quite different to be on the stage rather than down below."

"We welcome commentary of all sorts," Lear said. "Though we find clapping the most congenial."

Everyone dutifully clapped as Lear withdrew. A moment later, he reappeared, holding a lantern in his hand. He was followed by a young girl, wrapped in a purple mantle that was around a foot too long for her, who tripped into the center of the stage. She struck a pose. "This is old Ninny's tomb. Where *is* . . . my love?" It was immediately clear that Thisbe, unfortunately, was no great actress.

A lion entered, roaring. At least, Hugh thought it was a lion, given its rather furry appearance and its throaty roar.

"Oh!" shrieked Thisbe, running from the stage.

Hugh took a look around the circle. Everyone was staring at the stage in horror. The costumes were dreadful, and the acting was worse. Georgina looked up at him in desperate entreaty. He had to do something.

"Well roared, Lion!" he called, lifting his glass in a salute to the players. He nudged Georgie, who looked startled, then blurted out, "Oh! Well run, Thisbe."

Hugh glanced around the circle again. Everyone appeared nonplussed, except for his sister, who was smiling beatifically. She was holding out her hand for another glass of champagne.

"Well shone, Moon," Carolyn called, sounding a little tipsy. She looked up at her husband. "Truly, the Moon is very graceful." She turned to Gwendolyn, seated on her other side. "Didn't you think that was a graceful moon?"

"No," Kate said, from the other side of the stage. Captain Oakes clapped a hand over her mouth. The Lion picked up Thisbe's cloak in its mouth and shook it about with a good deal of emphasis before padding off the stage.

"The barn cat couldn't have done a better job," Kate said.

Her betrothed gave her an approving glance.

Pyramus pranced from the wings, wearing a magnificent curly wig that made him look like a poodle. "Sweet Moon, I thank thee for thy sunny beams," he said. "I thank thee, Moon, for shining now so bright." Having got the courtesies out of the way, he struck a pose. "For, by thy gracious, golden, glittering gleams, I . . . I . . ." An agonized look crossed his face. "O dainty duck! O dear!"

Gwendolyn turned to Alec. "Where did the duck come in?"

"There is no duck," Kate said flatly.

Oakes started laughing, but Pyramus had snatched the mantle and fallen to his knees. "Stained with blood," he informed the audience. "I am crushed, concluded, quelled!" There was a pause as everyone tried to figure out what he was talking about. "Thisbe must be dead," he told the audience in a faintly scolding tone.

"Ohhhh," Carolyn said, finishing her glass. "Thisbe's dead. That's awful. Poor Thisbe."

"Poor duck," Kate said dryly.

"Poor us," Alec put in.

"Come death, thou faithful friend," Pyramus

roared, obviously trying to override his audience.

"Can't come soon enough," Captain Oakes said.

"I find myself pining for the duck," Gwendolyn said. "Poor duck."

Georgie pulled Hugh's ear down to her lips. "Just when did Gwendolyn turn out to be so witty? My impression was that she was too shy to utter a word."

Carolyn turned to Gwendolyn. "What duck?" she said, utterly befuddled. "I don't see a duck!"

Her husband gestured for some more champagne. "Don't worry, dear. If you want a duck, I'll get one for you later."

She looked delighted.

Pyramus pulled himself away from contemplation of Thisbe's cloak and drew out his sword. "Come, tears, confound," he cried. "Out, sword, and wound the left breast of Pyramus. Ay, that left breast where his heart doth hop."

He stabbed himself. In fact, he stabbed himself more than once, which seemed to make Georgie nervous, so Hugh took advantage of the moment to pull her closer. "I love the breast where your heart hops," he whispered into her ear. "And the other one too."

"Thus die I, thus, thus, *thus*," Pyramus shouted, falling in a heap of flailing limbs. Hugh nodded to Alec, acknowledging a hearty death scene. When they were boys, they used to regularly fight duels, and Alec, in particular, could stretch his death to at least five minutes.

Pyramus clearly understood the value of a protracted death. He started up from the floor, and shouted, "Now am I dead," before collapsing again.

"We got that," Hugh said into Georgie's hair.

But Pyramus still wasn't done. "Now am I fled. My soul is in the sky. Moon, take thy flight."

The Moon seemed to have lost concentration, since Mr. Lear didn't move until Pyramus glared at him. Finally he trotted off the stage, and Pyramus rose just far enough to give his final speech.

"Now die, die, die, die, *die*!"

Thisbe rushed onto the stage and caught sight of Pyramus right away, though it would have been hard to miss him, given the sword sticking straight out of his armpit. "Asleep, my love?" She fell on her knees and shook him. "What, dead, my dove?"

"Doesn't this remind you of *Romeo and Juliet*?" Carolyn asked Gwendolyn.

"I prefer happy endings myself," Gwendolyn responded.

"Me too!" Carolyn said. She clapped her hands. "May we have a happy ending, please?"

There was a moment of silence on the stage.

"Did I say the cloak was covered in blood?" Pyramus cried, sitting up. "My Thisbe must have brought a jug of wine with her. Oh, Thisbe, give me a sip!"

Thisbe rose nimbly, politely kicking the sword into the wings, and hauled Pyramus to his feet.

"Sip wine from my ruby lips," she said with rather surprising eloquence.

"Live, live, live, live, live!" Pyramus shouted.

"Love . . . love . . . love . . . love . . . love," Thisbe said, throwing herself into Pyramus's arms.

"Now that's a happy ending," Carolyn said, with a sigh.

When the evening started, there were those in the audience who likely expected the performance to be ill received.

But the truth was that, in the end, when the players gathered together for their final bow, the audience rose to their feet and howled their appreciation.

Especially Carolyn.

Who never forgot her twenty-fifth birthday, and always told her husband, and then her children, and then her grandchildren, about the most romantic evening of her life. About the play that was practically written for her. And about the best present her darling husband ever gave her.

"You just didn't understand it," she would tell a polite, but disbelieving Piers, every year on her birthday. "It was about life, and death, and love . . ."

"And the duck?" he would ask, every time.

"The mystery of life and art," she would say with a sigh. "You just have to accept that we're not meant to understand everything."

"There's that one thing I do understand," he would say, pulling her close.

And she would smile up at him because the gift he gave her on her twenty-fifth birthday, and her thirtieth, and her fiftieth, and her seventieth was always the same, and they both knew it.

Love was the best present of all.

Do you love historical fiction?

Want the chance to hear news about your favourite
authors (and the chance to win free books)?

Suzanne Allain
Mary Balogh
Lenora Bell
Charlotte Betts
Manda Collins
Joanna Courtney
Grace Burrowes
Evie Dunmore
Lynne Francis
Pamela Hart
Elizabeth Hoyt
Eloisa James
Lisa Kleypas
Jayne Ann Krentz
Sarah MacLean
Terri Nixon
Julia Quinn

Then visit the Piatkus website
www.yourswithlove.co.uk

And follow us on Facebook and Instagram
www.facebook.com/yourswithlovex | @yourswithlovex

PIATKUS